WEIRD HEROES

SCIEN[...]URE THAT
IS ENT[...]PLY, FUN.
HERE IS[...]PUBLISHED
WORKS BY SOME OF THE MOST POPULAR AUTHORS IN
THE FIELD, ILLUSTRATED WITH OVER 25 PAGES
OF FANTASTIC GRAPHICS

WEIRD HEROES

EDMOND HAMILTON

PHILIP JOSÉ FARMER

RON GOULART

BEN BOVA

RALPH REESE • ALEX NINO

ARTHUR BYRON COVER

CRAIG P. RUSSELL

TOM SUTTON

CARL POTTS • TERRY AUSTIN

WEIRD HEROES

VOLUME SIX
BYRON PREISS, EDITOR

PYRAMID BOOKS, NEW YORK
BYRON PREISS VISUAL PUBLICATIONS, INC.

Letters of comment are welcomed. Please address mail to WEIRD HEROES 6 c/o Byron Preiss Visual Publications, Inc., 680 Fifth Avenue, New York, New York 10019. We are interested in knowing which characters you would like to see in their own books. The next volume of WH, Eye of the Vulture, Quest of the Gypsy Book 2, will be available in October '77.

WEIRD HEROES VOLUME 6
© 1977 Byron Preiss Visual Publications, Inc.
All artwork and design © 1977 Byron Preiss Visual Publications, Inc.
The character SHINBET © 1977 Byron Preiss Visual Publications, Inc.
Shinbet b/w portrait © 1976 Carl Potts. Used with permission.

All rights reserved. No part of this publication may be reproduced or transmitted in any form or by any means, electronic, or mechanical, including photocopy, recording, or any information storage and retrieval system, without permission from the publisher. For information address: Pyramid Books, 757 Third Avenue, New York City 10017.

Pyramid Edition Published April, 1977

"The stories, characters, and incidents mentioned in this book are entirely fictional. No actual persons, living or dead, are intended or should be inferred."

ISBN 0-515-0437-1

Library of Congress Catalog Card Number: 77-73625

Printed in the United States of America

Pyramid Books are published by Pyramid Publications (Harcourt Brace Jovanovich, Inc.). Its trademarks, consisting of the word "Pyramid" and the portrayal of a pyramid, are registered in the United States Patent Office.

WEIRD HEROES is a trademark of
Byron Preiss Visual Publications, Inc.

For information on dramatic and translation rights address:
The Sterling Lord Agency, 660 Madison Avenue, New York City

For information on British Edition rights, address Pyramid Books

Typography and Production by Anthony Basile

Cover painting by Steve Hickman
based on a character designed by Carl Potts

Cover Logo by Richard Nebiolo

This book is dedicated to Thelma Kawesch

WEIRD HEROES

Other books from
Pyramid/Harcourt Brace Jovanovich
and
Byron Preiss Visual Publications, Inc.

Weird Heroes Volume 1
an anthology featuring Farmer, Goulart,
Goodwin, Nino, Steranko, Lieber and more

Weird Heroes Volume 2
an anthology featuring Farmer, White,
Swift, Reese, Fabian, Maroto, Nino

Weird Heroes Volume 3
featuring *Quest of the Gypsy*, a novel
by Ron Goulart, art by Alex Nino

Weird Heroes Volume 4
featuring *Nightshade*, a thriller by
Mecham/King, illustrations by Nebres,
introduction by Walter B. Gibson

Weird Heroes Volume 5
featuring *Doc Phoenix* in *The Oz Encounter*
by Marv Wolfman/Ted White, illustrated
by Stephen Fabian (Hugo-nominee)

Fiction Illustrated 1
Schlomo Raven, a detective comedy by
Byron Preiss and Tom Sutton

Fiction Illustrated 2
Starfawn, a full-color science fiction
novel illustrated by Stephen Fabian

Fiction Illustrated 3
a hard-boiled detective novel by
Steranko, *Chandler*. With an
introduction by Joe Gores

Fiction Illustrated 4
Son of Sherlock Holmes, a full-color
whodunit with art by Ralph Reese

All books $1.50 plus 25c postage except *Fiction Illustrated
Volumes 3* and *4*, which are trade paperbacks available for
$4.95 plus 50c postage and handling from Pyramid Books/
HBJ, 757 Third Avenue, New York City 10017 Att'n: Mail Order

SIX!

With this volume of *Weird Heroes*, we begin our second cycle of publication. As with the earlier volumes, *Six* undoubtedly brings with it a new circle of readers. For those of your who are discovering *WH* through this book, rest assured that you are not walking in on anything totally from the middle. As a matter of fact, this may be the closest thing to a beginning that we've had in almost two years.

Weird Heroes exists as a home for new heroic fiction. It is akin to the classic pulp magazines of America in the twenties, thirties and forties, publications whose *raison d'etre* was to entertain a nation going through the largest—and most painful—experiences of its existence. In the period between WW I and WW II, the pulps sprang forth with some of the most colorful, exciting and bizarre heroes in the history of adventure fiction. *Doc Savage* and his band of aides were introduced by Lester (*Kenneth Robeson*) Dent. *The Shadow* materialized in the typewriter of Walter B. (*Maxwell Grant*) Gibson. Edmond Hamilton unleashed *Captain Future* and Doc Smith launched *The Lensmen* series. The modern age of heroes was underway.

Simultaneously, such science fiction magazines as *Astounding* and *Amazing* were acting as showcases for some of the most remarkable fantasy graphics to emerge since H.G. Wells took his readers back through time. From *Virgil Finlay* to *Hannes Bok* to *Leo Morey* to *Schomberg* and *Cartier*, the sf pulps exploded with page after page of weird perspectives, aliens and epic confrontations between man and space.

These pulp artists, heroes and authors are to a large extent the literary heritage of *Weird Heroes*. The adventure pulps provided readers with characters that were *fun* to read, whose exploits invited the purchaser to immerse him- or herself in the story on hand. The sf pulps were a visual treat, giving the readers a glimpse of worlds as yet unseen, tantalizing them with panoramas of depth and movement which often excelled the stories themselves. If the pulps were to be criticized for anything, it was that in their zeal to entertain, they also lapsed into mindless use of racist, sexist and violent situations which, frankly, showed up in most media of the time.

So, our purpose: to develop a *new* showcase for heroic fiction in the seventies; to establish a place where characters reflecting current times could have their adventures; to lay the groundwork for a continuing publication which gives ample room for the presentation of new fantasy graphics.

The unlikely name: *Weird Heroes*.

In 1975, we released two anthologies of heroic fiction. Their contents ranged from *Quest of the Gypsy*, a science fiction mystery, to *The Camden Kid*, a western comedy. The books won your gracious approval (and criticism). Both are now in their second printings.

The mail on the series aided us in planning the future of the books. Our goals were honed, and in this, our first new anthology in over a year, we have focused in on primarily science fiction and fantasy-oriented stories, with an occasional vintage pulp-oriented piece injected to retain the dramatic flavor of our literary predecessors.

Beyond these guidelines, we have strived to present characters who are exciting to read, but who do not resort to violence to solve their problems.

I mentioned at the outset of this piece that this is the beginning of *Weird Heroes'* second cycle. The books are structured so that each anthology or "set" of anthologies is followed by three or four novels featuring characters introduced in the anthologies.

That's where *you* come into the picture. We'd like your opinion on the new heroes introduced here. Which heroes would you like to see in books of their own? Which illustrators and artists appeal to you the most? Please let us know.

Regular readers will note a number of changes in this book. The first, the cover, is the result of work by Pyramid's new Art Director, Harris Lewine, in conjunction with a noted designer/calligrapher Richard Nebiolo. Steve Hickman, a painter for Ace Books and Christopher Enterprises (his *Wizards, Elves and Things* is a hit in the fantasy community) makes his *Weird Heroes* debut with a cover based on Potts/Austin's *Shinbet.* Steve is being touted as one of the up-and-coming hotshots of the paperback scene and we're delighted to note that he'll be doing about a dozen new illustrations plus a cover for *Weird Heroes 8* next fall.

In keeping with change, I've taken the liberty of revamping our interior design with the able help of Basile Associates, who do the production work on all of our titles.

Finally, our emphasis on sf/adventure/fantasy as opposed to the more expansive mystery/western/sf/fantasy slant has given us more room to showcase some of the popular sf writers in the current field. Art Cover, Hugo-nominated author of *Autumn Angels* (Pyramid, 1975) is here with Franklin Davis, the hero who debuted in *Platypus of Doom* (Warner, 1976). Ben Bova, the most respected sf magazine editor in the field, introduces *Orion* in an unexpected *fantasy* series. Phil Farmer is back with *Greatheart Silver Episode Three*, another cast-of-thousands-style novella to delight his many (crazed) fans.

In addition to the over twenty-five pages of remarkable graphics in this book, there is one special prose feature: *The Edmond Hamilton Papers*. This section, a fitting exclusive for this new American pulp, is a remarkable look back at the heyday of sf and comics. Edmond Hamilton, one of the best-loved writers in the history of science fiction, author of series ranging from *Captain Future* to the *Legion of Super-Heroes*, has graciously granted us permission to print his reflections here for the first time. Accompanying them are the notes of Julie Schwartz, a prominent figure in the early days of science fiction and currently a Senior Editor at DC comics, Inc., where he is responsible for the firm's major characters, Superman and Batman. Alex Nino, noted Filipino illustrator, has contributed some smashing pictures to top it off and old friends of Ed—Bob Bloch and Forrest Ackerman—have added their embellishments, too.

The stories in this book are "popular fiction" in the accepted sense of the phrase. They are entertaining fiction, "lighter" than some of our past pieces and—perhaps—they'll leave you at times with a smile on your face.

Now it's up to you. Let us know what you think of our new look, new direction, new series. We'll be back in the fall with *Volumes 7* and *8*.

Thanks for joining us again.

—Byron Preiss, Editor
New York City

SHINBET

RON GOULART • POTTS/AUSTIN

INTRODUCTION

Shinbet Investigates
A novelette by Ron Goulart
Based on a character developed by Ron Goulart, Byron
Preiss, Carl Potts, and Terry Austin
Illustrated by Carl Potts and Terry Austin

Talk about credits! Did you ever see such complications for a paperback book in which no film adaptation was involved? No? Neither have we. So sit back, relax, and hear a tale of collaboration involving two artists, one writer, and one editor (who should know better than to bother explaining all this).

Early in the spring of 1976, scouting new heroes for inclusion in this first of two new anthologies, I ventured downtown to Continuity Associates, the art/comics studio run by Neal Adams and Dick Giordano. Located in mid-Manhattan, Continuity doubles as watering hole, snack bar, and phone booth for the free-lance wing of the comics industry. It is also a reliable source for quick gossip and new, unsold *characters*. Although the former subject would undoubtedly have been cheaper, it was with the latter in mind that I scanned the walls and drawing boards of Continuity's "front office."

The "front office" of Continuity holds four drawing tables. As of this writing, the desk in the far left corner is occupied by a talented Californian named *Carl Potts*. Had Carl been seated in the second-slot position, currently held by Neal Adams (see *Weird Heroes*, Volume 2), this particular introduction might not have been written. Yet Carl *was* in the left corner, a spot which gave him the crucial "front office" *wall space*, on which he cleverly posted new illustrations as they evolved for his board.

On the day of my fateful visit, Carl's piece-of-the-rock held a new illustration. It depicted a new hero: not your basic shoot-'em-up vigilante, not your copy-the-Batman derivative crusader, nor your 38-inch starlet-with-a-cape. This hero was half-humanoid, half-wormlike, and noble-looking. This hero was *weird*.

"Who is he?" I asked the Potts.

"I don't know," he answered, ever eager to impress.

I stood there for a minute looking at the picture. In the upper right was a joint Potts-Austin signature; Carl had *penciled* the drawing (rendered the illustration in pencil) and a meticulous illustrator named *Terry Austin* had *inked* it (embellished Carl's work with a reproducible black ink). "What did Terry say about him?" I asked.

"Not much. I don't think he had any specific ideas either." A natural salesman, that Potts.

We talked about the worm for a minute or two. Then I posed a question which brought out the El Camino car salesman in old C.P. "Does anybody *own* the rights to him (it)? Did you sell the character to anybody?"

Potts's speech suddenly became quicker, all posture problems disappeared, and the acne which may or may not have been challenging the slopes of his chin swiftly dried up into retirement. Potts smiled slightly, sincere. The worm was his to sell.

In a moment worthy of David Selznick, I told him not to do anything with the worm without getting back to me first.

That's somewhat how things stood for the next few months. Apart from a few comments to C.P.—"I still want the worm"—there was no *final* news until—late spring.

I had had a photostat made of the illustration. The worm and I became, uh, *intimate*. I looked at it, it looked back. Finally, one day, it made it clear that it was a detective. Not your ordinary "Book 'em, Danno" detective, not your live-on-a-houseboat shamus, but a sleuth on a far grander scale than we were used to seeing. A chap who could deal with a mystery on both *interplanetary* and *interpersonal* levels. In short, a consulting detective who would be as much at home on the Calais coach as a on a slow boat to Titan.

The worm fit in nicely with the theme of mystery and science fiction, a theme which was becoming a recognizable quality of the *Weird Heroes* series. Visually, he was weird enough. On a literary plane he offered an interesting opportunity for out-of-the-ordinary epic-style whodunits.

I called our resident Edgar-award-winning mystery writer of science fiction.

"Hello, *Ron Goulart* here."

I told him of our newest property. He reacted with his usual enthusiasm. "A worm, huh? Half-humanoid, half-worm? All right, sent it up. I'll take a look."

"His name's *Shinbet*."

"Shinbet? Uh-huh. Is that permanent?"

"Unless you have something better."

He had *Windershin*, but I wasn't buying. So Ron concentrated on the character. I mentioned that I would like the initial adventure to set up a larger mystery linked to an interplanetary puzzle—a Moriartyesque web into which Shinbet and his talents would travel.

In a fit of cleverness, Ron evolved *Shinbet Investigates*, and in doing so established the slithering sleuth in a manner that made Carl smile. Even the skeptical Terry Austin displayed an upturned lip.

This is the first outing for one of Barnum's most talented visitors in a story by Barnum's most distinguished historian. We think you'll like him.

Shinbet Investigates
Ron Goulart

I was getting used to that damned catman giving me the finger every time we encountered each other, but then he started sending his camera to tail me.

That's the reason I finally, on that especially inappropriate night, told the fat, shaggy bastard I'd throttle him if he didn't quit. Well, actually, according to what the witnesses later related to the police, I threatened not only to throttle Prof2 Deel Zimmer but to cut him in quarters, string his innards from the light fixtures in Lecture Dome 26 of Taberna Territory Multiversity, and thereafter dance a jig on his remains. If you've ever taught at a university, especially on a planet like Murdstone in the Barnum System, you know how easy it is to grow excessive when you get in an argument with one of your colleagues. The most I probably would have done to Zimmer was poke him a few times on the snout. I didn't get a chance to do even that the last time I saw him. Of course since I had broken both legs of his robot camera and knocked off its wig, I had some difficulty trying to convince the police I'm not really much of a violent personality.

It was raining that night. Had it not been raining, a steady downpour, I wouldn't have left my cottage in the Liberal Arts Tract when I did to make an attempt to sneak over to Gwen's cottage in the Life Science Tract. Rainy nights her husband, Prof3 Milos Tennant, always went out to stun frogs at the lake on the edge of the TTM campus. Gwen, already wearing only a Lycra pajama top, had pixphoned me moments earlier to let me know Milos had grabbed his stungun and hopped into his skycar. I paused long enough to put on a raincape and a

beard. The beard, as I subsequently learned from the police, didn't fool anybody. Coming originally, though, from a planet even more conservative than Murdstone I was really unable to skip over to meet Gwen without making some attempt at disguise.

I was crossing the decorative neowood bridge which connected my tract with Gwen's when I became aware of a faint whirring noise behind me. I halted, spinning to confront what appeared to be a little old lady following in my wake.

"All my money's in compscript," she announced in a squeaky voice.

"You've got wheels." I pointed at the hem of her long pseudogingham skirt.

"How rude, to discuss a person's limbs."

"Wheels." I cocked my head, trying to see into the neocalico bonnet which hid the face. "And a lens."

"When you get up in years you'll need a few replacements yourself, young fellow. The sort of life I've led, it's a wonder—"

"You're not a little old lady, you're a robot camera." I snatched at the skirt.

"Help! Sexual assault!"

Bong!

The damned camera had cracked me one across the nose with its metal right hand. Blinking, tears spurting, I let go and hopped around on the wet bridge. Bumping into the railing, I stumbled and my shoulder jammed into the machine.

"Help! Rowdy conduct!"

The wheels skidded on the slick bridge surface, the camera went rolling back, smacked into the low railing, and fell over into the decorative moat fifteen feet below. The bonnet spun free, sailing through the rain to be swallowed by darkness. The wig flew next and I got a glimpse of the one-eyed face of Zimmer's robot camera before the whole gadget hit the water and sank.

Splash! Klong!

"Why'd you toss the old girl into the drink, Kilby?"

I turned, then shuddered. It was Prof1 Meshing, a lizard-man in the Mind Science Department. Lizards make me feel very uncomfortable; I always break out in bumps when I meet one. Snakes hit me the same way. Meshing contends it's a common reaction, since many nonreptilian races associate lizards and snakes with the reproductive organs. I never saw a reproductive organ that was six feet tall, wearing a checkered suit and a neoglass derby, but I find you can't argue with anyone in MSD.

"It was a camera," I told him.

After getting down the rainbow-pattern suitcase he had been carrying, Meshing removed his glass derby, rolled it down his arm, fluttered it, and returned it to his scaly green head. "Ah, there's an association I haven't hit up against before. Why, Kilby, does dunking a motherly old bimbo make you think of—"

"It *is* a camera. It's Zimmer's robot camera, the thing he sends to check up on me. Some nights it dresses up like a landscape gardener, some nights like a delivery boy from an all-night synfood service, once like a hussar."

"We don't," Meshing pointed out, "have any hussar barracks hereabouts."

"Which is exactly why I originally tumbled," I told him. "See, Zimmer is competing with me to become head of the Earth Culture Department next semester and—"

"I know that, know all about it." The rain was making finger-tapping sounds on his glass hat.

"Then you know that furry son of a bitch will go to any length to damage my reputation. His camera keeps trying to get some compromising footage of me, to show to the Regent Machines."

"You'd better hope they haven't got any shots of you in the sack with Gwen Tennant." The lizard psychiatrist picked up his suitcase, rested it on the bridge rail.

"You know—"

"Know all about that, all about it."

"Don't tell Milos Tennant, huh? He's sort of violent; most Valorians are."

"I don't inform on my colleagues," Meshing assured me, "especially to a man who stuns frogs. As I was telling Prof1 Shinbet only this—"

"That guy," I said, shivering. "How can you stand to hang around with him? I mean, teaching Earth Culture for six years now I've had to learn to accept some fairly odd things . . . but *Shinbet*. I know they all think he's brilliant over in the Criminal Science Department, but still he's—"

"Shinbet is one of the most brilliant criminologists in our system of planets. Why, when he practiced as a private investigator out on Barafunda the results were amazing. He's a smart cookie."

"I'd never consult a . . . well, I think I'd better go have a talk with Prof2 Zimmer."

Meshing put a scaly hand on my arm. "Leave him be, Kilby. Forget that the lousy bastard's making every effort to ruin you and cheapen your name. Forget he's fouling up your chances for a little nookie. Let him gloat, you get on over to your assignation."

"No, I have to tell him what I did to his camera, what I'm going to do to him if he keeps on interfering with me." I was standing there on the bridge with fists clenched, gasping in air through my open mouth.

"Back on my home planet," said the lizard psychiatrist as he gathered up the rainbow suitcase, "I learned if you count to ten before doing anything foolish, it helps. Of course on my home planet each of the numbers is composed of innumerable syllables so by the times you've reached, say, six or seven, much of the initial fire . . ."

I about-faced and went jogging back toward Lecture Dome 26. Zimmer was delivering an evening lecture there on Hard-boiled Films of the Twentieth Century, his favorite branch of Earth Culture. With any luck I'd catch him just as he was finishing.

". . . and thus you see why I don't agree entirely with the justly famous Avallone List of the Ten Best Hard-boiled Films," the shaggy Zimmer was saying. He had the unsettling habit of nibbling on pickled mice while he lectured and he was crunching up his last one when I came in at the back of the slanting pastel-colored lecture dome. After dipping his fat furry fingers into his snackbox, Zimmer gave a sad shake of his huge cat head on finding it empty and then said, "There are those, alas, some of them my very colleagues in this department, who will tell you that Humphrey Bogart was a major talent in the hard-boiled pantheon of mid-twentieth-century Earth cinema. Flapdoodle, is my only reply." He bowed toward his class of sixty-some and then noticed me. The beard didn't hinder his identification, because his right paw came up and he threw me the finger.

I might have stayed where I was, following Meshing's advice about counting to ten, except for that finger. I went running down the aisle. "Listen, Zimmer!" I shouted while I was still fifteen feet from the lecture dais. "I just dumped your damned robot into a moat. You're going to join him unless—"

"Who can this be?" He pressed his paws to his plump whiskered cheeks, feigning surprise. "Who is this bearded intruder who—"

"If you don't quit riding me I'm going to throttle you!" I hopped onto the dais. "Then I'm going to chop you into chunks, I'm going to decorate this place with your inner workings, and then I'm going to perform a simple but effective tap dance on your skonce. After, that is, disconnecting it from your neck."

About seventy percent of the students cheered my threats. Zimmer, though, did have some followers.

"Sour grapes, Prof2 Kilby!"

"Poor sport!"

"Don't you touch our Zimmy!"

I felt at my beard, realizing again it wasn't adequate. I took another of those deep, body-shaking breaths. "A word to the wise, Zimmer," I told him. I went striding away across the stage to a back exit. Glancing once over my shoulder, I was just in time to see the grinning catman give me the finger yet again.

Going through the arched doorway I nearly bumped into Prof1 Horn, a human-type from the Life Science Department.

"Happened to be passing, heard a frumus," he said. "Anything wrong, Kilby?"

"Nothing more than a lively debate." I didn't want to hang around chatting to anybody from the same department as Gwen's damned husband. I hurried away.

I was almost clear of the campus when I was hailed by the voice of old Jimphix of the Academic Conduct Team.

"Could you *breep breep* drop into my office for a moment, Kilby *breep*?"

He'd sent one of his little flying voxboxes to track me down. It hovered just above my head. "Can't this wait until—"

"Now would be *breep* best, Kilby."

Reaching up, I gave the little box a slap. "Your crownwheel is malfunctioning, which is why you make that *breep* sound," I told the gadget.

"Not the box's fault, Kilby," old Jimphix informed me. "It's *breep breep* mine. My new electronic upper bridge needs a bit more adjusting. In fact, these new teeth are a mite too aggressive and of late I find myself compelled to take bites out of furniture, wall hangings, even the—"

"Listen, I really have a couple of important engagements to—"

"You really better *breep* come see me now."

I sighed, crossed a rain-swept entryramp, headed for his office. The box, making lazy circles around me, tagged along.

Most everything in Jimphix's office was lopsided, tipped, fallen. "I won't invite you to sit down, Kilby, since the chairs are too nibbled, I fear." He was human, small, and much-freckled. His new front upper teeth gleamed and whirred when he gave me a careful smile.

His ball-television set was on, floating above a filing cabinet which had a few bites out of its edge. " . . .program that pulls no punches in its dedicated pursuit of the truth! Yes, it's the 'Shoveling Muck Show' . . . with H.L. Rover!"

"Grruff," said the dog-headed newsman on the screen. "Tonight we're going to dig into the shocking boondoggling and featherbedding which so flagrantly exists at Taberna Territory Multiversity. My special guest this evening is employed at that institution, but I can assure you he is one of the very few honest men in the teaching profession. Known in several planet systems for his feisty integrity and probing mind . . . he is *Shinbet*."

"Him again?" I looked elsewhere. "Can we turn that thing off while we have our chat, Jimphix?"

"I have to *breep* monitor this, Kilby. Part of my duties," he said. "Now what about these death threats?"

"What death threats? No one's made any death threats against me."

"No, no, I refer to the death threats you're making against others."

On the floating TV screen Rover was reading from a thick stack of blue and green papers. "Rrruff! Here we have only a partial listing of the unnecessary research projects going on at TTM. There is Prof3 Goedewaagen's vastly overbudgeted study of vegetarianism in dogs . . . everybody knows dogs love lean red meat . . . Grruff, wufff, grrr . . . but I digress. Another waste of tax money is Prof1 Horn's foolish delvings into reanimation of defunct animals and people. Then there is Prof2 Reisberson's researches on frontal nudity as a political weapon, Prof1 Meshing's ridiculous researches into teleportation . . . well, there are but a few. What light can you cast on all this frightful waste, Professor Shinbet?"

Shivering, I walked away from the dangling set and dropped into a sling chair. "I haven't been making any death threats," I told old Jimphix.

"I do believe you've chosen one of the pieces of furniture my new choppers compelled me to munch at—"

Crunch! Thump!

The chair legs gave way; I thunked to the floor.

"Yes, it certainly is," Jimphix said.

Shinbet's voice, rasping and unpleasant, was pouring out of the set. "These little halfwit peccadillos are a mere weep in the bucket," he was saying. "The real problem at TTM, as it is most everywhere else in the universe, is the growing influence of the Basher Society."

Rover said, "I don't believe I know what the Basher Society is, Professor."

"Of course you don't," said Shinbet, "because you're

just as big a halfwit as the rest of the supposed investigative journalists on this backward planet."

"Grr rowr ruff!"

Sounds of struggle and toppling furniture came out of the set's speakers.

I got myself up. "If you Academic Conduct people weren't a bunch of ... of halfwits, you'd look into Zimmer's actions and not mine. He's got cameras following me, he—"

"Hush a minute," requested Jimphix. "I want to find out myself what this Basher Society is."

"Sorry I took a nip at you, Shinbet," Rover was apologizing. "When I get riled up—and calling me a halfwit will surely do that—I get a little snappish. I feel foolish, needing three of our technicians to pull me off you."

"Not the first time I've been attacked by my inferiors," Shinbet assured him, "nor the last."

"Grr grr."

"Easy, H.L., easy now," cautioned an unfamiliar voice.

"Suppose ... grr grr ruff ... ah, suppose you explain what this Basher Society is, exactly."

"The Basher Society is a galactic criminal syndicate which practices crime and evil on an interplanetary scale," explained Shinbet in his unnerving voice. I still didn't feel up to watching his image. "I've been able to thwart and expose their operations on other planets, and I'll continue to combat them."

"You mean to imply that this vast criminal conspiracy operates here on Murdstone as well?"

"That is exactly what I do mean, you halfwit."

"Grr rowrr woof!"

"Easy, H. L., back, sit."

I moved closer to Jimphix's desk. "You'd better tell

Zimmer to lay off me. Otherwise he's . . . well, *you* tell him."

"I do hope you'll, after this *breep* talk of ours, come to your senses. Violent behavior on the part of a faculty member can often lead to serious trouble."

"Especially for that furry bastard," I told him as I went stomping out.

Actually I saw Zimmer once more that night. It was a somewhat odd encounter, and I attempted to tell Gwen about it when I finally reached the Tennant cottage.

"He didn't flash me the finger," I said as I unseamed my trousers.

"Come on, Jed, come on. Less talk, more action." Gwen was already naked, sprawled on her circular airfloat bed in the one-way dome bedroom above the cottage.

The rain was still drumming down. "I suppose it doesn't sound odd to you," I continued, stepping out of my trousers and my allseason briefs. "The point is, Gwen, there I was coming along Lane 16 from my place and there was Zimmer walking to his cottage and he didn't react to me at all."

"Maybe your new disguise fooled him." She jabbed an impatient elbow into the allseason sheet beneath her long, slim body. "Now let's proceed to the dirty work. Come on, come on. You're an hour late."

"Zimmer always sees through my disguises. I did go back to my place for a new beard because all the damn kids at his lecture penetrated my other disguise. Even Profl Horn knew it was me, when I came barging—"

"Oh, don't talk about him. All he ever talks about is that project of his to revive the dead. Frogs are bad enough, but when you have a dinner party and Horn gets into corpses it—"

"You know it could be that my confrontation with Zimmer has scared the fat bastard into—"

"Let's go, Jed. Are we going to bang or not? Milos may be home at any moment. Let's go, hop on."

"Wait, Gwen—any *moment?*"

"You never know with Milos. He loves stunning frogs, but sometimes he gets suddenly bored." She sat up, her breasts wobbling into each other to produce a soft, provocative smack. "Let's roll." She reached up to clutch the back of my neck. "Come on, come on. Quick."

"Let me at least take off this beard. It's sort of—"

"Frig the beard, Jed. Let's bang!"

"You know, Gwen, as fond as I am of you, I sometimes wish we'd go a little slower." I sat beside her, stroking her smooth stomach with one hand and trying to tug off my latest beard with the other.

"Living with a man like Milos, there's no time for leisure."

"At least a little foreplay might—"

"Okay, okay. There!" Her lovely head ticked forward, and she kissed me once on the cheek. "So much for foreplay, let's get down to the screwing."

I was really fond of her, so I complied. We made love her way.

Afterward we both, lulled by the fall of the night rain, dozed off, arms around each other.

Kablam! Wham! Kaboom!

"Milos!" I hinged upright, wide awake.

"No, that was someone busting down the front door. Milos wouldn't do that."

I leaped from the bed, found my briefs and trousers, and commenced tugging them on. "He might be in an irate mood, angry enough to make an entrance which—"

"Not Milos." She, too, was off the bed. "He'd creep in

at a window and stun you before you knew what was what. Which reminds me." Still naked, Gwen knelt and reached under the floating bed.

I recalled what I was doing, ceased watching her backside, and located the remainder of my clothes.

"Prof2 Jed Kilby!" An amplified voice came blaring from downstairs.

"Does that sound like Milos?" I was having some difficulty, because of the still-attached beard, pulling my tunic on over my head.

"No, it doesn't." There was a stungun in her hand.

I noticed it when my head emerged from the tunic neck. "Better give me—"

"Prof2 Jed Kilby! We request your surrender. This is your Territorial Police."

"Police?!" Gwen had been about to pass the weapon to me. She allowed her hand to drop to her naked side.

"They should have knocked first." I crossed to the bedroom door.

"Be careful, Jed." She thrust her fingers into the print lock on the wall beside the bed.

The door slithered open and I peered out. There were three Territorial Policemen, in bright scarlet and gold uniforms, arranged on the ramp leading up to our doorway. One human, one catman, one lizardman. The lizard cop was closest and I developed goosebumps when he took a step toward me.

He held a scaly fistful of faxpaper permits and forms. "You admit to being Prof2 Jed Kilby?"

"I'm Kilby, yeah. What's the—"

"Here you see our Door Busting Permit, our Window Smashing Permit (which we, now that I think about it, never got around to using, more's the pity), and here, this nice one with the big crimson seal, is a Warrant for your arrest."

"Arrest?"

"Arrest?" echoed Gwen back inside her bedroom. "Adultery isn't a crime on Murdstone, which is one reason I coaxed Milos into transferring from the Barnum Advanced Frog Study Institute."

"You are the prime suspect in a murder case," the lizard cop informed me. "Will you dress yourself and accompany us to an Interrogation Office, please?"

"I am dressed."

"You lack footwear."

I glanced down. "Oh, I forgot to . . . oof." Gwen had come up behind me and poked my boots into my back. I brought them around in front of me.

The TP reached for his stunrod, then relaxed. "Would yo ca e re tte tte tto too to to to to to to to to to to to ccc confess?" He waved a pink sheet of papesub at me. "This is a Plea Bargain Form. If you'd care to fill it out we can promise you a twenty-five-year sentence rather than lifetime at—"

"Who'd he kill?" Gwen stepped out from behind me.

"Aiii!" The lizardman smacked his paper-filled hands up against his eyes. "The humanoid form unclothed."

"Don't do that, lady," cautioned the catman. "A liz can't stand to look at a naked human."

"Ugh! Ugh!" The green cop was doubled up, his black tongue coiling and uncoiling.

"Clothes—put them on," I told her, moving so I blocked the cops' view of her. "Now, who am I accused of killing?"

"Ugh! Ugh!" The lizard policeman was working at straightening up, eyes still masked by his thick green fingers.

"He's got your Charge Sheet," explained the human cop, bending to try for a last glimpse of the retreating

Gwen between my legs. "I think it's one of your colleagues."

I had a sudden awful hunch. "Which one?"

The lizard man had himself under control. After swallowing and dabbing at his face with a scarlet and gold handkerchief, he read from a slip of blue paper. "You are the prime suspect in the murder of Prof2 Deel Zimmer. Sure you don't wish to confess?"

I didn't say anything.

When Inspector Quirk joined the other policemen and detectives in my Interrogation Suite I started to feel hopeful. A lanky catman, Quirk headed up the Improbable Investigations Division of the TP. I heard enough about him to realize they wouldn't have called him in unless they didn't have a clear-cut case against me.

I relaxed a little in the neoskin loungechair and sipped from the glass of pink lemonade they'd placed on the stand by my chair.

Inspector Quirk strolled right up to me, the others moving out of his way. Even Inspector Bukka, the chunky Earthman who'd been hollering at me for more than two hours, stepped aside.

"Good morning, Professor." Quirk came originally from a territory on Barnum which had been settled by colonists from a section of Earth known as England. Because of my study of twentieth-century Earth culture I recognized his accent as distinctly upper-middle-class English. "I trust, old chap, they haven't made things too bally rough for you, eh?"

"I didn't kill Zimmer."

Removing his checkered cap, Quirk seated himself in a glass chair facing me. "If you are responsible for doing the bloke in, old fellow, you're deuced clever."

"Didn't kill him."

"You weren't fond of the blighter, eh what?"

"Couldn't stand him. Mostly because he and I were competing for the same job," I said. "I've been here six years, Zimmer only three. Naturally I figure I'm better qualified to head a department."

"You, rather rashly, threatened the chap last evening in front of an audience. You vowed to do a series of vile, as well as fatal, things to him."

"I was angry."

"Over this rivalry business?"

"Well, that and the damned camera he had following me."

"Ah, yes," said Quirk, "the unfortunate robot camera."

"He murdered the gadget," put in Inspector Bukka. "He admits that."

"One cannot murder a mechanism," reminded Quirk, "although, Professor, you did do considerable violence to this particular robot. Had it been a living being—"

"It wasn't, it was a snooping robot camera," I told him. "Anyway, I bumped into it and the damned thing went toppling into the moat. An accident really, you can ask Profl Meshing if—"

"Its legs got broke," said Bukka. "Its head is just a gob of scrap now."

"It was following me, I bumped into it. It fell."

Quirk smiled, his prickly tongue touching at the fur around his mouth. "I'm not exactly clear, old thing, as to how this unfortunate device fits into the rivalry between you and your late colleague."

"Kilby was shacking up with that bimbo," explained Bukka. "Zimmer was getting pix."

"Is there some sort of affair of the heart involved as well?"

I said, "You must know about that, too. Since your people broke into Mrs. Tennant's house in the middle of the night."

"You and young Mrs. Tennant are amorously involved?"

"Yes."

Quirk nodded slowly. "So that exposure by Zimmer would affect not only your academic standing, old boy, it might also cause you to be the victim of Milos Tennant's wrath, eh?"

"I suppose that's possible," I admitted.

Resting a furry hand on his knee, Inspector Quirk leaned closer to me. "Am I correct in assuming, old thing, you are aware of the department in which I serve?"

"Improbable Investigations."

"Let me be absolutely frank with you," he said in a low, confiding voice. "I've dealt with a great many improbable crimes in my day, but this one I'm very tempted to label impossible." He leaned back, steepling his fuzzy fingers. "You're aware that in a planet system such as ours, even more so than in the neighboring Earth System, there is an infinite variety of people. Some of them—too blooming many, to my way of thinking—have what you call wild talents. The police, especially an efficient organization such as we have in Taberna Territory, can cope with and solve almost any crime of a relatively normal nature. However, every now and then a crook with a wild talent comes along and then it's time for IID to lend a paw. We have a knack for solving the odd cases, old chap, for catching the unusual criminals. You may recall the recent Stonebridge murder case, which turned out to involve a lycanthrope with the additional ability of levitation. I solved that."

"Damn fine police work," asserted Inspector Bukka.

"Is there something odd about the circumstances of

Zimmer's death?" I asked.

Several of the gathered police laughed.

Inspector Quirk said, "Your late associate retired to his cottage at approximately 9:26 last evening. You are probably aware he kept a large and valuable collection of motion pictures in his cottage."

Zimmer was always crowing about it. "I'm aware, yeah."

"Your colleague made a practice of taking several safety precautions to guard his collection," said Quirk. "Around his cottage, on all four sides, was installed an invisible force screen which rises twenty feet straight up. Furthermore there is a stun-system which will knock out anyone who attempts to enter the place without the permission of the householder. Therefore, even if you were able to *fly* over the force screen, there would be that stun setup to overcome. As an additional safeguard, Zimmer had six photorobots stationed in the various rooms of his cottage. Anyone who reaches the doors and windows and attempts to enter is photographed and the pictures sent instantly to Zimmer in his tamperproof film-study room. The room where he was found dead is also equipped to record all visitors on vidisc."

"How was Zimmer murdered exactly? Did someone really throttle him?"

"The bloke was shot with a blaster pistol," replied the inspector. "The weapon was not in his film-study room, nor anywhere else in the home."

I was trying to figure why Quirk had been called in at all. "Where's the improbable angle? Don't his cameras show you who visited him last night, who shot him?"

"According to the film and vidisc records, old boy, Prof2 Zimmer had no visitors at all. And the mechanisms appear not to have been tampered with in any way," said the inspector slowly. "In other words, no one visited the bloke once he'd fortified himself in the blinking cottage. His neighbors confirm that. He was seen to enter the cottage alone, no one dropped in, and nothing unusual was heard. Yet this morning when his robot valet went to wake him, Zimmer was dead in his film room."

"Maybe the robot did it," I suggested.

"We've investigated the possibility, old thing, and ruled it out."

"Well, it looks like an impossible crime, sure enough."

"It looks improbable, rather," said Inspector Quirk. "I can guarantee you, old chap, I'll find a solution and bring the killer to justice."

"He hardly ever fails," Bukka told me.

Quirk stretched up out of his chair. "Would you care to tell me how you did it, Prof2 Kilby? It would save us all a bloody lot of work."

"Didn't do it," I repeated again. "I did not kill Zimmer."

"Perhaps," said Quirk, fluffing his whiskers. "You may go now, Professor. I shall, old dear, be talking to you again."

A Tenure Committee android was sitting in my oval parlor when I got back to my cottage. One of those chrome-plated ones with the blond wavy hair. "Well, how's every little thing?" he asked.

Slumping into an aluminum replica of a bentwood rocker, I answered, "Splendid, absolutely splendid. Why did you break in here?"

From the breast pocket of his white jacket, the andy drew a slip of yellow realpaper. "Here's my Walk-Right-In Permit, Professor." His head gave off a faint pinging noise when he smiled across at me. "First off I wanted to tell you how sorry the university is you committed this murder. We—"

"Didn't commit any murder."

"You are the chief suspect, though, aren't you?"

"Probably, from what Inspector Quirk implied. Why are you here?"

"Ah, so they have called in IID."

Ping!

"Your cheeks need adjusting," I mentioned after his newest smile. "We used to have a mammy android back home on Barnum who developed the same problem. Every time she clapped her hands and—"

"Murdering Prof2 Zimmer puts you in an awkward position vis-a-vis the university," the Tenure Committee android said. "While it does eliminate your main competitor for the post you covet, the action at the same time rules you out of the running."

I left the rocker. "What the hell does that mean? I haven't murdered anyone. Whoever knocked off that shaggy bastard, it wasn't me. You trying to tell me simply because I happen to be a suspect, an innocent bystander almost, I'm not going to get a job I've worked six long—"

Ring! Ring! Ring!

The android whacked his temple with the heel of his hand. "There goes that strange noise inside my gear box again. It's enough to—"

"My pixphone. Excuse me." I crossed to the phone alcove. "Yeah?"

Gwen, still naked apparently, bloomed on the round screen when I flipped on the switch. "Are you out on bail pending trial, Jed?"

"I'm out because Inspector Quirk of IID and Inspector Bukka of plain everyday TP can't prove I killed Zimmer."

"You didn't murder him, did you?"

"Don't you know me well enough to—"

"I see you're mostly in bed."

"Why are you still unclothed, Gwen?"

"I'm not still," she explained. "I was completely dressed till Milos came home and tore the clothes off me. A good night of stunning frogs always stimulates him. When he's in such a mood I must submit. Submit to the caress of his coarse hairy hands, still thick with froggy slime, submit to having my most intimate—"

"Okay, okay," I said. "Listen, Gwen, there's a TC andy here. I better call you later to—"

"No, don't phone me. Not until this murder blows over." She glanced back over her bare shoulder. "Jed, I have a feeling Milos suspects our relationship."

"That's possible, since the entire police force knows."

"I wanted to warn you to be careful, and alert. Milos may try to sneak up on you."

"Okay, thanks for the warning." I turned off her image and backed out of the pixphone alcove. "I think the Tenure Committee is being damned unfair. You'd better tell them I plan to protest their—"

"Your best bet is to find out who killed Prof2 Zimmer . . ." said the blond mechanism, "if, which seems hardly likely, you really and truly aren't the murderer." The android stood up.

Pung!

"You ought to have them look at your knee when you go in for your smile adjustments," I advised. "The left one is—"

"Have you considered Shinbet?"

I shuddered. "For what?"

"He's reportedly a brilliant detective." The android headed for the door. "You may be sure the police won't be consulting him, since, to a man, they find him repellent."

"So do I."

"He may be your only hope," said the android.

He left and my phone sounded again.

Ring! Ring!

Inspector Quirk was on the screen. "A few more questions, old bean."

"I didn't knock off Zimmer."

"Yes, yes, to be sure," said the lean catman. "You didn't mention you'd encountered the unfortunate Prof2 Zimmer twice last evening."

"Thought I had. Yeah, the second time was on Lane 16, around 9:15 or so. He was on his way to his cottage, I guess."

"Did you make any further threats?"

"We didn't exchange a word, or even a gesture. You see, usually Zimmer would make an obscene—"

"Let us get along, old thing." Quirk's eyes seemed to be glowing, staring into mine. "Did you see anyone else? With Zimmer, or following him perhaps?"

"Nope, nobody."

"Not even . . . a midget?"

"Especially not a midget. Is there a midget involved in this case?"

"This particular midget has several wild talents. One of which is the ability to walk through . . . Ah, but no sense in taking up any more of your time."

"Okay, I'll—"

"Should it develop, old thing, that you know this gifted little nipper, things shan't go easy with you. Would you care to tell me about him?"

"I didn't kill Zimmer and I don't know any midgets." I cut off the call.

Pacing the pseudohook-rug in my parlor, I tried to convince myself I ought to go consult Shinbet. His cottage was only a mile or so away, in the Criminology

Tract. I couldn't, though. The idea of—

Buzz! Buzz!

Someone on the porch. I eased over to the spyhole, pushed the once-over button.

"Uck," I said aloud.

Shinbet was standing out there. Not standing exactly, since he didn't have any legs. *Arched*, I suppose, *coiled*.

"I'm no fonder of you than you are of me," he said in that rasping, grating voice of his. "Still I can't sit back and allow them to ruin even a halfwit like you, Kilby. Let me in."

"Why?"

"So I can save your halfwit life."

I poked my fingers in the control box. Recognizing my prints, the door opened. "I was thinking about consulting you, Shinbet."

"Couldn't bring yourself to do it." He came slithering across the threshold.

Shinbet hails from a remote planet in a system beyond ours. He's . . . well, mythological in appearance. From the waist up he's humanoid, and not a bad-looking guy. Somewhere in his forties, thin, sharp-featured, wearing a plaid tunic. The lower part of his resembles a snake, one very large snake. He can ride around on that tail, move on one of the coils of it as though he had a single leg—no, more gracefully than that. Usually he was, counting his human torso and the length of the serpent tail he stood on, about six feet high. Though if he extended that scaly green tail to stand on the very tip of it he'd be near ten feet tall.

"They're retractable," he said.

"Huh?"

"My sexual organs. You were wondering, since I don't wear trousers, where they were."

I was. "Down in the snake part?"

"There is no snake *part*, halfwit. I am a total entity. He rolled across my rug. "I'm not a snail, either."

I'd been watching the rug, worrying he might leave a trail of some sort of slime. "I'm sorry, I'm not used to dealing with visitors from your planet sys—"

"You're not used to dealing with anything," Shinbet assured me. "You really have god-awful taste in women, Kilby. Gwen Tennant, for crying out loud." He reached up an arm, removed his softbrim hat.

"She's very affectionate."

His laughter came rasping out of him. "Maybe I ought to let them put you away from a dozen years or so. Trouble is, halfwits usually never mature. They simply become older and older halfwits."

"Do you know who killed Zimmer? Or did you come over just to blacken the name of—"

"I don't as yet know the name of the killer," Shinbet said. "I'll find out. My principal purpose in dropping by was to inform you that I believe you to be innocent."

"I appreciate that." In my gratitude I actually held out my hand to him.

He ignored it. "A halfwit like you couldn't have brought off such a murder."

"Inspector Quirk thinks a midget did it."

"He thinks *you* did it, Kilby—with the help of, among others, a matter-displacing midget." Shinbet flipped his hat down onto a lamp table. "Bukka's men are hunting for this talented little fellow, even though he had nothing to do with Zimmer's death."

"If he had walked through a wall into Zimmer's place, the cameras would have taken his picture, wouldn't they?"

"Not if he materialized through the ceiling after landing on the roof." Shinbet made a dismissing gesture with his right hand. "A halfwit theory, but what can you expect from the likes of Quirk."

"You don't think it was this midget?"

"Aren't you paying attention? There's *no midget* involved. The only reason Quirk thinks so is because he's got the wrong suspect, the wrong method of murder, and the wrong motive."

I blinked. "What was the reason for killing him?"

"The exact motive is something I'm not yet certain of. But it's going to have something to do with the fact that Prof2 Zimmer was not really a catman."

"He wasn't? Inspector Quirk didn't mention that."

"Quirk won't know until the autopsy reports are in. Still you'd think he could spot a phony. I noticed it the second time I saw Zimmer."

"He was disguised, huh?"

"Yes, Kilby, and a good deal better than you are on *your* nocturnal rambles."

"What was he, underneath all that fur, if he wasn't an obese catman?"

"Zimmer was an obese human." Shinbet's green tail flicked against the leg of a rocker as he rolled across the room. "Now'd I'd like you to tell me everything that happened to you last night, everything you saw, everything you sensed. Try not to be such a halfwit."

"If I'm negligible, why bother to help?"

"I have a very strong sense of justice," answered Shinbet. "And the problem tickles me. Sit down and tell me."

I sat down and told him.

Rain again that night. It pounded on the shingle roof of the band pavilion, insinuated down through several cracks to pat on the heads and shoulders of the robot musicians. Although there was no concert tonight, nobody'd bothered to carry the musicians into the Robot Storage Rooms across the deserted park.

Ping!

A drop of rain hit the bell of the bandleader's cornet.

Ping! Ping!

More fat drops slapped the glistening black visor of his scarlet cap.

I was standing in a dry place on the stand, watching the dark trees a hundred yards off. I was excited, scared some. This was going to be the first time in months I'd meet Gwen outdoors.

There she was now, a blur of white moving carefully across the thick black lines of trees. Leaving the shelter of the woods, she looked swfitly to the left and right before dashing across the grass and up to me on the stand.

"Gwen!" I hugged her.

"Okay, Jed, let's get to it," she said as she wriggled free. "I'm not wearing anything under this plyoponcho. So we can commence banging in about ten seconds." With one sweep of her slender hand she unseamed the opaque cloak.

"Right here? I thought we'd talk about all the—"

"I can always talk to you when you're in the jug. Let's get on with the boffing." She flapped her arms once, causing the poncho to fall free of her body. She really was naked under there. "Come on, come on, let's roll. I—"

Bzzung! Zzum!

Gwen gave one pained gasp and stumbled for an instant before tumbling down atop the discarded rain cloak.

I ducked down beside her, which is what kept me from taking the next blast of the stungun.

Kachowie! Wuzzz!

An accordionist rattled, but I was safe, shielded by the

low wall of the pavilion.

"Gwen, hey, are you all right?"

She was alive, only stunned. I rubbed at her wrists, urging her to arise even though I knew the effects of a stungun jolt usually lasted an hour or more. Although maybe a stungun intended primarily for frogs wouldn't be so effective with people.

See, I was assuming it was Gwen's lunatic, frog-stunning husband out there in the woods, hellbent on revenge. He'd obviously been aiming at me and bopped Gwen instead. When you aim at a cluster of frogs it doesn't matter which one you hit.

Okay, Gwen would recover even if I left her slumped there. The important thing was to get myself out of there and away. I struggled out of my tunic, glad I hadn't worn a disguise for this rendezvous. Very cautiously I reached over and proceeded to unseam the band jacket of the nearest trombone player. By dressing up in these clothes, I figured to elude Gwen's vengeful husband.

Doowah! Doowah!

The start button got nudged while I was working at disrobing the trombone player. He was puffing into the damned instrument.

I decided to abandon my quick-change plan. Draping the trombonist's bright-buttoned jacked over the naked Gwen, I backed away, on hands and knees, from her stunned form. I backed smack into the harpist andy and, five second later, his harp.

The glissando was still fading into the rainy air when I felt the barrel of a damp stungun pressed into my un-clothed back. For a big burly guy, Milos moved very quietly.

Only it wasn't Gwen's husband.

"Hate to do this, Kilby. You can imagine all the con-flicting ideas rattling around in my coco at this moment."

There was Profl Meshing, the lizard Mind Science instructor, standing over me with his stungun prodding my spine. "Don't tell me you don't approve of—"

"Nothing to do with your adventures between the sheets," he said, with a clucking sound which might have been meant to convey sympathy. He urged me to my feet. "The way things turned out, this is the sensible way to resolve this situation."

"What situation? How does knocking out Gwen make—"

"The idea, kiddo, is that you are filled with remorse over icing Zimmer," Meshing began explaining in his lecture-room voice. "You get in touch with the cupcake tonight and the pair of you decide on a suicide pact. You leave a note confessing all—I've got it in my pocket and it's a masterpiece of both imitative penmanship and Kilby style. You swear the death of Zimmer is all your fault, and simply another academic feud murder having nothing to do with the Basher Society or—"

"Suicide pact? That's only for people who are—"

"You're going to knock yourself off." Meshing had a second gun. With a scaly green hand he yanked it from beneath his slicker. It wasn't another gun, it was a blaster. "First the jane and then yourself. Ties up all the loose ends, gets us off the hook. Inspector Quirk is just dense enough to buy the suicide angle and close the case. He'll make Shinbet quit investigating, too. So I hope you'll forgive me, Kilby, because you're not really a bad—"

By throwing myself against the piano I was able to shove it right into him.

Zizzle! Bap! Zzum!

Both the lizardman's guns went off. Fortunately both into the ceiling of the band pavilion. More rain was let in.

The piano had by this time nudged Profl Meshing against the pavilion's low wall.

Splunk! Crackle!

The neowoods gave way, the piano drove off the stand and dropped to the wet grass four feet below, taking Meshing with it.

Bong! Slush! Tinkle!

"Very well, you chaps. There's been enough destruction and violence," boomed a familiar voice. Inspector Quirk and three plainclothes investigators came walking through the rain, umbrellas in one hand, blasters in the other. The inspector, fur beaded with rain, swung up onto the bandstand. "I've had you under surveillance since your release, Kilby. Jolly good thing for you, eh what?"

"Yeah, I don't like the general notion, but it did come in handy tonight." I glanced down to the spot where Meshing had landed. He was flat on his back, arms spread wide, unconscious and half under the piano. Two of Quirk's men were attempting to extricate him. "He was going to kill me and Gwen, make it look like suicide."

"So we heard whilst lurking, old thing," the inspector said. "When thieves fall out, what?"

"What do you mean? Don't tell me you're still idiotic enough to think—"

"We've picked up the midget, old cork. Soon as the little beggar cracks we'll—"

"I'm not in cahoots with any damn midgets," I insisted. "I'm nothing but a . . . a victim of circumstances."

Quirk's whiskers quivered as he chortled. "Very droll, Kilby, very—"

"Knock off the halfwit snarfling," suggested a rasping voice down in the rain. There was the sound of slithering on grass. "I've collared the other one."

"Jove!" Quirk's fur stood. "Bless me if it isn't that

snake chappy."

It was indeed Shinbet, rolling on his coiled tail, a black raincloak over the human part of him. He was dragging, by the collar, Profl Horn. The resurrectionist was unconscious.

With amazing ease Shinbet tossed Horn up onto the bandstand. Then, in a crawling, wriggling manner I'd rather not describe, he came up and joined us. "You now have the two perpetrators," he told the inspector. "If you'll refrain from making any halfwit snorts, chortles, and other feline outpourings, I shall explain the entire Zimmer murder case to you in some detail and with total clarity."

"Eh?" Quirk, scowling, forced himself to approach the criminologist. "Ah, yes, my men have informed me you've been sucking around headquarters, sneaking looks at the autopsy reports, the crime scene materials, other restricted—"

"I warned you about interrupting," said Shinbet. "Now sit on that piano stool there and be still."

Quirk, swallowing hard and brushing at his whiskers, obliged. It mean shoving the android pianist off.

Gong! Bumb!

Rain dripping down through the ceiling onto his cloak, Shinbet continued, "Do you know why your autopsy report states Zimmer died an hour before he entered his cottage last evening?"

"Very difficult to pinpoint the time of death in cases like—"

"Not at all. In fact, Quirk, when I gleaned that single fact from your halfwit report I saw at once the only possible solution." He chose this moment to drop Profl Horn to the puddled bandstand floor.

"Murf wuzzle," murmured the professor, stirring.

"Bluff and bluster, old chap," said Inspector Quirk to

the snake investigator.

"I can also tell you why Zimmer, a human, was masquerading as a catman."

The inspector's yellow eyes went wide. "What? I say, Shinbet, old bean, how'd you bloody well know about that? I had the autopsy johnnies delete the fact from the report until such time as—"

"I don't need scraps of paper to help me reach most of my conclusions." Swaying on his green tail, Shinbet laughed one of his chalk-on-slate laughs.

I remembered my abandoned tunic, snatched it up, and got into it.

Shinbet said, "The simplest *careful* observation of the late professor should have told you he was no more a catman than I am. Why, then, did he pick such a repugnant disguise for himself?"

"Half a mo, old top," protested Inspector Quirk. "There's nothing repugnant about being a catman. The fact of the matter is I'm bloody glad I'm one and not a blinking . . . well, no matter. Why do you think this Zimmer bloke resorted to a disguise and a spurious identity? Not that it matters, since we've sent his prints and patterns to Interplan Police and should have proper ident—"

"Zimmer's real name was Richard Dahlgren," Shinbet informed him. "The reason for his whole masquerade had to do with the suitcase Kilby here told me about."

"Meshing's suitcase?" I said. "Is that why he tried—"

"I suggest we adjourn to my cottage," said Shinbet, "and bring most of these strewn halfwits with us."

Inspector Quirk was stroking his cheek whiskers with a furry paw. "Very well, old thing. We may as well submit to one of your blinking charades."

"Halfwit." Shinbet went slithering away into the rain.

I was standing as far from Shinbet as the steamy parlor allowed. There were no chairs, no divans. Since Shinbet never sat himself, he'd had all that sort of furniture removed from his cottage. There were mats on the floor, a few scattered cushions. Inspector Quirk was squatting, uneasy, on a green and orange cushion. Two of his men waited outside. Gwen, still stunned, had been hauled home in a police hopper by the third policeman. I tried not to think about how her husband would react to that.

Sharing the parlor with us were Meshing and Horn, both relatively conscious now.

Shinbet himself was pacing, after a fashion, back and forth in front of the special steam-producing unit he'd had installed in the fireplace. "You'll find," he was saying, "that Zimmer, alias Dahlgren, dropped out of sight on the planet Esperanza some four years ago, after making off with $760,000 belonging to the Basher Society."

Quirk bounced on his cushion, brushing against the drooping leaves of the lush potted plant beside him. "You mean to imply we're dealing with interplanetary organized crime here?"

"Obviously," replied Shinbet. "Since my sources of information are speedier than yours, I found out several hours ago the true identity of Zimmer. Even a halfwit, Quirk, should be aware that the Basher Socity never forgets, never forgives, never gives up. Some time over a year ago they traced Zimmer to this university. Their next stop was to alert their agents here, and to plant a new man to help get rid of Zimmer. Once the stolen money was found and retrieved, that is."

"Was part of their plot," I asked, "to make it look like I killed him? From the start, I mean." I glanced over at Meshing, who avoided meeting my eyes.

"The Basher Society doesn't care about you. But

Meshing realized if he could tie it all to you, thanks to your halfwit antics, he'd be home free." Shinbet swayed so he was facing Horn and Meshing. "Profl Meshing did some interesting work with telekinesis before coming to TTM."

"What's that got to do with anything?" the lizardman demanded. "Simply because I happen to get a kick out of forging suicide notes, purely for prankish purposes as I tried to tell the inspector, is no—"

"The Basher Society dispatched an assassin here, though they already had an agent on campus," said Shinbet. "You were that agent, Meshing."

"Typical scapegoating tactic."

"Once you and your assassin associate made certain the stolen Basher Society dirty money—what was left of it—was in an arcoris-skin bag under the flooring of Zimmer's movie room, you used your telekinetic abilities to heist it. To whisk it out without ever having to enter the place."

"I'm not really an agent of any—"

"Unfortunately for you, Kilby saw you that night immediately after you'd caused the bag to teleport out of Zimmer's cottage into your hand," Shinbet went on. "It was his remembering the rainbow-hued bag, meaning it was made of the skin of the arcoris, which made me initially curious about you. As you may know, Meshing, articles made of that particular kind of skin, because of the remote possibility of rainbowpox, are not allowed on this planet of Murdstone. Zimmer no doubt smuggled his bag in."

"Kilby must be mistaken."

"No," I said directly at him. "I had a similar suitcase when I worked on Esmeralda one—"

"We'll be wanting to have a look-see at that blinking bag," said Quirk. "Taken along with this blinking fake suicide note we caught you in the act of trying to make come true, Professor . . . well, things don't look good for you." Quirk, whiskers flickering, turned again toward Shinbet. "You say, Shinbet, this bloke snitched the alleged money. Who did Zimmer in, then?"

Shinbet inclined his thin face in the direction of the remaining professor. "That was Horn."

Profl Horn chuckled. "Really, Shinbet, this grows more and more ridiculous. It's bad enough you fell me with some kind of bizarre off-planet wrestling blow while I was taking a perfectly innocent stroll near the—"

"You went along with your accomplice," said Shinbet, "to make sure the faked suicides came off." He slithered to a new swaying position, closer to the steam unit. "You see, inspector, the reason there was no record of any visitors to Zimmer's cottage last night is simple: there were no visitors. Zimmer wasn't murdered in his cottage."

"Eh, what?" Quirk popped to his feet. "The bloke had to be. He was seen entering the blinking place, alone, and he never came out again. Not alive."

"He was seen entering the cottage, yes. He was, however, already dead when he did that. Which is why your autopsy boys gave you such a puzzling report, Quirk."

Quirk was worrying an ear with his paw. "Dead already? Then how'd the ruddy beggar walk?"

Shinbet jerked a thumb at Horn. "Only one man on this campus could bring off that stunt," he said. "A man who just happened to be outside Zimmer's lecture hall last night. A man, who, since he arrived at TTM last year, has received research grants totaling over two million dollars to work on his resurrection process. In addition to being an agent of the Basher Society, he's an excellent reanimation man."

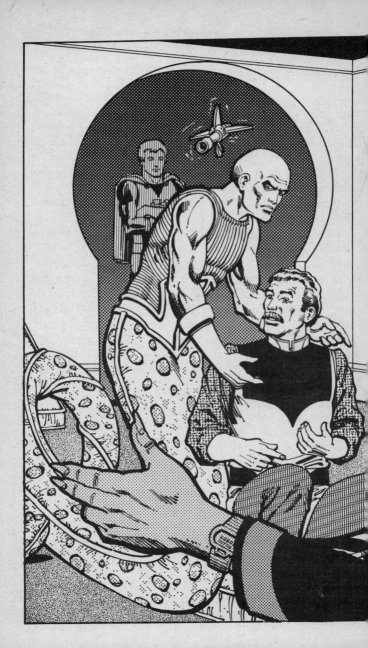

"Really now, old bean," protested Quirk, "we all know Horn hasn't succeeded as yet. Why, the best he's been able to do with a dead chap is get the poor devil to rise up and walk around for an hour or so, then the poor lad is once again dead and . . . Jove!" The inspector slapped himself on the jaw. "Gad, that's all he'd need to do."

"Exactly," said Shinbet, with a particularly grating laugh. "Horn induced Zimmer to visit his lab, shot him, and then brought his dead body back to life. He instructed the zombie-like Zimmer to return home and go through his usual routine. Therefore, people saw Zimmer afoot and moving after he was actually dead. Since Horn's reanimation process involves chiefly electronic devices and not drugs, only a very astute reading of the autopsy report reveals what was actually done to him. Once locked in his cottage, the process, as usual, wore off and there you had a dead man inside a sealed house with no sign of a weapon about."

"An insane story," said Horn. "One which, further, you can't prove at all, Shinbet. I'll be talking to the Tenure Committee about—"

"I've got this however." The snake detective pulled a blaster pistol from his pocket.

Horn sprang upright. "You couldn't have retrieved that. I tossed it down the drainoff pipes under my lab. No man could . . ."

"Precisely," said Shinbet. "I slithered down that pipe, Horn. You were so confident you even left a few prints on this." He dropped the weapon to a cushion near the tip of his tail.

Inspector Quirk addressed the two accused professors. "Well, gents, what have you got to say for yourselves?"

"You don't intend to buck the Basher Society?" asked the lizard psychiatrist.

"Done that before, old thing." He crossed to the door, jerked it open and summoned his men.

"Thanks," I said toward Shinbet. "I appreciate what—"

"How many times do I have to tell you I didn't do this for you? It was simply the problem, plus the chance to give the Basher Society another kick in the slats. You can go home now."

Keeping out of Quirk's way, I moved to the doorway. "Okay, see you later."

"Yes, I'm afraid we will be seeing each other," said Shinbet, with a hissing sigh. "Oh, and one other thing."

"Yeah, what?"

"See if you can't upgrade your romantic life."

I gave Shinbet a halfhearted salute and left his cottage. It was still raining.

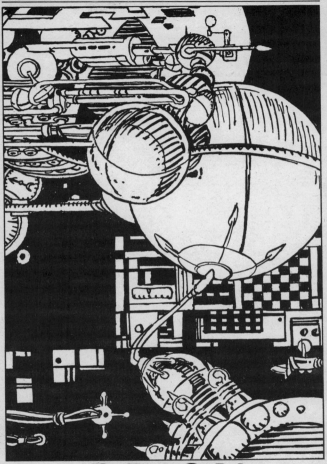

ORION

BENJAMIN BOVA • CRAIG P. RUSSELL

INTRODUCTION

Orion
by Ben Bova
Illustrated by Craig P. Russell

There's a better-than-even chance that this will be the favorite story of those of you reading this volume. Of course, I'd say that about practically *all* the features in *Weird Heroes Six*, but award-winning *Analog* Editor-in-Chief *Ben Bova* has outdone himself.

Orion is *not* the sort of piece you'd find in *Analog*. Although the "hard science" within the story is accurate and an integral part of the plot, it is far from being the focal point. Our story concerns a superman, a hero, a strange and, at first, faceless man. His name, pulled from the stars, is Orion.

Without spoiling Ben's surprises, let me say that this first element of the planned Orion series serves to lay the groundwork for an epic tale, a struggle across space with mythic and classical fantasy overtones. This is *fantasy* at its most fantastic.

Those of you unfamiliar with Ben Bova's other works are urged to run to your nearest bookseller and search out copies of *Millennium* (Random House/Del Rey Books) and *The Starcrossed* (Pyramid), the latter a funny, ficitonalized version of how a *Starlost*-type television program is put together in the future. I also recommend *The Quest of Quasars,* an NAL paperback which is a remarkably good handbook on basic cosmology.

Craig Russell, who undertakes the task of visualizing *Orion*, is no stranger to readers of Marvel Comics. His highly acclaimed work on their *War of the Worlds* and *Doctor Strange* series is known as much for its adaptation of the art nouveau line to heroic fantasy as it is for its legendary completion time. Craig has been known to labor over a single "job" for months—*years*—and *Orion* is no exception. Somewhere in New York City lies the first piece of *Orion* art, beautiful in its own right, but discarded by mutual decision with Craig as not quite appropriate for the purpose.

So here are the other four, a variety of Craig's styles, from the simple/kinetic entry shot to the Lang-lit office scene. As these go to press, Mr. Russell occupies himself with a visualization of Wagner's *Ring* cycle, surely a task of herculean proportions.

ORION
By Ben Bova

I am not a superman.

I do have abilities that are far beyond those of any normal man's, but I am just as human and mortal as anyone on Earth.

The core of my abilities is apparently due to the structure of my nervous system. I am in complete conscious control of my entire body. I can direct my will along the chain of synapses instantly to make any part of my body do exactly what I wish it to.

Last year I learned to play the piano in two hours. My teacher, a mild, gray little man, absolutely refused to believe that I had never touched a keyboard before that day. Earlier this year I stunned an akido master by learning everything he had absorbed in a lifetime of work in less than a week. He tried to be humble and polite, but it was clear to me that he was furious with me and ashamed of himself for it. I left his class.

My powers are growing. I have always been able to control my heart rate and breathing. I thought everyone could, until I began reading about yogas and their "mystical" abilities. For me, their tricks have been literally child's play.

Four months ago I found myself sitting in a midtown Manhattan restaurant. I tend to be a solitary man, and usually take my lunch hour late enough to avoid the noisy crowds. It was nearly 4:00 P.M. and the restaurant was almost empty. A few couples sitting at scattered tables, speaking in hushed tones. Waiters standing back near the kitchen. One customer sitting at the bar—a strikingly handsome, gold-maned man. Even though he was wearing a conservatively dark business suit, he looked more like a movie idol or an ancient Greek god than a Manhattan executive who was getting an early start on the cocktail hour. There was an aura about him; the air almost seemed to glow where he was sitting.

Another man entered the restaurant and sat at the opposite end of the bar. If the first one was a golden angel, this second one had the presence of a dark netherworld figure. His face was heavy and thick; his muscular body bulged his clothing, his hair, his eyes, even his voice seemed dark and heavy with anger.

I was sitting not far from the bar, finishing my coffee and starting to look for my waiter to ask for the check. That's what saved me.

At the rear of the restaurant, a bald little man in a black coat popped out of the kitchen's swinging door momentarily and threw a gray egg-shaped object up toward the bar. A hand grenade.

I saw it all as if it were happening in slow motion. I realize now that my reflexes were suddenly operating at an incredibly fast rate. Maybe it was adrenaline. Every nerve in my body went into overdrive.

I could see the man ducking back inside the kitchen. The waiters stiffening with surprise. The couples at the other tables still talking, not realizing that death was a second or two away. The bartender stared at the grenade as it sailed the length of the restaurant and thunked on the floor about five feet from my table.

The two men at the bar were as fast as I was. The golden one dived over the bar like a trained acrobat. The dark one merely ducked down behind it. I was trying to shout a warning as I slid off my chair to the floor, pulling the table over to make a shield for myself.

The clatter of the dishes hitting the floor was lost in the roar of the explosion. The room flashed and thundered. It shook. Then ... smoke, screams, the heat of flames.

I got to my feet, unharmed. The table was splintered and the wall behind me was shredded by flying shrapnel. Smoke was filling the room. Through it I could see people mangled and bleeding, laying on the floor, slumped against the walls.

I had carried two of them out to the sidewalk and was going in for a third by the time the police, firemen, and ambulances arrived. Eight people were already dead.

"Goddam IRA," a plainclothesman grumbled.

"Cheez—they tossin' bombs around here now?"

"Maybe it was the PR's," another cop suggested.

They questioned me for a few minutes, then turned me over to the medics for a quick checkup.

"You're lucky, mister," said the white-jacketed doctor. "Didn't even get your hair mussed."

I hardly paid him any attention. The important thing to me was that there was no sign of either the golden man or the dark one. They had disappeared. The bartender had been decapitated by the blast. His two customers had vanished.

Once the police let me leave, I pushed through the crowd that had been drawn by the excitement and walked back to my office. By the time I reached the corner of the street there were only the usual throngs of a late Manhattan afternoon.

As evening fell, I was still sitting in my office, wondering why the grenade was thrown and how I had escaped being killed by it. Which led me to wondering why I have such abilities, and whether those two strangers at the bar have the same powers. Which, in turn, led me to wonder who I really am and where I came from.

The externals are easy. My name is Gilbert P. O'Ryan. I realized that my name had always made me feel uneasy, as though it wasn't the proper name for me, not my real name at all. Gil O'Ryan. It didn't feel right, somehow. I am an assistant to the director of marketing for Continental Electronics Corporation, an international company that manufactures lasers and other high-technology equipment. My personnel folder says that I'm thirty-six, but I've always felt more like thirty . . .

Always?

I tried again to remember back to my thirtieth birthday, and found that I still couldn't picture it. My thirty-third birthday was clear in my mind: that was the night I spent with Adrienna, the boss's private secretary. But beyond that my memory was a blank. I frowned in concentration so hard that my jaw muscles started to ache, but still I couldn't remember anything more than three years back! No knowledge of who my parents were. No memories of childhood. I didn't even have any friends outside the small circle of acquaintances here at the office. Cold sweat broke out all over my body.

Who am I? *Why* am I?

I sat in my office for hours, as evening deepened into darkness, alone in my quiet, climate controlled, chrome-and-leather office, behind my sleek Brazilian mahogany desk, and stared at my own personnel file. There wasn't much in it. Names. Dates. Schools. None of them made any sense to me.

I looked up at the polished chrome mirror across the office. Dark hair, undistinguished face with a slight Mediterranean cast to it (but why O'Ryan, then?), medium build, light-colored jacket and slacks. The personnel file said I had been a good athlete at school. I still looked solid and trim. But totally "average." I could fade into a crowd and become invisible quite easily.

Who am I? I couldn't escape the feeling that I had been put here, placed in this life, by some power or agency that was beyond my knowledge and experience.

I had to find out who, or what, had put me here. And I

realized, with the total certainty of truly inbuilt instinct, that to try to discover my origins would mean mortal danger for me. Death. That grenade was meant for me and no one else.

But I couldn't turn back. I had to find those two other men—the angel and the dark spirit. One of them, or perhaps both of them, knew the what and why of O'Ryan.

How do you find two individual men in a city of eight millions? And what if all my certainties were wrong, and I was merely an amnesia victim, a paranoid, a madman building fantasies in his mind?

The answers to both questions were the same. It took me a sleepless night of thinking to find the single answer I needed, but I have never been much of a sleeper. An hour or two has always been sufficient for me; often I have gone several nights in a row with nothing but an occasional catnap. My fellow workers often complained, jokingly, about the amount of work I take home with me. Sometimes the jokes were bitter.

The morning after the restaurant bombing, I strode into my office exactly at nine, just as usual. I had to brush aside questions from my secretary and several of my co-workers, who had either seen the bombing on the evening TV news or were brandishing morning newspapers with my photo on the front page.

I sat at my desk and immediately called the company physician. I asked him to recommend a good psychiatrist. On the phone's small, flickering videoscreen, the doctor looked slightly alarmed, slightly puzzled.

"Is this about the blast you almost got caught in yesterday?" he asked. He had read the papers, too.

"Yes," I said. "I'm . . . feeling a little shaky about it."

Which was no lie.

He peered at me through his bifocals. "Shaky? You? The imperturbable Mr. O'Ryan?"

I said nothing.

"Hmm. Well, I suppose having a hand grenade go off in your soup would shake up anybody."

He gave me the name of a psychiatrist. I called the man and made an appointment for that afternoon. He tried to put me off, but I used the company's name and our doctor's, and told him that I only wanted a brief, preliminary talk with him.

The talk was quite brief. I outlined my lack of memory, and he quickly referred me to another psychiatrist, a woman who specialized in such problems.

It took many weeks, going from one recommended psychiatrist to another, but I finally reached the one I wanted.

He was the only specialist who agreed to see me at once, without argument, the day I phoned. His phone had no videoscreen, but I didn't need one. I knew what he looked like.

"My schedule is very full," his rich tenor voice said, "but if you could drop by around five-thirty or six o'clock, my office ought to be empty by then."

"Thank you, Doctor. I will."

His office was indeed empty. I opened the door to the anteroom of his suite, and no one was there. It was already getting dark outside, but there were no lights on in the anteroom. Gloomy and dark. Old-fashioned wood furniture. Bookshelves lining the walls. No nurse, no receptionist. No one.

A short hallway led back from the anteroom, and a glow of light came from its end. I followed the light to a partially closed heavy wooden door.

"Doctor . . . ?" I didn't bother saying the name that

was on the door. I knew it wasn't the true name of the man inside the office.

"Mr. O'Ryan," that same warm tenor voice called. "Come right in."

It was the golden man from the restaurant. The office was small and oppressively overfurnished with two couches, a massive desk, heavy window drapes, thick carpet. He sat behind the desk, smiling expectantly at me. The only light was from a small floor lamp in one corner of the room. But the man himself seemed to glow, to radiate golden light energy.

He was wearing a simple open-neck shirt. No jacket. He was broad-shouldered, handsome; he looked utterly capable of dealing with anything. His hands were clasped firmly together on the desktop. Instead of casting a shadow, they seemed to make the desktop slightly brighter.

"Sit down, Mr. O'Ryan," he said calmly.

I sat in the leather armchair that was in front of the desk.

"You said you have a problem with your memory."

"You know what my problem is," I told him. "Let's not waste time."

He arched an eyebrow and smiled more broadly.

"This isn't your office. It's nothing like you. So since you know my name, and yours isn't the one stencilled on the door, who are you?"

"Very businesslike, O'Ryan." He leaned back in the swivel chair. "You may call me Ormazd. Names don't really mean that much, you understand, but you may use that one for me."

"Ormazd."

"Yes. And now I will tell you something about your own name. You have been misusing it. Your name is Orion . . . as in the constellation of stars. Orion."

"The Hunter."

"Very good! You *do* understand. Orion the Hunter. That is your name and your mission."

"Tell me more," I said.

"There is no need to," he countered. "You already know. But much of the information stored in your brain remains blocked from your active memory."

"Why is that?"

His face grew serious, as if he were pondering, trying to make a decision. "There is much that I cannot tell you. Not yet. You were sent here on a hunting mission. Your task is to find the Dark One . . . Ahriman."

"The one who was in the restaurant with you?"

"Exactly. Ahriman."

"Why? Who sent me here? From where?"

He sat up straighter in his chair, and something of his self-assured smile returned to his lips. "Why? To save the human race from destruction. Who sent you here? Your own people. From where? From about fifty thousand years in the future."

I should have been shocked, or surprised, or at least skeptical. Instead, I heard myself saying, "My own people. And they live fifty thousand years in the future."

Ormazd nodded gravely. "That is your time. You have been sent backward in time to this so-called twentieth century."

"To save the human race from destruction."

"Yes. By finding Ahriman, the Dark One."

"And once I find him?"

For the first time, he looked surprised. "Why, you must kill him, of course."

I shook my head. "No."

"You don't believe what I have told you?"

I wished I could truthfully say that I didn't. But somehow I knew that he was speaking the truth.

"I believe it. But I don't understand it. Why can't I remember any of this? Why . . . "

"Temporal shock, perhaps," he interrupted. "Or maybe Ahriman has already reached your mind and blocked its capacities. Do you have any idea of what you can *do*?"

"Some," I said.

"Do you know the capacities of your mind? The training that you've had? Your ability to use each hemisphere of your brain independently?"

"What?"

"Are you right-handed or left-handed?"

That took me off-guard. "I've always been . . . both."

"You can write with either hand? Throw a ball with either hand, play a guitar either way?"

I nodded.

"You can also use both sides of your brain independently of each other," he said. "For example, you could run a computer with one hand and paint a landscape with the other. Simultaneously."

That sounded ridiculous. "So I could get a job in a freak circus, is that it?"

He smiled again. "Far more than that, Orion. Far more."

"What about this Ahriman?" I demanded. "What danger does he pose to the human race?"

"He seeks to destroy the entire race. He would scour the Earth clean of human life, if we allowed him to."

Strangely, my mind was accepting all this and working at it very logically. "But . . . if I actually came here from fifty thousand years in the future, that means that the human race still exists at that time. Which means that the human race was not destroyed here in the twentieth century."

"Precisely," Ormazd said. "It was not destroyed

because you saved it."

"But if I fail to?"

He stared at me for a long moment, and his aura seemed to glow brighter. He radiated light, like a miniature star. "You cannot fail to. *It has already happened*. There remains nothing for you to do but to play out your part."

"I can refuse. I can turn my back on all of this nonsense."

"You won't!" he snapped.

"How do you know?"

The light around him seemed to pulse, as if in anger. "As I told you . . . it has already happened. You have found Ahriman. You have saved the human race. It is inescapable! All that you need to do in this time era is to play out your part."

"But if I refuse?"

"That is unthinkable."

"If I refuse?" I insisted.

He glittered like a billion fireflies. His face became grim. "If you do not play out your predestined role . . . if you do not stop Ahriman . . . the very fabric of time itself will be shattered. The human race will die. All of time will be shifted to a different track, a different continuum. Perhaps the entire planet Earth will be dissolved. This whole universe of space/time could disappear—vanish —as though it had never existed."

It had the ring of truth in it.

"And if I do cooperate?"

"You will find Ahriman. You will save the human race from destruction. The time continuum will remain on its present track. The universe will continue."

"I will kill Ahriman, then?"

He hesitated a long, long time before answering. "No," he said slowly. "You will stop him. But . . . he will kill you."

"That has also already happened?"

"Yes."

Suddenly I stood bolt upright, leaned across the desk, and reached for Ormazd's arm. My hand went right through his shimmering, gleaming image.

"Fool!" he snapped. And he faded into nothingness.

I was alone in the psychiatrist's office. I had seen holographic projections before, but never one that looked so convincingly solid and real. It was the scintillations that gave it away. But even though I searched that office until dawn, I could find no lasers or other projection equipment of any kind. Nothing that could produce a hologram.

It was a wisp of memory that put me on Ahriman's trail.

By the time I returned to my own dark and quiet apartment that dawning morning, I had remembered (*remembered!*) the origin of the names the golden man had used: Ormazd, the god of light and truth; Ahriman, the god of darkness and death. They were from the ancient religion of Persia, Zoroastrianism, founded by the man the ancient Greeks called Zarathustra.

So the Golden One considered himself a god of light and goodness. Was he a time traveler? Obviously so. Was he indeed Ormazd? Did he appear to Zarathustra long eons ago in Persia? Was he struggling against Ahriman even then? Of course. Then and now, future and past, all are the same in time.

The memory that started my hunt for Ahriman was a different one, however. I sat in my apartment and watched the dawn slowly brighten the city, thinking back over every scrap of memory I could coax from my mind.

And at last it came. I knew why I had been placed in this time era, why I had come to this particular company and this exact job.

I closed my eyes and recalled Tom Dempsey's long, serious, hound-dog face. It had been at the office Christmas party last year that he had told me, a bit drunkenly, "Th' lasers, man. Those goddam big-ass ol' lasers. Most important thing th' company's doing. Most important thing goin' on in th' whole wide world!"

The lasers for the thermonuclear fusion reactor. The lasers that would power a man-made sun, which in turn would provide the permanent answer to all of the human race's energy needs. The god of light made real in a world of science and technology. Where else would the Dark One strike?

It took me nearly a week to convince my superiors that I should be assigned to the laser project. Continental Electronics was producing the lasers for the world's first CTR—Controlled Thermonuclear Reactor. By the end of the week I was on a company plane bound for Ann Arbor, Michigan, where the fusion reactor and its associated power plant had been built. Tom Dempsey was sitting beside me as we watched the early winter clouds forming along the shore of Lake Erie, some thirty thousand feet below our speeding jet.

Tom was grinning happily at me.

"First time I've seen you really take an interest in this fusion project. I always thought you couldn't care less about this work."

"You convinced me of its importance," I said, not untruthfully.

"It *is* damn important," he said, unconsciously playing with his seat belt as he spoke. Tom was the kind of engineer who kept everything neat, polished, in its place. His hands were never still.

"The fusion reactor is ready for its first test?" I led him on.

"Yep." He nodded emphatically. "You put in deuterium, which you get from ordinary water, zap it with our lasers, and out comes mucho *power*. Megawatts of power, man. More power in a bucket of water than all the oil fields in Iran."

It was a slight exaggeration, but not much of one. I had to smile at his mention of Iran—modern-day Persia.

The flight was smooth, and the company had a car waiting for us at the airport. I was surprised at the small size of the fusion lab building, but Dempsey kept telling me that CTRs could be made small enough to fit into the basements of private homes.

"No need for electric utility companies or any other kinds of utilities, then, except for water. Turn on the tap and filter out enough deuterium in five minutes to run your house for a year."

He was a happy engineer. His machines were working. The world was all right.

Except that as we came up to the front gate of the lab, we saw there were pickets marching along the wire fence. Many of them were young, students most likely. But there were plenty of older men and women who looked like teachers, housewives, and even blue-collar workers. The placards they were carrying were neatly printed:

WE DON'T WANT H-BOMBS
IN OUR BACKYARD!

PEOPLE YES! TECHNOLOGY NO!
FUSION POWER HAS TO GO!

RADIATION CAUSES CANCER

The car slowed down as we approached the gate. Our driver, a company chauffeur, said over his shoulder to Tom and me, "The lab security guards don't wanna open the gate. They're afraid the pickets will rush inside."

There were only a couple of dozen of them, but as we got closer to the gate they seemed like a larger mob. They crowded around the car so that we couldn't move and shouted at us:

"Go back where you came from!"

"Stop poisoning us!"

In a flash they were all chanting their "People yes! Technology no!" slogan and pounding the car with their fists and placards.

"Where are the police?" I asked the driver.

He merely shrugged.

"Shit on this," Dempsey snapped. "I'm not gonna let a bunch of punk kids keep me out of the lab."

Before I thought to stop him, he pushed open the car door on his side and got out, shouting, "Get the hell out of our way! Go on, get lost! There's nothing for you to be afraid of. Get out of here!"

The demonstrators wouldn't move. Dempsey shoved one of them, a frail-looking boy who seemed no older than high school age. An older one, football-player size, pushed Dempsey against the side of the car.

I began to get out as Dempsey grappled with the football player. The driver opened his door suddenly and hit somebody hard enough to make him or her scream with pain. Someone else swung a fist at me. I blocked it automatically, while out of the corner of my eye I saw a girl crack Dempsey on the head with the corner of the placard she was holding. He went face down on the grimy pavement. The chauffeur grabbed at the girl's placard. She yelled and tried to squirm out of his reach. Another guy socked the chauffeur and suddenly a half-dozen angry young men were yelling at me.

"Let's teach 'em a lesson!"

They tried to pin me against the side of the car. I moved sideways to straddle Dempsey's body. I could see a thin trickle of blood coming from his scalp.

I took a punch on the side of the face. Before the youngster could pull his arm back I had him by the wrist and elbow. I flung him against the others, lifting him off his feet and knocking them down like tenpins. With two short steps I was on the goons beating the chauffeur. Everything happened very quickly. Suddenly they were gone, except for the five on the ground with various concussions and fractures. The rest of them were running down the street.

In the lab's infirmary I spoke with the security chief, a waspish little man named Mangino, whose skin was the color of cigarette tobacco.

"I don't understand it," he muttered, as Dempsey's head was being bandaged. "We never had a speck of trouble until today. This bunch of nuts just pops outta nowhere and starts parading up and down in front of the main gate."

They were meant for me, I knew. But I said nothing.

"Our public relations people have been telling everybody that this reactor isn't like the old fission power plants. There's no radioactive waste. No radiation at all gets outside of the reactor shell. And it can't explode."

Dempsey, tight-lipped, said, "You can't talk sense to those people. They get themselves all worked up and they don't want to listen to facts."

"No," I corrected him. "They don't get themselves all worked up. Somebody works them up."

They stared at me.

"And I think it might be a good idea if we found out who—and what—that someone is."

Mangino said, "I guess so. It could be Arabs, or oil companies, or any one of a dozen nut groups."

Or, I added silently, *Ahriman*.

It wasn't difficult to find the local headquarters of the demonstrators. It was an organization that called itself STOPP, an acronym for Stop Technology from Over Powering People.

STOPP's headquarters was an old four-story frame house across the main avenue from the university campus. I parked my rented car in front of the house and sat watching for a while. Plenty of students walking by; more congregating around the pizza and fast-food shop on the corner of the street. This side of the avenue was strictly urban: houses and shops packed side by side, right down the street for block after block. Across the avenue was the campus: tall green hedges, trees reaching bare branches toward the gray, early winter sky, big, brooding stone buildings set off by spacious lawns and walkways.

And all the noise of city traffic honking, growling, clattering along the main thoroughfare itself. Trucks, cars, buses, motorcycles, even a few electrically powered bikes.

I got out of the car and decided the best approach was the direct one. I walked up the wooden steps and across the porch that fronted the house, pushed the antique, rusting bell button, opened the front door, and stepped in.

The outside of the house looked Victorian, turn-of-the-century, Middle American tasteless. Inside, it was decorated in late Student Activist style. Yellowing posters covered most of the walls in the front hallway. A library table was heaped high with pamphlets. I glanced at them; none of them mentioned the fusion laboratory.

Doors were open on the right and left of the hallway. I looked left first, but the big, high-ceilinged room was devoid of people. A couple of old sofas, three tattered army cots, a big square table with a typewriter on it. But no people.

I tried the room on the right. A bright-looking young woman was sitting behind an ultramodern portable phone switchboard, which rested incongruously on a heavy-legged Victorian mahogany table. The girl had an earphone-and-pin-mike arrangement clamped over her short-clipped blonde hair. Without breaking the conversation into the microphone, she waved me into the room and pointed to one of the frail plastic chairs that lined the wall.

I sat and waited while she finished her conversation and switched off. Their phones had no videoscreens.

"Welcome to STOPP," she said cheerfully. "What can we do for you, Mr. . . . er?"

"Orion," I said. "I want to see the chief of this organization."

Her pert young smile clouded over. "You from the City? Fire Marshall?"

"No. I'm from the CTR facility. The fusion lab."

"Oh!" That took her by surprise. The enemy in her boudoir.

"I want to see the head person around here."

"Don Maddox? He's in class right now."

"Not him. The one he works for."

She looked puzzled. "But Don's the chairperson. He organized STOPP. He's the . . ."

"Is he the one who decided to demonstrate against the fusion lab?"

"Yes . . . " It was an uncertain answer.

"I want to know who put him up to it."

"Now wait a minute, mister . . . " Her hands began

fidgeting along the switchboard buttons. A barely discernible sheen of perspiration had broken out along her upper lip. Her breathing was slightly faster than it had been a moment earlier. A very highly trained interrogator might have noticed these reactions of fear. I recognized them immediately.

"All right then," I said easily. "Who first suggested demonstrating at the fusion lab? It wasn't one of the students, I know that."

"Oh, you mean Mr. Davis." She sat up straighter; her voice took on a ring of conviction. "He's the one who woke us up about your fusion experiments, and all that propaganda you people have been handing us!"

There was no point in arguing with her. Davis. I smiled inwardly. With just a slight change in pronunciation I came up with *Daevas*, the gods of evil in the old Zoroastrian religion.

"Mr. Davis," I agreed. "He's the one I want to see."

She was instantly suspicious. "Why? You trying to arrest him or something?"

I had to grin at her naivete. "If I were, would I tell you? No one got arrested at the lab this morning, did they?"

Shaking her head, she said, "From what I heard, they had a platoon of Sonny Chibas out there breaking heads."

"Whatever. I'd still like to see Davis. Is he here?"

"No." I could easily see that it was a lie. "He won't be around for a while . . . maybe tonight. I don't know."

With a shrug I said, "All right. Try to get in touch with him. Tell him Orion wants to see him. Right away."

"Mr. O'Ryan?"

"Orion. Just plain Orion. I'll be waiting in my car outside. It's parked right in front of the house."

She frowned. "He might not be back for a long while.

Maybe not even tonight."

"You just try to contact him and give him my name. I'll wait."

"Okay," she said in that tone that implied *"but I think you're crazy."*

I waited in the car less than an hour. It was a cold, gray afternoon, but I adjusted easily enough to it. Clamp down on the peripheral blood vessels, so the body heat isn't radiated away so fast. Step up the metabolic rate a bit, so that some of the fat stored in the body's tissues gets burned off. This keeps the body temperature up despite the growing cold. I could have done the same thing by going to the corner and getting something to eat, but this was easier and I didn't want to leave the car. I did begin to get hungry after half an hour. As I said, I'm no superman.

The blonde girl came out on the porch, shivering in the cold. She had thrown a light sweater over her shoulders. She stared at my car. I got out and she nodded to me, then ducked back inside.

I followed her into the house. She was waiting in the hallway, her arms clamped tight across her body.

"It's really cold out there," she said, rubbing her arms. "And you don't even have an overcoat!"

"Did you reach Mr. Davis?" I asked.

Nodding, she replied, "Yes. He . . . came in through the back way. Down at the end of the hall. He's waiting for you."

I thanked her and walked to the door at the end of the hall. It opened onto a flight of steps leading down to the cellar of the house. *Logical place for him*, I thought, wondering how many legends of darkness and evil he had inspired over the span of eons.

It was dark in the cellar. The only light came from the hallway, at the top of the stairs. I could make out a bulky, squat, old-fashioned heater, spreading its pipes up and outward like a metal medusa. Boxes, packing crates, odd-shaped things hugged the shadows.

I took a few tentative steps into the dimness at the bottom of the stairs and stopped.

"Over here." The voice was a harsh whisper.

Turning slightly, I saw him, a darker presence among the shadows. He was big: not much taller than I, but very broad. Heavy, sloping shoulders; thick, solid body; arms bulging with muscle.

I walked toward him. I couldn't see his face, the shadows were too deep for that. He turned and led me back toward the heater. I ducked under one of the pipes . . .

And was suddenly in a brightly lit room! I squinted and staggered back half a step, only to bump against a solid wall behind me. The room was warmly carpeted, paneled in rich woods, furnished with comfortable chairs and couches. There were no windows. No decorations on the walls. *And no doors*.

"Make yourself comfortable, Orion," he said, gesturing to one of the couches. His hand was thick-fingered, blunt and heavy.

I sat down and studied him as he slowly eased his bulk into a soft leather reclining chair.

His face was not quite human. Close enough so that you wouldn't look twice at him on the street, but when you examined him carefully you saw that the cheekbones were too widely spaced, the nose was too flat, the eyes a reddish color. His hair was gray and cropped so close to his broad, flat skull that he almost looked bald. His chin sloped and quickly vanished into a bulllike neck.

But it was the color of his skin that startled me most. It

was gray. Not black or any mixture of negroid. Gray. Almost like the color of an elephant's skin. The color of ashes.

"You are Ahriman," I said at last.

He almost smiled. "You don't remember me, of course. We have not met before." His voice was a whisper, like a ghost's, or an asthmatic's tortured gasping.

"We have?"

With a slow nod, "Yes. But we are moving in different directions through time. You are moving back toward the War; I am moving forward toward the End."

The War? The End? But I said nothing.

"Back and forward are relative terms in time travel, you understand. But the truth is, we have met before. You will come to those places in time and remember that I told you of it."

"You're trying to destroy the fusion reactor," I said.

This time he did not smile. It was not a pleasant thing to see. "I am trying to destroy your entire race."

"I'm here to stop you."

"You may succeed."

"Ormazd says that I will . . . that I *already have* succeeded." I didn't mention the part about being killed. Somehow, I couldn't.

"Ormazd knows many things," Ahriman said, "and he tells you only a few of them. He knows, for example, that if I prevent you from stopping me this time . . ."

This time? Then there have been other times!

" . . . then not only will I destroy your entire race of people, I will smash the time continuum and annihilate Ormazd himself."

"And demolish this whole planet," I added.

"Phfft! This one planet? I will bring down the pillars of the universe. *Everything* will die. The whole space/time continuum will come crumbling down. Stars, planets, galaxies . . . everything." He clenched his massive fists.

He believed it. He was making *me* believe it.

"But why? Why do you want to . . . "

He silenced me with a gesture. "You will find out. You will learn. But not now. Not here. Not this time."

I tried to see past his words, but my mind struck an utterly blank wall.

"I will tell you this much," Ahriman whispered. "This fusion reactor of yours is the third nexus in your race's development. If you make the fusion process work, you will be expanding out to the stars within a generation. *I will not allow you to accomplish that.*"

"I don't understand."

"How could you?" He leaned closer to me, and seemed almost glad of the chance to explain it to someone, as if he'd been alone for eons and needed a companion, a listener, even if it was an enemy.

"This fusion machine—this CTR, as you call it—is the key to your race's future. If it is successful, within ten years fusion power plants will be supplying energy everywhere on Earth. The fuel comes from the sea. The energy is limitless. Your people could stop playing with their puny chemical rockets and start building real starships. They could expand throughout the galaxy."

"They *have* done so," I realized.

"Yes they have. But if I can change the nexus here, at this point in time . . . if I can destroy that fusion reactor . . . He smiled again.

I shook my head. "I don't see how one machine's failure can kill the whole human race."

"It is simple, thanks to the inherent manic nature of your race's mentality. The fusion reactor explodes . . . "

"It can't explode!" I snapped.

"Of course not. Under ordinary circumstances. But I

do have access to extraordinary means, you must realize. I can create a sudden surge of power from the lasers, strong enough to detonate the lithium shielding that surrounds the reactor's ignition chamber. Instead of a microgram of deuterium being fused and giving off its energy, a quarter-ton of lithium and heavier metals will explode."

"That can't . . ."

"Instead of a tiny, controlled, man-made star radiating energy in a manageable flow, I will create an artificial supernova, a lithium bomb. The explosion will destroy Ann Arbor totally. The fallout will kill millions of people from Detroit to New York."

I sagged back, stunned.

"Your people will immediately react against the very idea of fusion power. Their reaction against the uranium and plutonium fission power plants will be as child's play compared to this. Their reaction will be swift, violent, and total. There will be an end to all nuclear research everywhere. You will never get fusion power. Never."

"But even so, that won't kill off everyone."

"Not at once. But I have all the time in the world to work with. As the next few years go by, your increasing energy needs will go unmet. Your mighty nations will continue to struggle against each other for the possession of petroleum, of coal, of food resources. There will be war, inevitably. And for war, you have fusion devices that *do* work—H-bombs."

"Armageddon," I said.

He nodded triumphantly. "At the time when you should be expanding outward toward the stars, you will destroy yourselves with nuclear war. Your planet will be scoured clean of life. The fabric of time itself will be so twisted that the entire universe will collapse and die. Armageddon indeed."

I wanted to stab him, to silence him. I grabbed for his arm. It was real enough: strong and alive. But he easily pulled away and got to his feet.

"Despite what Ormazd has told you, I will succeed in this. You will fail. You are trapped here, and will remain here while I destroy your precious CTR."

"But why?" I asked, my voice pleading—not so much in fear as in desperate curiosity. "Why do you want to wipe out the human race?"

He stood a moment, staring at me. "You really don't know, do you? They never told you . . . or they erased your memory of it."

"I don't know," I said. "Why do you hate the human race?"

"Because you wiped out *my* race," Ahriman replied. "Your people killed mine. You annihilated my entire species. I am the only one of my kind left alive. And I will avenge my race by destroying yours—and your masters, as well."

The strength left me. I sat weakly on the couch, unable to challenge him, unable to move.

"And now good-bye," Ahriman said. "I have much to do before the first test run of your fusion reactor. You will remain here . . . " He gestured around the tiny room. It had no windows or doors. No exits or entrances of any kind. *How did we get in here?* I wondered.

"You will be comfortable enough in here," he went on. "If I succeed, it will all be over in a few hours. Time itself will stop and the universe will fall in on itself like a collapsing balloon. If I fail, well . . . " that ghastly smile again, . . . you will spend the rest of your life in this room. It will not be long, I promise you. The air will give out long before you starve."

"The air will give out? We're in space, in a satellite?"

"Hardly," he answered. "We are thirty miles underground, in a temporary bubble of safety and comfort created by warping the energies of the atoms around us. Think about it as you suffocate—you are only a step away from the house in Ann Arbor. One small step for a man . . . if he truly understands the way the universe is constructed."

He turned abruptly and walked *through* the wall and disappeared.

For long minutes I sat on the couch, unmoving, my body numb with shock, my brain spinning in turmoil.

You wiped out my race . . . your people killed mine . . . and I will avenge my race by destroying yours—and your masters, as well.

It couldn't be true. And what did he mean by all that talk about him and me moving on different time tracks, of having met each other before. *Our masters?* What did he mean by that? Ormazd? But he said *masters,* plural. Is Ormazd a representative of a different race, an alien race from another world that controls all of humankind? Just as Ahriman is the last survivor of an alien race that we humans battled so long ago?

How many times had we met before? Ahriman said that this point in time, this first test of the fusion reactor, marked a nexus for the human race. If it succeeded, we would use fusion energy to reach out to the stars. If it failed, we would kill ourselves within a generation. There must have been other nexuses back through time: the discovery of electricity, perhaps; Columbus's voyages; the invention of steel tools; the discovery of language; agriculture; the taming of fire.

Somewhere back along those eons there was a war, The War, between the human race and Ahriman's kind. When? Why? How could we fight invaders from another world back thousands of years ago?

All these thoughts were bubbling through my brain until finally my body asserted itself on my consciousness.

"It's getting hot in here," I said aloud.

My attention snapped to the present. To this tiny room. The air was hot and dry. The room was now hot enough to make me sweat.

I got up and felt the nearest wall. It was almost too hot to touch. And although it looked like wood paneling, it felt like stone. It was an illusion, all of it.

One small step for a man . . . if he truly understands the way the universe is constructed.

I understood nothing. I could remember nothing. All I could think of was that Ahriman was back on the Earth's surface, in Ann Arbor, working to turn the CTR test run into a mammoth lithium bomb that would eventually destroy the entire human race. And I was trapped here, thirty miles underground.

You are only a step away from the house in Ann Arbor, he had said.

"One small step for a man," I muttered. How *is* the universe constructed? It's made of atoms, I answered myself. And atoms are made of smaller particles. These particles are made of energy, tiny bits of frozen energy that can be made to thaw and flow and surge . . .

This room was created by warping the energies of the atoms in the Earth's crust. Those energies were now reverting back to their original form; slowly the room was turning back into hot, solid rock. I could feel the air congealing, getting hotter and thicker by the second. I would be embedded in rock, thirty miles below the surface; rock hot enough to be almost molten.

Yet I was only a step from safety, according to Ahriman. Was he lying? No, he couldn't have been. *He* walked directly through the rock wall of this room. He must have returned to the cellar of the house in Ann Arbor. If he could do it, so could I. But how?

I already had!

I had stepped from the cellar into this underground dungeon. Why couldn't I step back again?

I tried doing it and got nothing but bumps against hot solid rock for my efforts. There was more to it than simply trying it.

But wait. If I had truly traveled thirty miles through solid rock in a single step, it must mean that there is a connection between that house and this room. Not only are the atoms of the Earth's crust being warped to create this room, but the geometry of space itself is being warped, to bridge a thirty-mile distance by a human step.

I sat down on the couch again, my mind racing. I had read stories about space warps, where futuristic starships could cover thousands of light-years of distance almost instantaneously. And astrophysics had discovered "black holes" that warped space with their titanic gravitational fields. It was all a matter of geometry, a pattern, like taking a flat sheet of paper and folding it into the form of a bird or a star.

And I had seen that pattern, I had gone through it, on my way into this room. But it all happened so quickly that I couldn't remember it in detail.

Or could I?

Data compression. Satellites in orbit can accumulate data on magnetic tapes for days on end, and then spurt it all down to a receiving station in a few seconds, on command from the ground. The compressed data is played out at a lower speed by the technicians, and all the many days' worth of information is intact and usable.

Could I slow down my memories to the point where I could recall, microsecond by microsecond, what happened to me during that one brief stride from the house to this underground burial chamber? I leaned back in the couch and closed my eyes.

A thirty-mile stride. A step through solid rock. I pictured myself in the cellar of that house. I had ducked under a heating pipe and stepped into darkness . . .

And cold. The first instants of my step I had felt a wave of intense cold, as if I had passed through a curtain of liquefied air. Cryogenic cold. The kind that physicists use to make superconducting magnets of enormous field strength.

In those few microseconds of unbearable cold I saw that the crystal structure of the atoms around me had been frozen, almost utterly stopped. Nearly all the energy of those atoms had been frozen down into stillness, close to absolute zero temperature.

All around me the atoms glowed dully like pinpoints of jeweled lights, but sullen and almost dark because nearly all their energies had been leached away from them. The crystal latticework of the atoms formed a path for me, a tunnel, as my body moved in slow motion in that one thirty-mile-long step through the darkness of a place where space and time had been frozen, suspended, warped out of their natural flow and shape.

I opened my eyes. The tiny room was glowing now, the walls themselves were radiating heat. It was difficult t to breathe. But I understood how I had gotten there.

There was a crystal lattice of energy connecting this room with the house in Ann Arbor. A tunnel that connected *here* with *there*, using the energies stolen from the atoms in between to create a safe and almost instantaneous path between the two places. But the tunnel was dissolving just as this room was dissolving; the energies of those tortured atoms were returning to normal. In minutes, all would be solid rock once again.

I understood now the connection, the tunnel. But how to find the opening? I concentrated again, but no sense of it came through to me. I was sweating, both from the heat and from the effort of forcing myself to understand. But it did no good at all. My brain could not comprehend it.

My brain could not . . . *Wrong!* I realized that so far I had been using only half my brain to attack the problem.

Every human brain is divided into two hemispheres, left and right. I remembered Ormazd telling me that I could use both halves simultaneously, something that most humans cannot do. So far, I had been using one half of my brain to see the geometrical patterns of the energy warp that connected my underground chamber with the Earth's surface.

But this half of my brain could *only* perceive geometrical problems, relationships involving space and form.

With a conscious effort, I forced the other half of my brain to consider the problem. I could almost hear myself laugh, inside my head, as the unused portion of my mind said something like, "Well, it's about time."

And it *was* about time. The solution to the problem of how to find the gateway to the crystal latticework of atoms was a matter of timing. All those dully glowing atoms were still vibrating: slowly, unnaturally slowly, because most of their energies had been drawn from them. But still they vibrated, and only when they were all in precisely the exact positions was their alignment such that the tunnel's entrance could open. Most of the time they were shifted out of phase, as unaligned and mixed-up as a crowd milling through a shopping mall. But once every minute or so they reached precisely the right arrangement necessary to form the tunnel that led back to safety. Like a swarm of meandering ants that suddenly arrange themselves into an exact battle formation, the atoms would "get together" for a bare microsecond or two to form the tunnel I needed.

Only during those incredibly tiny moments of time was

the tunnel open. I had to step into the crystal lattice-work, through the searing hot wall of the room, at the exact moment—or not at all.

I stood and forced myself close to the wall. The heat was enough to curl the hair of my eyebrows and the backs of my hands. I kept my eyes closed, simultaneously picturing, with one side of my brain, the crystal pathway itself, while calculating with the other side of my brain the precise moment when the lattice would be open for me to step through.

With my eyes still closed I took a step forward. I felt an instant of roasting heat, then cold beyond the most frigid ice fields of Antarctica. Then nothing.

I opened my eyes. I stood in the cellar of the STOPP house. For the first time in what seemed like years, I let out my breath.

I found a back door to the cellar and stepped out into the cold night air. It felt beautiful. There was an alleyway between the house and its next-door neighbor, leading to the street. My car was still parked out there, adorned with a yellow parking ticket affixed to the windshield wiper. I stuffed the ticket into my pocket and got behind the wheel. I was glad that no one had towed the car away or stolen it.

It took me twenty minutes to get back to the fusion lab. I didn't even think about speed limits or highway police. Once in the deserted lobby of the building I phoned for Tom Dempsey, Mangino the security chief and the lab's director of research. It was close to midnight, but the tone of my voice must have convinced them that something important was happening. I got no arguments from any of them, although the phone's computer system had to try three different numbers before it located Dr. Wilson, the research director.

They all arrived in the lab within a half-hour; thirty

minutes during which I checked with every security guard on duty. No one had reported any problems at all. They were on constant patrol around the entire laboratory, inside and out, and everything seemed quiet and normal.

Dr. Wilson was a lanky, long-faced Englishman who spoke quietly and seemed completely unflappable. He arrived first, but as I was explaining that someone might try to detonate the fusion reactor—and he was smiling patiently and saying it was totally impossible—Dempsey and the security chief came into the lobby together.

Dempsey looked more puzzled than angry, his dark hair an uncombed tangled mess. He must have been asleep when I called and had merely pulled on his clothes helter-skelter. Mangino was definitely angry; his deep-set brown eyes snapped at me.

"This is a lot of hysterical nonsense," he said as I repeated my fears. I didn't tell them about Ormazd and Ahriman, of course; nor about the underground chamber I'd just escaped from. It was enough to convince them that a real danger existed. I didn't want them to bundle me off to a psychiatric ward.

Dr. Wilson tried to explain to me that the reactor simply could not be turned into a bomb. I let him talk; the longer he explained, the longer we stayed on the scene, available to counter Ahriman's move.

"There simply isn't enough deuterium in the reactor at any given moment to allow an explosion," Dr. Wilson said in his soft, friendly voice. He was slouched on one of the plastic couches that decorated the lab's lobby. I was leaning against the receptionist's desk. Dempsey had stretched out on another couch and apparently gone back to sleep. Mangino was behind the desk, checking out his security patrols on the videophone.

"But suppose," I stalled for more time, "there was a way to boost the power of the lasers . . ."

"They'd burn out in a minute or two," Dr. Wilson said. "We're running them at almost top capacity now."

". . . and an extra amount of deuterium was shot into the reaction chamber," I went on.

Dr. Wilson shook his head. "That can't happen. There are fail-safe circuits to prevent it. Besides, even so, all that would happen is that you'd get a mild little *poof* of a detonation—not a hydrogen bomb."

"What about a lithium bomb?" I asked.

For the first time, his brows knit worriedly. "What do you mean?"

"If things worked out the right way, couldn't that *poof* of a detonation trigger the lithium in the shielding around the reactor chamber? And wouldn't the lithium go off . . . ?"

"No, no. That would be imposs . . . that would be very unlikely. *Very* unlikely. I'd have to work out the calculations, of course, but the chances against it are . . ."

"Forty-four, *report*." Mangino's voice broke into our conversation.

I turned and looked at the security chief. He was frowning angrily. " dammit, forty-four, answer me!"

He looked up at me, eyes blazing. As if I were responsible. "One of those outside guards doesn't answer. Patrolling the area around the loading dock."

"Good grief!" Wilson was on his feet. I could sense his body trembling. "The loading dock . . ."

Mangino held up a hand. "Don't get excited, Doc. I've got the area on one of the outside TV cameras. Everything looks normal. Just no sign of the guard. He might be sneaking a smoke somewhere . . ."

I went around the desk and peered at the TV screen. The loading dock area was brightly lit. There were no cars or trucks anywhere in sight. All looked quiet and calm.

Just the same, "Let's take a walk down there," I said.

We roused Dempsey and told him to stand guard over the phones and TV screens. He rubbed his eyes sleepily and nodded okay. Then Dr. Wilson, Mangino, and I hurried down the building's central corridor toward the loading dock. Mangino reached inside his coat and pulled out a slim, flat, dead-black pistol. He hefted it once as we quick-stepped down the corridor, then slipped it into a hip pocket.

Lights turned on automatically ahead of us as we hurried along the corridor, and switched off behind us. The loading area looked like a miniature warehouse. stacked cardboard cartons, steel drums, all sorts of exotic-looking equipment wrapped in clear plastic.

"You could hide a platoon of men in here," Mangino grumbled.

"But everything seems to be in order," said Dr. Wilson, looking around.

I started to agree, but felt the slightest trace of a breeze on my face. It was coming from the direction of the loading dock doors, big metal roll-up doors that were shut and locked. Or were they?

I walked slowly toward the doors and saw a man-sized doorway that had been cut into one of them. A single person could slip in or out without raising and lowering the big doors. This smaller door was windowless and tightly shut. I reached for it.

"It's locked," Mangino said. "Electronic lock . . . if anybody tried tampering with it . . ."

I pulled the door handle and it swung open effortlessly. Mangino gaped.

Kneeling, I saw that the area around the edge of the lock had been bent slightly, as if massive hands had pried it open, bending the metal until it yielded and opened. The slight breeze I had felt came through the bent area after the door had been carefully closed again.

"Why didn't the electronic alarm go off?" Mangino wondered out loud.

"Never mind that," I said. "He's inside the lab! Quick, we don't have any time to lose!"

We ran to the fusion reactor area, Wilson protesting breathlessly all the way that no one could tamper with the lasers on the reactor in any way that could cause an explosion.

We skidded to a clattering halt in front of the doors to the laser control room. They should have been shut. They were open. A quick look inside showed us that no one was there. The control boards seemed untouched.

Mangino was yelling into his palm-sized radio, "All security guards, converge on the fusion reactor area. Apprehend anyone you see. Shoot if he resists. Call the police and the FBI, at once!"

We entered the big double doors that led into the long, cement-walled room where the lasers were housed. Again, the overhead lights snapped on automatically as soon as we crossed the doorway.

"Those doors should have been closed, too," Dr. Wilson said. "And locked."

The lasers were long, thin glass rods, dozens of them, mounted on heavy metal benches, one behind the other, like a series of railway cars. In between each pair of lasers were lenses, Faraday rotators, all sorts of sensors. The double line of lasers marched down the room for nearly fifty feet and focused on a narrow slit cut into a five-foot-thick cement and steel wall at the far end of the chamber. Beyond that slit was the reactor itself, where the deuterium pellets received the energy from the lasers.

The three of us stood there uncertainly for a moment. Then the lasers began to glow greenish, and an electrical hum vibrated through the air.

"They're turning on!" Dr. Wilson shouted.

Mangino and I swung our attention to the far end of the room, where the control section was. In the shadows up there, behind the thick protective-glass window, bulked the heavy dark form of Ahriman.

Mangino pulled out his gun and fired. The glass starred. He fired again and again. The glass shattered, but by then Ahriman was gone.

The lights went out. All we could see was the green glow of the lasers, twin paths of intense green light aiming at the slit. And beyond that was the reactor.

We stumbled out into the hallway. It was dark everywhere. From somewhere far off I could hear running footsteps. Then shots.

"They've got him!" Mangino yelled. But to me it sounded as if the running and shooting was going in the direction away from us. The shots grew fainter. As long as they continued, they didn't have Ahriman, I knew.

"I'm going after him," said Mangino, and he moved off into the darkness.

"We've got to stop the lasers," I said to Dr. Wilson, "before they build up enough power to detonate the lithium."

"I told you that can't happen!" he insisted.

"Let's stop them anyway." With that he didn't argue.

But the laser control room was now in a shambles. In the eerie green light of the lasers themselves, we could see that the control panels had been smashed, dials shattered, metal paneling bent out of shape. Wires sagged limply from broken consoles. It was as if an elephant had gone berserk in the tiny room.

Wilson's jaw hung slackly. "How could anyone . . ."

The electrical whine of the lasers suddenly went up in pitch several notches. The lasers glowed more fiercely. I heard a glass lens pop somewhere down on the floor of the laser room.

I pulled Wilson out of the control room and we stumbled down the darkened hallway toward the reactor chamber.

"How do we turn the darned thing off?" I shouted into his ear.

He seemed dazed, bewildered. "The deuterium feed . . ."

"That's been jury-rigged and smashed, too, I'll bet. We won't be able to turn it off any more than we can turn off the lasers."

I could sense him shaking his head in the shadows as we stumbled to a step in front of the reactor room.

"Main power supplies," he mumbled. "I could get to the main power switches and shut down everything . . ."

"Okay! Do it!"

"But . . . it'll take time . . . five, ten minutes at least."

"Too long! By then it'll be too late. She'll blow up in another minute or so."

"I know."

"What else can we do?"

"Nothing."

"I don't believe it! There must be *something* . . ."

"Damper," he muttered. "If we could place a damper between the deuterium and the lithium shielding . . ."

I knew enough about the fusion reactor to understand what he meant.

The deuterium fuel for the fusion reaction was in tiny lexan pellets that dropped out of a tube like water droplets leak from a faucet. Ordinarily the pellets dropped one at a time, once a second. And the laser pulses were timed to flash exactly when the pellets were at the focal point of the laser beams. The laser energy smashed the pellets flat; the deuterium was squeezed and instantly heated to the hundred-million-degree temperature where

fusion processes take place. Energy came out—some of the energy was heat; most of it was fast, deadly neutrons, subatomic particles that could kill a man very quickly if they ever got outside the five-foot-thick shielding around the reactor.

Under ordinary circumstances, the neutrons impacted against the inner wall of the reactor chamber, which consisted of hundreds of pipes carrying liquefied lithium. The neutrons transmuted the lithium into more deuterium, providing fresh fuel for the reactor. The lithium absorbed the neutrons and made the outside of the reactor completely safe.

Under ordinary circumstances.

What was happening now, though, was that the deuterium pellets were being forced into the reactor at an insanely fast rate, and the lasers had been jury-rigged to zap them just as fast as they entered the reactor. Thousands of times more neutrons were boiling off the deuterium pellets and hitting the lithium; within a minute or less, the lithium would be energized to the point where it would explode.

How many megatons of energy would be released in that explosion? Enough, I knew, to destroy much of the human race.

We needed a damper, some sort of material that could be inserted between the deuterium pellets and the lithium pipes. Or better yet, something that could block off the incoming laser energy.

"A damper," I snapped at Wilson. "Okay . . . you find the main power switches. I'll find a damper."

"But there's nothing . . ."

"Get moving!" I commanded.

"You can't get anything in there without going inside the reactor itself! That'll kill you!"

"Go!"

I pushed him away from me. He staggered off, then hesitated as I yanked open the door to the reactor room.

"For God's sake . . . don't . . .!" Wilson screamed.

I ignored him and stepped inside.

The high-ceilinged room was bathed in the greenish light from the lasers. In its center was the round metal reactor already beginning to glow a deep red. It looked like a bathysphere, but it had no portholes in it. There was no way to interrupt the laser beams from the outside; they were linked to the reactor chamber by a thick quartz light pipe. I couldn't break it, even if I had the time to try.

There was only one hatch in the metal sphere. I yanked it open and was literally pushed back by the overwhelming intensity of light and heat blazing inside. A manmade star was running amok in there, getting ready to explode.

My burning eyes squeezed shut, I grabbed the hot edges of the metal hatch and forced myself inside the chamber. I flung my body in front of the laser beams.

I knew then what hell is like.

Pain. Searing agony that blasts into your skull even though your eyes have been burned away. Agony along every nerve, every synapse, every pathway of your entire body and brain.

All the memories of my mind stirred into frantic life. Past and present and future. I saw them all in that instant, that never-ending infinitesimal flash of time.

I stood flayed and naked and burning as my mind saw tomorrows and yesterdays.

Newspaper headlines blaring ATTEMPT TO SABOTAGE FUSION LAB FAILS.

Puzzled FBI agents searching for some trace of my body as Dr. Wilson is wheeled into an ambulance, catatonic with shock.

Ahriman's presence looming over my horizon of time,

brooding, planning vengeance.

Ormazd shining against the darkness of space itself.

And me. Orion the Hunter. I see all my pasts and futures. At last I know who I am, and what, and why.

I am Orion. I am Zeus. I am Krishna. I am Zarathustra. I am the Phoenix who dies and is consumed and rises again from his own ashes, only to die once more. The never-ending agony of life and death and renewal.

From fifty thousand years in Earth's future I have hunted Ahriman. This time he escaped me, even though I thwarted his vengeance. Humankind will have fusion power. We will attain the stars. That nexus has been passed successfully, just as Ormazd told me. It required my death, but the fabric of time and the continuum has not been broken.

I have died. And I live. I exist, and my purpose is to hunt down Ahriman, wherever and whenever he is.

I will live again.

AFTERWORD

Orion was written as a self-inflicted challenge, on many levels.

First, it is an attempt to write a story that captures the flavor and sense of wonder of the earliest types of science fiction—while still keeping the technical accuracy and writing style of modern sf. Second, both the protagonist and the author are engaged in an odyssey through time; Orion doesn't know where he is going to end up, and neither do I. Most stories are written with at least a general idea of how the ending will go. This enables the author to keep the story in line. But Orion's story is open-ended. His adventures will depend on how he develops as a character in future installments, and how the characters around him develop. Finally, if all goes well, this series of stories should link up thematically with the threads I developed in earlier novels, such as *As On a Darkling Plain*.

So, in a very real sense, *Orion* is an adventure—for the writer as well as the reader.

Ben Bova
Manhattan
November 1976

(Author's note: All references to the laser-fusion energy system and the Controlled Thermonuclear Reactor (CTR) in this story are based on fact. The first successful laser-fusion laboratory reaction took place in 1974, at the KMS Fusion, Inc., laboratory in Ann Arbor, Mich.)

HAMILTON

THE EDMOND HAMILTON PAPERS

INTRODUCTION

Fifty Years of Heroes
The Edmond Hamilton Papers
A Memoir
with supplementary material
by Julius Schwartz, Forrest Ackerman
and Robert Bloch
Illustrations by Alex Nino

When, in the spring of '76, Edmond Hamilton wrote to me saying that he would be willing to pen a 6,000 or so word memoir for inclusion in *Weird Heroes*, I was delighted. Hamilton had not only written some of the best heroic fiction to emerge in the pulps, but he was also the man responsible for a healthy share of the most literate, interesting and memorable comics stories to appear in America in the 1940's and 1950's. This was ideally suited for our readers' experience.

Those of you who are new to the field may not immediately recognize the stories and authors who Ed mentions in his article. Haimlton himself, however, has probably occupied your time somewhere along the line with his tales of world-saving, fantasy and adventure. His *Star Kings*, still in print from Warner Books, is one of a select list of 'classic' s.f. heroic novels which still elicit respect from the ever-changing list of current s.f. luminaries. His *Captain Future* was the prototypical space adventurer, cut from the same cloth as Flash Gordon and Buck Rogers and written with panache and intelligence that put it in many readers' minds above the others.

When the following piece had reached its final stage, I sent a copy of it along to an old friend of Hamilton, Julie

Schwartz. The result is a lengthy sub-memoir that begins at the conclusion of Ed's article. Julie was Hamilton's agent and his memories of the s.f. heydays sweeten this entire feature.

Had time permitted, there would not be *three* but probably *thirty* comments such as the pieces herein by Bob Bloch and Forry Ackerman. Both men are old, dear friends of the world-saver and were delighted to add their postscripts to *Fifty Years of Heroes*. There are literally scores of other s.f. titans that Ed counts among his friends and all, no doubt, place their sentiments with Bloch and Ackerman.

So here is a small dose of the life and times of Edmond Hamilton, writer, raconteur, husband of Leigh Brackett, and the man behind hundreds of beloved fantasy tales. In the words of Alex Nino (the famous Filipino fantasy illustrator who provides four plates to embellish this tale), "Mabuhay!"

Which means "Cheers!"

FIFTY YEARS OF HEROES
by Edmond Hamilton

*"I get enough of ordinary people in my everyday life
. . . when I read fiction, I want to read about heroes!"*

I can't remember who said that, but I've always thoroughly agreed with it . . . not only as regards reading fiction, but also in writing it.

My first science fiction story, a serial entitled, "Across Space," appeared in *Weird Tales* magazine in the summer of 1926. In it, evil Martians attempted to take over the Earth by means of a great machine on Easter Island. Their plans were defeated by a scientist who perished heroically in the struggle . . . and who was memorialized as the man who saved the whole Earth.

The readers liked that story. So did I. Therefore, being a new and very young writer, I wrote basically the same story over and over again fourteen or fifteen times. In each tale, a scientist-hero saved Earth from a terrible menace.

The dooms that poured upon the hapless Earth from the Hamilton typewriter made the atom bomb puny by comparison. Colossal metal robots, directed by a malefic computer-brain, mucked about stamping the cities of America flat. Seallike aliens from the depths of the ocean tried to drown the world by the simple expedient of pumping vast quantities of seawater to double the ocean depth. Menaces poured in on the hapless Earth from every quarter . . . from the depths of the ocean, from under the polar ice, from the other side of the moon, from the planet Saturn, from a subatomic universe. And in each case the Earth was saved by some noble-minded scientist-hero who outfoxed the hellish invaders at the last moment.

It is not surprising that I soon became known among the readers and fans as "World Saver Hamilton." In fact, in 1930 in one of the earliest issues of *Astounding Stories*, the letter section carried a long, not-too-serious poem of tribute to Hamilton the World Saver, written by a young reader named Mort Weisinger. Chuckling over that, I little dreamed that Mort and his young pal, Julius Schwartz, would in days to come be foremost among my editors.

I wound up the world-saving with a long story that appeared in *Weird Tales* as a four-part serial in late 1927. Its title was "The Time Raider," and this story, which has never been reprinted, was a wowser. The Raider of the title was a mysterious entity of mind and force that could travel into the past and future, and could drag people along with him from other ages.

Intent upon a total conquest of Earth, the Raider brought thousands of fighting men from past ages and penned them up, until he needed them, in a vast underground pit. This story really had five heroes instead of one . . . the young chap of our present-day era made fast friends with four other fighting men . . . a centurion of ancient Rome, a seventeenth-century French musketeer, an Aztec warrior, and a noted English swordsman of the late eighteenth century.

At the climax of this tale, the five friends, by dint of heroic swordsmanship, held a stair that was the only exit from the pit, preventing the ravening hordes of the past from surging out to attack all Earth. There, I tell you, was a fight!

When the story was published, it troubled me a bit that I had unconsciously modeled some parts of it after the fantastic novels of A. Merritt, which I had always admired greatly. Several years later when I met A. Merritt, I earnestly apologized for this. But Merritt simply waved

aside my apology and assured me that he had enjoyed my tale very much. He was a prince among men.

By this time I was getting tired of writing stories about the doom menacing Earth (and no doubt my readers were tiring of them, too). So in 1928 I struck out in a new line. My heroes were now officers of the Interstellar Patrol. These stories were laid in the far future, and postulated a galaxy ruled by the Federated Suns. The law-and-order arm of this vast federation was the Interstellar Patrol, the officers of which came from many different star-worlds. Only one of these officers was a human man of the future Earth. The others were nonhumans but intelligent aliens from many far stars . . . a metal-bodied chap from Antares, an insect-man from Procyon, a great furry, four-armed person from Betelgeuse, and so on. They were a colorfully variegated lot, with complete loyalty to each other and to the traditions of the great Patrol.

The chief heroes of these tales were Dur Nal, an Earthman, Korus Kan, a nonhuman Antarian, and Jhul Din, a huge alien from Spica. Their adventures took them into all sorts of places across the galaxy . . . into a gigantic comet, to the surface of a dead star, to the perils of a gigantic sun, and so on. They faced all sorts of terrific cosmic menaces in carrying out the mission of the Interstellar Patrol.

I wound up this series with a novel-length story of the Patrol entitled "Outside the Universe." In this long story, the heroes of the patrol ventured clear outside the galaxy to distant Andromeda galaxy to foil a cosmic plot against our own island-universe. In the finale, the star-fleets of e galaxies had at each other in an epic fight.

I remember that I was so excited when I wrote that final space battle, and punched my little portable typewriter so hard, that the machine "walked" all over the surface of my old flat-topped desk—and I sort of followed it, banging away at it as I finished my climactic scene.

These wild tales were quite popular with the readers. And I was immensely pleased that my hero, A. Merritt, liked them and wrote in praise of them . . . not only to me but to *Weird Tales* magazine, where his letters were published. He even tried to get his own publisher, Horace Liveright, to publish them in book form, but Mr. Liveright did not think they would sell, and doubtless was quite right.

But eventually they were published in two paperback volumes. A young reader of the magazine, Donald Wollheim, was a great admirer of these tales, and when long years later he became editor of Ace Books, he published the old stories. Also Don, in his recent history of science fiction, *The Universe Makers*, devoted a chapter to the Interstellar Patrol stories, saying that they were the first stories ever to visualize a future universe ruled by intelligence and law of many different life forms.

Another young reader who liked them was a lad in Cleveland who started writing to me early in 1930. He was instrumental, by his letters, in bringing together Jack Williamson and myself in a long friendship. He wrote me that he had an idea for hero stories himself, and that he and a friend were going to try to work up a new character. This youngster's name was Jerry Siegel, and the hero character he and his friend eventually created was . . . Superman!

At that time in the early '30s I made the acquaintance of a lot of other science fiction, adventure, and fantasy writers. The first I met, at the Chicago home of Farnsworth Wright, editor of *Weird Tales*, was E. Hoffman Price, a flamboyant and colorful writer of Oriental adventure and fantasy. I am glad to say he is still my friend and at least once a year comes zooming down from the San Francisco Bay Area where he lives, to spend a week here with us in the southern California desert where we stay in the winter, and to talk far into the night about the old days.

Jack Williamson and I pooled our resources in those Depression years to make some forays together ... a long trip down the Mississippi River in a skiff, a winter on the beach at Key West, travels around his native New Mexico and Arizona. Jack was at the time just beginning his great "Legion of Space" adventure series.

And how we could talk in those days! I remember a wintry night in 1933 when Jack and I and Price went to the home of Otis Adelbert Kline for dinner. Harold Ward, who was then writing the "Dr. Death" series, was there, and Gordon Gurwit, and Wright and others. We talked stories, editors, publishers, and more stories. Mrs. Kline courteously bade us goodnight and retired, but when dawn came we were still sitting there at the table, talking away.

Kline was a big, hearty man, with shoulders like a professional wrestler, and a genial, friendly manner. He had sent me an inscribed copy of his first novel, and I met him in June, 1931, in Farnsworth Wright's Chicago apartment. He and E. Hoffman Price came in together ... they had been combing rug merchants in search of treasures, Price, whom I also met then for the first time, being an Oriental rug collector.

Price waved triumphantly to a rather grimy swatch of carpet which he declared would be of surpassing beauty when clean. "I'll just wash it out now in your bathtub," he said. Marjorie Wright, doubtless thinking of her spotless bathroom and what this grimy carpet would do, suggested, "It's too big for a bathtub, isn't it?" Price waved her objection aside. "Hell, I once washed a thirty foot runner in a bathtub," he retorted, and departed for

the bathroom with a worried Marjorie trailing him.

Kline looked across at me and grinned, and I grinned back . . . and we were friends from that time on.

At about the same time I was meeting a good many of the writers based in New York. In 1934 Mort Weisinger, my one-time fan, was working for Standard Magazines' editorial department, and he and the editorial director, Leo Margulies—alas, it is now the late Leo Margulies —acquainted me with many of the great group in New York. Among them was Lester Dent, author of *Doc Savage*; Arthur Burks, "the king of the pulp magazines" as he was rightly called; Norvell Page; and many others, including Eando Binder ("Otto") and Henry Kuttner and his wife, C. L. Moore.

The NY sf scene in the later '30s and early '40s was a yeasty and exciting one. New magazines were appearing, new writers popping up, and we were all fascinated by the field. Every Friday an unofficial meeting of sf writers was held at Steuben's Tavern in mid-Manhattan, and when I was in town I enjoyed it very much. Henry Kuttner, Alfred Bester, Manly Wade Wellman, Otto Binder and many others were regulars. We had great discussions and hot arguments about new developments in sf. Julie, Mort and David V. Reed were also regulars. Lester Dent did not attend these . . . I met him at the old Tale Twisters group of pulp writers who foregathered at the Algonquin. Lester was a heck of a nice guy . . . big, genial and friends with everyone. I remember a period when he got a consuming interest in photography, and would rather use a camera than a typewriter. Others at the Tale Twisters gatherings were many of the old Black Mask writers . . . Carrol John Daly, Theodore Tinsley, Steve Fisher, Frank Gruber. They were all old friends and welcomed an infrequent out of town writer like myself in the friendliest fashion. Leo Margulies and Mort got me into the group.

All through the '30s I kept trying my hand at various different kinds of fiction . . . mystery and detective stories, supernatural stories, and also science fiction of a more serious sort. One such sf story that I wrote in 1934 was a grim, realistic account of one of the first expeditions to Mars. It was so harrowing that no magazine would publish it then, and not until the mid-1950s was it published, under the title of "What's It Like Out There?"

But adventure science fiction was still my chief interest, and I wrote a lot of it for Leo Margulies and Mort Weisinger, especially after Standard Magazines started *Thrilling Wonder Stories* and *Startling Stories*. In 1938 I wrote for the latter magazine a novel entitled "The Three

Planeteers," about a trio of comrades—an Earthman, a Venusian, and a Mercurian—who adventured across the solar system. This novel led them to ask me to do a series for a science fiction hero magazine they planned to begin publishing the following year.

Their first title for it was "Mr. Future, Wizard of Science." And the chief character was to be a small man with a big head and brain. Leo decided that was too freakish a lead character, and so he became Captain Future, a red-haired scientific adventurer. They sent me their ideas about the series and I went to New York and talked it out at length.

Their original prospectus—I still have it—outlined three comrades Captain Future would have. One was Simon Wright, an elderly man who was a sort of living memory—that is, he could remember every scientific fact in existence but could do nothing else; Otho, a warrior from Ganymede, who was to be a living jewel set in a ring worn by Captain Future; and the third, an automaton —not an intelligent robot, but a sort of manlike machine.

I convinced Leo and Mort that these three characters would be very hard to use in a story, and suggested changes in them. Simon Wright became an aged scientist who, about to die, had his living brain transferred into an artificial serum-case, and was known as the Brain. (At first, he could not move around at all, but after doing a few of the novels I found this was too hampering a restriction, and gave him powers of movement.) Otho became an android, a living man of synthetic flesh created in their moon laboratory by the Brain and Captain Future's father. And the automaton became Grag, the intelligent robot, who was not very brilliant but was immensely strong and very faithful.

There were seventeen of the Captain Future novels in

all, before the wartime paper shortage killed the magazine. Of these, I wrote fourteen; "Worlds to Come" and "Days of Creation" were written by William Morrison and "The Solar Invasion" by Manly Wade Wellman. What happened was this: I wrote all the Captain Future novels until Pearl Harbor in December 1941. As I was then a bachelor and figured I'd soon be in the army, I notified Leo I wouldn't be able to write any more, so he got two other writers and changed the authorship of the magazine to the pseudonym "Brett Sterling." But in 1942 the army ruled they would not accept men over thirty-eight years old, so, on the verge of being inducted, I was ruled out, and went back to writing Cap. Future again. Some of my stories then appeared under the "Brett Sterling" byline, and others under my own name; but aside from the three I've listed, I wrote them all.

I enjoyed doing the stories. They were not too serious science fiction, but they were a lot of fun to do. At first, because the editors thought they shouldn't go too far out, the stories were confined to the solar system. But after doing five or six, in "The Quest Beyond the Stars" I got the Futuremen out into deep space, and after that, not even the sky was the limit.

One story about the Captain Future novels remains in my mind. In the winter of 1943 I lived for a few months in Monterrey, in old Mexico. I wrote there the Captain Future novel called "Magic Moon." When I returned into the States, the wartime customs inspection of all papers and written material was very strict. Now, I always did the two "departments" of the Captain Future magazine . . . one called "Worlds of Tomorrow," with a map of the planet on which the action took place. The Customs men seized upon my map of a totally imaginary world, and seized with it the whole manuscript of the

novel and sent them to Washington for closer examination. It was months before I got them back, and in the meantime I had to write another Captain Future novel in a great hurry to fill the schedule.

Years later, in the 1950s, *Thrilling Wonder Stories* revived the old Captain Future stories as a series of ten-thousand-word novelettes. I did all these stories, and in them I was able to take a more subtle approach to the Futuremen. At that time Sam Merwin was the editor, one of the best science fiction editors I ever worked for, and he gave me a freer hand with the stories than I had had before.

The Captain Future novels were published in Sweden, in translation, back in those days . . . and to this day there is a Captain Future Society in Sweden. They were youngsters when they read the stories and they have a nostalgic thing about them. They publish a Captain Future Fanzine, which they send me along with a synopsis of its contents in English. They are a great bunch of guys, and I was delighted when one of them, Bertil Falk, visited me here in California not long ago. There's also a group of Captain Future fans in Japan—the stories were issued in translation here some years ago—and now Kouichi Yamamoto and Masuro Noda of Kyoto are preparing to publish a *Captain Future Handbook*. So the old Captain and his dauntless trio of comrades live on, in a way.

While I enjoyed doing the Captain Future novels, by the time I had done fourteen of them I was weary of editorial limitations. I remember one night in the summer of 1941 some of us were up at Bob Heinlein's house and he told me he had read my latest Cap Future novel, "The Lost World of Time." (I expect he only read it out of friendship's sake.) He said, "It's a good story, but if you ever waste my time again with a juvenile thing

like a baseball game on the moon, I'll disown you, Ed!" I told him, "That wasn't my idea; the editors demand I put some kind of a futuristic game in each novel."

But, being tired of a set pattern, I decided to write a star-adventure novel completely on my own, with no editorial suggestions whatever. All through the winter of 1944–45 I worked on this, and to this very long novel I gave the title "The Star Kings." There was no market for it at all in those days, because of the paper shortage, so when I finished it, all I could do was put it away in my file. Not until 1947 did markets reappear, and Ray Palmer then published it in *Amazing Stories*.

While I don't think it was my best story, "The Star Kings" has been far and away my most successful one. It has been continuously in print for almost thirty years, in one or another edition. It has been translated into a lot of foreign languages and has been published in such unlikely places as India and Brazil. No less than three editions, by different book clubs and publishers, have appeared in France. In fact, for the French book club edition I wrote a sequel to the story, "Return to the Stars," which Jacques Sadoul, the editor, published with the first story in a lavish hardbound volume. *(Also published in the U.S. by Lancer Books in 1966 or 1967.)*

I think the reason for the surprising popularity of this story is that it is my ultimate wish-fulfillment hero story. The main character, John Gordon, is a young insurance clerk who is bored with his job and his life. One night he receives a telepathic message from Zarth Arn, a man of two hundred thousand years in the future, who has a scientific method of exchanging bodies and minds, across time. To his suggestion of such an exchange, Gordon agrees . . . and wakes up in the body of Zarth Arn, two thousand centuries in the future. He finds that in that future day, the galaxy is divided up into many independent star kingdoms and that he, Zarth Arn, is heir to the throne of the mightiest of all those warring star kingdoms.

This brief summary, I think, will give an idea of why this story has been so popular. There isn't a one of us in everyday life who doesn't get bored now and then with ordinary existence. The thought that one could suddenly wake up and find himself a heroic and important figure in the glamorous universe to be, winning the love of star princesses and leading great hosts of mighty ships in colossal space battles for the dominance of the universe . . . who could resist such a daydream as that? Certainly not, I, which is why I wrote it and why, I'm sure, it remains such a perennial favorite of readers.

I ended this novel with Gordon's return to everyday Earth, but there were so many protests from readers that the story shouldn't end there that I wrote a sequel. Cele Goldsmith, then editing *Amazing Stories*, wanted some stories from me, so I did four fifteen-thousand-word novelettes which ran together to make a novel, *Return to the Stars*. In this, Gordon went back to the future universe to stay, and this seemed to make the readers happy. I agreed with them . . . after all, a man who had led the hosts of the Mid-Galactic Empire in terrific battles would never be happy as an insurance clerk!

About this time, in 1946, I heard again from Mort Weisinger. He had returned from his war service to take up his job again at National Comics Publications, as DC Comics were known at that time. He and Jack Schiff had left Standard Magazines in 1941 to work in the comics field, and later on Julie Schwartz had joined them at DC.

We were old friends by then. Julie and I in 1941 had driven out to California and spent a summer there, living in a rented bungalow which we made into a sort of hospitality center for the whole Los Angeles science fiction gang. (The kid who sold newspapers on our corner there, and who had ambitions to be a science fiction writer, was Ray Bradbury. He would come often to our cottage after selling papers. Julie would read his stories in mss and give helpful criticism.)

Mort wanted me to write comic scripts for DC magazines, to start with Batman. I had some doubts at first, as the format was quite different from fiction stories. But in those days after the war, the pulp magazine market was very poor, and so I decided to try it. I went up to New York and had long conferences with the boys. They were very helpful, realizing that this was a new form of writing for me, but even so, I had to write a few very poor scripts before I began to catch on to the ways of comic writing.

But once I started, I found that it wasn't really too different from fiction writing. In fact, comic scripts are very much like movie screenplays. I never had anything to do with the films myself, but my new wife, Leigh Brackett, had done a lot of screenplays, from Humphrey Bogart and John Wayne movies on, and looking at her scripts I discovered a great similarity.

For the first year or two, all my scripts for DC were Batman stories. As I learned the ropes, they became fun to do. But anyone who thinks comic scripts are just dashed off any old way is totally wrong. Mort and Jack Schiff were the nicest guys in the world to work for, but they took their work seriously, and if I made a stupid error or scuffed over anything, they told me so at once, and loudly.

It was fun to think up new wrinkles for the character. Most of them Mort thought up himself, but I did have some ideas which were used. If I remember rightly—and it's hard to be sure after all this time—I thought up some things like Batwoman, the Batman of the future, and so on. But Batman was a valuable character and no quick, off-the-top-of-my-mind ideas were taken. I would say that generally, Mort was more gag-minded on the stories and that Jack was more logical-minded. Together, they made a great editorial team.

After a year or two I started to do Superman stories also. Here I was, working on this immortal character dreamed up by my young fan-reader who had written me back in 1930! I think I did better on Superman than on Batman, simply because it was more science-fictional. But on the other hand, Superman could present some knotty problems in plotting.

Recently, somebody—I think it was Julie Schwartz —said that kryptonite, the substance which makes

Superman vulnerable, was just a crutch for the writer. This is absolutely true. On the other hand, the writer needs such a crutch. It's difficult to make up a suspenseful story about Superman, who's invulnerable to ordinary harm, unless he's vulnerable to *something*. And green kryptonite is a great help, as is the fact that Superman loses his powers when he is under the rays of a red sun.

In fact, my favorite of all the scripts I wrote was one entitled "Superman Under the Red Sun." In that story, Superman traveled into time by using his superspeed to "burst the time barrier." But unwittingly he went too far, into a time when Earth's sun had become old and *red*. The result was that he had no superpowers—and couldn't get back. Earth was dead, and he was condemned to wander alone upon it. Mort objected to the fact that, being alone on Earth, Superman wouldn't have any companions to talk to, and the pictures, always an important element, would be dull. I got around this by having Superman, in his loneliness, constructing robots who were doubles of Lois Lane, Perry White, Jimmy Olsen, and his other pals.

Another I liked was "When Superman Was Superbaby"—I believe the first of the Superbaby yarns. I always remember that as the only script I ever wrote in one day, the reason being that, as a baby, he couldn't talk very well . . . he could just say things like, "Pretty . . . bright . . ." "Bad mans!" and so on. This made dialogue writing a breeze.

I have to admit that the villains of the Batman and Superman stories interested me more than the heroes themselves. The Joker was my favorite Batman villain . . . he had a flair for zany crime that I liked. I also was fond of Catwoman, but I never did too many scripts with her as villainess. In the Superman characters, Luthor the evil scientist was a favorite . . . I suppose, again, because he was more science-fictional. The Superman villain I hated to write about was the zany Mr. Mxyzptlk . . . not only because I could never spell his name right, but also because it was hard to think up tricks to make the imp spell his name backwards . . . that being the only method of sending him back to his own dimension.

I also did some of the Superboy stories, although someone else did most of those. Later on, when Mort launched the "Legion of Superheroes" series, I did a lot of those. Superboy was one of them, but all the superheroes had some terrific superpower or other. One of them was a girl, Shrinking Violet, who could make herself tiny at will. That wasn't so hard to use. But one character I found it the devil and all to use: the girl called Triplicate Girl. Her power was that she could split herself into three different girls, all exactly alike. You think that's easy to use in a story? Triplicate Girl was one character who consistently baffled me.

Julius Schwartz first edited the science fiction magazines at DC—*Strange Adventures, Mystery in Space*, and so on. I did a good many sf stories for those, and when I started doing them I thought, "This will be a breeze . . . writing for an old pal like Julie will be no trouble." I was wrong! Friendship cut no ice when Julie read a story, and he was as strict with me as with anyone else. I guess that's why he became one of the greatest editors in the business.

I didn't like to live in New York, as most of the writers for the comics did. So I worked at home in our little 150-year-old farmhouse in rural Ohio, which is still our home for half the year. Mort and I worked out our plots on the phone. But for the first year or two we lived there, we couldn't get a private phone line. There were nine different parties on that country line! Not only did that make it hard getting through, but also some nice old ladies on our line who happened to overhear our conversations really got an earful. Mort would say, "Then we tie this fellow hand and foot and lock him in a safe and drop it into the ocean . . ." and so on, detailing a plot sequence he wanted. I would hear one of the old ladies on the line say, "Ulp!" I sort of got some queer looks around the village in those days. But after we got a private phone line, my reputation improved.

I wrote for DC Comics from 1946 to 1966. During that time, I was still writing science fiction and produced a good many sf books and magazine stories. Working on both projects sometimes kept me hopping. When I resigned from comic work in 1966, it was only because Leigh and I were about to go on some long-deferred world travels—to Egypt, India, and so on—and I would not be able to fill any schedules. But I always enjoyed working for the hero comics, particularly for such a great bunch of guys.

After we returned from our travels, I wrote three novels for Ace Books on a new science fiction hero . . . the "Starwolf" series. These were science fiction star adventures about two heroes . . . one of them being John Dilullo, an aging veteran of the starways of the future, the other being a younger man, Morgan Chane, who had been brought up as one of the Starwolves, a race of cosmic robbers with special capabilities in space.

My Morgan Chane character was of Earth descent, being of Welsh extraction. In one novel I had Chane go back to Carnarvon, in Wales, looking up his ancestors. I had visited Carnarvon and liked it very much. And I was able to put into the story all the Welsh boys who were my pals when I was a youngster . . . the western Pennsylvania town where I spent my boyhood was full of Welsh people who had come there to work in the tin mills, and remembering my old boyhood buddies, I put them into this yarn.

Looking back on the more than three hundred stories I have published, I find that with a few exceptions, it is the stories of heroic adventure that are foremost in my affection. I think that is true also of the readers. Back in 1940 I had a novel in *Startling Stories* titled "A Yank at Valhalla" about a modern-day chap who finds a lost land in the Arctic, in which still live the great gods and villains of Norse mythology: Odin, Thor, Loki, and the rest. That story was all swords and sorcery, ending up with Ragnarok, the twilight of the gods. I thought everyone had forgotten it, but a few years ago an old-time reader in Hawaii called it to the attention of Fred Pohl, then editing Ace Books, and he reprinted it as a paperback novel.

And sometimes something that happens in the news will recall an old story sharply to mind. In 1970 when *Apollo XIII* got into trouble on its way to the moon and it was feared that it might pass the moon and go on forever into space, the news hit me hard. The reason was that in 1959 I'd published a book, *The Star of Life*, in which that identical situation had happened . . . except that there was only one astronaut in the rocket, not three. And my hero had frozen to death in space, only to be revived many ages later to find himself in a strange future universe.

I have always been proud that one of my very old stories contained one of the first descriptions of the modern space suit used by astronauts. That story was "The Sargasso of Space," printed in *Astounding Stories*' September 1931 issue. It had a beautiful cover by Wesso, showing two men in space and wearing very present-day space suits, with transparent helmets, built-in radio-phones, and so on. When I saw the first "space walk" on television several years ago, I had a strong feeling of *déjà vu*. We science fiction writers, in imagining the possibilities of the future, make many wrong guesses. So when we make a guess that comes true, it's a highly gratifying thing.

I should say that my fascination with adventure stories still extends to my reading as well as my writing. In our old farmhouse in Ohio we have about three thousand books. A very large portion of this library consists of history, especially ancient history and the history of the American West, which subjects increase in interest to us as the years go by. But one large room up under the eaves, my workroom, contains mostly fiction.

Beside the classic authors, down to Proust and Joyce, stand shelves upon shelves of the great adventure novels. We have a complete Rider Haggard, a complete Edgar Rice Burroughs, a nearly complete Edgar Wallace, all the novels of John Buchan, and many other classics. Also, I have gathered together a complete file of the old *Adventure* magazines of the 1920s and 1930s . . . probably the greatest pulp magazine ever published.

The treasure of our collections is, of course, the volumes inscribed to us over the years by friends and fellow authors. These include many books by Otis Adelbert Kline, Sprague De Camp, Henry Kuttner, and C. L. Moore; a great set of novels of Dr. E. E. ("Skylark") Smith presented to us by Doc years ago; a complete set of Ray Bradbury's first editions; and books by Michael Moorcock, Otto Binder, and many others.

I am glad to say that among these volumes by right of worth stand the adventure novels of my wife. I have always counted myself lucky that I not only married a gal who is a professional writer, but also one who loves adventure stories and has written a great many of them.

Before I ever met Leigh Brackett, she was an established science fiction writer. Like myself, she preferred adventurous stories, and through the years has continued writing them, though turning now and then to work in Hollywood. Her screenwriting began with the Bogart-Bacall version of *The Big Sleep*, continued through several big Westerns and adventure films for John Wayne, and a few years ago she wrote the film for another of Raymond Chandler's Philip Marlowe stories, *The Long Goodbye*, with Elliott Gould playing Marlowe this time.

A short time after we were married, Leigh did a lonr story for *Planet Stories* about Eric John Stark, a man of Earth extraction who had his childhood on the wild planet Mercury. He became her favorite character, and she has written many stories about him, notably the three-volume series beginning with *The Ginger Star*, about Stark's adventures on the planet of a distant star. Stark is also one of my favorite all-time characters.

While we have in the past done a little unofficial collaboration, we never collaborated on a story that was to bear both our names as authors. A couple of years ago Harlan Ellison suggested that we do such a story, for a collection he has planned. After deliberation, we decided that such a story should be about our respective favorite heroes.

So the story is "Stark and the Star Kings"; it begins with Eric John Stark ridinr at night down the Great Rift Canyon of Mars, and it ends thousands of years in the future, with the redoubtable Stark going into battle at the side of the Star Kings.

In recent years, there has been much talk of "serious" science fiction, and adventure stories have been decried. I dissent from this absolutely. To my mind, the core of

science fiction is the great theme of the coming conquest of space. And, as I have asked before, if that is not adventure, what is? Armstrong and Aldrin taking the first steps upon the surface of the moon, the crew of *Apollo XIII* fighting to get back to Earth with their crippled rocket—these are stories more adventurous than any we science fiction writers ever dreamed.

No, I remain convinced of the value of hero stories. I could cite Thomas Carlyle's great essay "On Heroes and Hero-Worship" to support that belief. But I think the best defense of the great adventure stories was that given by G. K. Chesterton, the famous English critic of a generation ago. When someone sniffed at "blood-and-thunder stories," Chesterton roared, "I *like* blood-and-thunder stories . . . for they are about the blood of man and the thunder of God!" And he added, "Mankind still drives its dark trade in heroes, in many little-known publications, and I hope it always will."

So do I.

Julius 'Julie' Schwartz, innovative and respected Senior Editor of Superman, Batman *and many other DC Comics for over thirty-two years, was Edmond Hamilton's first agent. As co-producer of* The Time Traveler, *the legendary first sf fan magazine, Julie became acquainted with most of the sf writers of the day. This led to his role as their author's representative, a job which Julie found most rewarding. Few clients gave him more pleasure than the champion of disasters, Ed Hamilton. In this section, recorded and embellished with Julie in his New York office, he reminisces about the old days with Ed, sf, and the comics.*

****

"In partnership with Mort Weisinger, I started the first magazine about science fiction, which as you mention, was called *The Time Traveler*. The first issue of this 'fanzine' came out in January, 1932. It was mimeographed, six pages, ten cents and contained news and gossip on the writers and stories of the day. Eventually a fan with access to a printing machine, Conrad Rupert, offered to run the magazine for us. *"TTT"* thus evolved into the better-looking "Science Fiction Digest" and finally, "Fantasy Magazine."

In the history of the magazine, one of the most exciting things we ever did was a 'round robin' serial to which most every famous sf writer of the time contributed. It was an epic story with sections by A. Merritt, Otto Binder, Doc Smith, Ralph Milne Farley, Dr. David H. Keller, even John Campbell.

The story appeared in 1933 in seventeen or eighteen chapters—a feat which has not been topped to this day! When we got to the end of this epic, we dumped the story into the typewriter-hands of Ed "World-Saver" Hamilton, who was, by reputation, everybody's choice to save the planet from sixteen other chapters of invasion and chaos.

Of course, he proved worthy of the task!

****

"As Ed's agent in the mid-thirties, I would meet regularly with him and my other clients at Steuben's Tavern in Manhattan. Each week the likes of Manly Wellman, Hank Kuttner, Otis Kline, Eric Frank Russell, Fran B. Long, Otto Binder, and Robert Heinlein would descend on the restaurant for hours of talk about the s.f. field. In retrospect, it was really a mini-convention, held weekly—a marvelous gathering point for storytelling and conversation—not to mention business.

"In the summer of 1941, Ed and I drove cross-country to Los Angeles. Along with other celebrities in L.A., we'd make several trips up to Bob Heinlein's house atop Lookout Mountain. Driving down that winding road at night was a harrowing experience. For that reason, Bob never served hard liquor. Looking back on it, Heinlein was more than a considerate, generous host. He could have wiped out half his s.f. competition with a few bottles of Scotch!

****

"On that same trip out in '41, an incident occurred which to this day, Ed has not let me forget. We were driving out to sell Hamilton's car in California. We met in Pittsburgh and journeyed West, making a side-trip along the way to see an s.f. writer named Ted Sloat. I think he lived in Iowa. At the time I was 26 and Ed was in his mid-thirties. We went to a local (*Elks?*) club and—for the first time in my life—I got loaded. So bombed, in fact, that when we returned to our hotel room, neither of us could maneuver the key into our door. Ed had to call the bellboy to do it. To this day, Hamilton never fails to remind me of the comment he made as we finally fell into the room. *"Wellman would be proud of you!"* he shouted, alluding to Manly Wade Wellman, another s.f. writer who knew how to hoist a few.

****

"Still another memory from that summer of '41, was the visit paid to Ed and I by a local contingent of s.f. fans headed up by Ray Bradbury. To prepare for the visit, we went out and bought about two *dozen* cans of *beer* and *one* can of *Coke!* The cola was for Bradbury, who didn't drink. Much, much later, in the summer of '76, when I spent some time in California with Ed and Ray, it was *Bradbury* who drank more beer than any of us!

****

"In my entire career as a s.f. literary agent, one of the high points was selling a story of Hamilton's entitled, "The Accursed Galaxy". I remember the kick I had from reading that story. It dealt with the theory of all galaxies receding from Earth. I was so impressed with it, with the principle, which had never appeared in s.f. before, that I rushed it off to *Astounding*, which in those days paid the highest rates in the field. Ed had been receiving a half-cent per word from *Amazing* and *Wonder* (on *publication*) but *Astounding* bought the story for a "whopping" one cent per word on *acceptance*! We were both thrilled. (*Astounding* is currently published as *Analog* magazine, still the most prestigious magazine in the field. "Accursed Galaxy" the story mentioned here, was reprinted in Isaac Asimov's series, *Before the Golden Age*.)

****

"Ed mentions that kryptonite was a crutch for the writer. It was! In 1970, I succeeded Mort Weisinger as *Superman* editor and my first act was to wipe out kryptonite. It was my trademark at DC to make changes in whichever magazines I edited. With *Batman*, I started the 'New Look' in the early nineteen-sixties. In 1950, with Ed, we introduced the first of many 'series' to appear in the DC s.f. comics line. Called "Chris KL-99", the "Columbus of Space", as the character was known, ran for several issues to favorable fan response. DC was one of the first companies in the business to give cover credit for stories and Ed's by-line appeared on many an issue of *Strange Adventures*. (*Sherman did some of the art on that KL-99 series*).

****

"I had driven out to see Hamilton in his (and Leigh Brackett's) home in Lancaster, California. Both Leigh and Ed had been asking Ray to come up for years and I had managed to pick Bradbury up as a surprise visitor. Of course, Leigh and Ed were expecting to see me, but when they saw Bradbury, casually sitting in my car in tennis shorts as we drove up, she did the biggest double-take I've ever seen!

"Ray had been best man at their wedding and, to the best of my memory, Leigh first met Ed during that eventful 1941 trip, when she came to visit me as a client.

****

"Ed Hamilton has a remarkable memory. He can remember almost *every* story that happened to us back in those days—and I have trouble remembering *yesterday!* Ed's an old, dear friend—a great guy!"

Forrest Ackerman, famous editor/agent in the field of s.f., has known Ed Hamilton since the early days of the pulps. His anecdotes below give further evidence of the warmth and talent of the man.

EDMOND HAMILTON: THE WORD-SAVER
By Forrest J Ackerman

A typographical error, you say? Isn't he famous as "The *World*-Saver"? Well, that too; but about 1932 I sent him a snapshot signed "Your greatest admirer", and 45 years later he is wont to produce that picture from his wallet at world sf conventions and regional conferences to show fans who weren't born at the time what a percipient youngster Mr. Science Fiction was.

I have always had a special fondness for the first stf story by Edmond Hamilton that I ever read, "The Comet Doom" in the January 1928 *Amazing*. It was also his first story in a stf magazine. Later I discovered his "Crashing Suns" et al in *Weird Tales*. I probably have read about every word that Ed ever wrote—except, of course, his love letters to the lady he was courting, who quickly became Mrs. Edmond Hamilton—Leigh Brackett. My principal claim to fame, Hamilton/Brackett-wise, is that Ed borrowed my copy of the fantasy classic *cum* collectors' item, Eddison's "The Worm Ouroborous", with which to woo Leigh. (Wooed by a worm? Now how can you squirm out of that?)

The most extraordinary thing that ever happened to me Hamiltonwise was running into Ed & Leigh on a crowded New York street when neither they nor I had any idea the other was in town.

Funniest story Ed ever told me: Phone rang. "Hi, Ed, howya doin'?" "Fine, fine—yourself?" And 5 minutes of pleasantries passed while Ed was desperately trying to figure out who he was talking to. Finally the issue was forced when the unidentified voice said, "Hey, how about you and the wife coming over for dinner tonight?" At this point Ed was embarrassedly forced to admit he didn't know who he was talking to! That's alright: at that point it developed the other party was speaking with the wrong Ed!

But Hamilton for 50 years has been the right Ed for me. I especially thank him for "Cities in the Air", "A Conquest of Two Worlds", "Cosmic Pantograph", "The Eternal Cycle", "The Hidden World", "Horror in the Telescope", "The Intelligence Undying", "Island of Unreason", "The Truth Gas", "The Space Visitors" . . . and for the contribution to my Science Fiction Museum of an original cover painting by Frank R. Paul. Hamilton has consistently been one of the best entertainers the science fiction field has ever had.

Robert Bloch, raconteur, novelist, world-famous short story writer and the author of Psycho, *concludes this section wih his short, touching memoir on Ed.*

"In *The Summing Up*, Somerset Maugham discusses his literary career as follows:

'In my twenties the critics said I was brutal, in my thirties they said I was flippant, in my forties they said I was cynical, in my fifties they said I was competent, and now in my sixties they say I am superficial.'

"Such critical changeability remains a constant for any writer whose career extends over a long period of time, and Edmond Hamilton is no exception. In more than a half-century of varied and prolific output he has been acclaimed as a brilliant new discovery, derided as a one-plot "world-saver, hailed anew as an innovator, dismissed as a hack, rediscovered for mature literacy—and now enthroned as science fiction's Grand Master.

"Let us hope that this enthronement is permanent. Certainly it is deserved—not just by reason of longevity and volume of published wordage, but by virtue of Hamilton's amazing versatility, imaginative range, and continual development of style and skill in a field whose growth he had done so much to stimulate.

"If this sounds stilted and pretentious, it was not meant to be. These are the last words anyone would associate with Ed Hamilton himself. He's perhaps the most modest and self-effacing author in the entire *genre*; certainly he's one of the warmest and kindest.

"It has been a great privilege to read him and an even greater privilege to know him. The world he has so often saved 'in fiction is a better place in reality because of Edmond Hamilton's presence."

We regret to say
that as this book went
to press,
we received word from
California on the passing
of Edmond Hamilton on
February 1, 1977.
The world of science fiction
and fantasy
has lost an irreplaceable talent.
Those that knew him mourn the
loss and those that love
his works will long remember
the hours of adventure that
the splendid
World-Saver continued to
provide for over fifty years.
His stories are a
legacy that will entertain for
years to come.

GREATHEART

PHILIP JOSÉ FARMER • TOM SUTTON

INTRODUCTION

Greatheart Silver in the First Command
A novella by Phillip José Farmer
Illustrated by Thomas Sutton

It is time for another memorable Greatheart Silver epic from the pen of *Phil Farmer*, who has already treated us to *Showdown at Shootout (or The Grand Finale)* in *Weird Heroes*, Volume 1 and *The Secret Life of Rebecca of Sunnybrook Farm* in *Weird Heroes*, Volume 2.

Those of you who missed both adventures, don't worry. Phil is no stranger to continuing series (the famed *Riverworld*, the *Continuum* tetrology, *Ralph Von Wau Wau*, etc.) and he'll make you feel at home right from the start.

As a matter of fact, Phil's vast knowledge of zeppelin lore and logic will make us all feel like passengers on the grand airship. With GS at the helm and Micawber behind the scenes, there's no question that danger's afoot, ahand, and ahead.

Regular readers are in for some surprises. Jill's back, in a new role, and Greatheart's command begins on a new ship. You can be sure that things won't stay calm for long.

Readers of *Weird Heroes* will be quick to recognize the art of *Tom Sutton*, who has also drawn BPVP's *Schlomo Raven* (see *Fiction Illustrated*, $1.00, Pyramid Books, 1976). Tom has adopted a new, somewhat starker style here (you can compare it to his earlier GS portrait, reprinted in full with this story) and it evokes a more dramatic, *pulpier* feeling.

Phil has managed to effectively blend the flavor of Errol Flynn, the Marx Brothers, James Bond, and Donald

Westlake within a crowded, Harvey-Kurtzmanesque milieu. There's the usual *GS* cast of thousands, raging chaos and claustrophobic calamities. Then there's a nefari—but enough teasers! On with the show!

As a Peoria scholar once wrote, "Gentlemen, please remove your hats."

GREATHEART SILVER
in *The First Command*
or *Inglories Galore*
by Philip José Farmer

1.

Whom the gods would destroy, they first make happy.

2.

A more jubilant man than Greatheart Silver on that fine evening probably did not exist. He was captain of the Acme Zeppelin Company Airship AZ-49. It was his first command, won after a long, hard, dirty battle against forces that seemed unbeatable.

Also won, and on board, was his bride, Jill Amber Silver, née Micawber. Though the captaincy had been squeezed out of her father through blackmail, Greatheart didn't feel guilty. The old crook had managed to blacklist Greatheart with every airship company in the Western world. He had done everything short of murder to keep his daughter and Greatheart apart.*

Through Micawber's malicious conniving, Greatheart had plunged from first mate of the AZ-8 to skid row in Los Angeles. But now he had overcome the biggest rapscallion and curmudgeon in the American business world. Old Micawber had been defeated on every front, including financial and personal.

Other men, faced with such failures, would have had heart attacks. His father-in-law had come down with a case of piles.

How symbolically appropriate, Greatheart thought, smiling to himself.

*See Volumes 1 and 2 of *Weird Heroes*, ed. Byron Preiss, Pyramid Books.

Silver looked out of the wide, curving windscreen of the navigating bridge, which was just below the radome bubble in the nose of the dirigible. Seven thousand feet below was the night-blanketed South Pacific Ocean. Above were stars undimmed by clouds.

God was in His Heaven, Silver was top dog of the AZ-49, and all was well with the world.

The zeppelin was making 100 miles per hour on a south-west course. Its nose was turned just enough to the northwest to counter a 10-mph wind. Two hundred miles to the northwest, over the Marquesas Islands, a typhoon was roaring at 110 mph, heading toward the airship. But the AZ-49 would have slipped by its main force by the time it arrived in this area. Nevertheless, there would be peripheral winds to battle against for an hour or so before a calm region was reached.

Greatheart had ambitions to be captain of one of the nuclear-powered air leviathans of the Acme fleet. However, there were no openings. In any event, it was company policy that the chief officer have at least five years' experience in freighters before assuming command of the superclass zeppelins. Not even Micawber could override this. Nor would Silver have wanted to be appointed through nepotism.

He was happy enough. The AZ-49 was a fine dirigible, primarily a freighter, but with accommodations for over thirty-five passengers. It bored through the skies now, a monster of conventional cigar-shape, 1345 feet or more than a quarter-mile long, with a midsection diameter of 224.16 feet. Its giant gas cells held 40,000,000 cubic feet of noninflammable helium. Ten diesel engines could, in still air, drive it at 125 mph. Two were in gondolas, one under the nose, one under the tail. The others were in the middle section, inside the hull, their power transmitted through gears in exterior housings. Their variable-pitch

propellers could be swiveled through 180 degrees to assist in hovering or upward or downward flight.

The twin cargo holds in the midsection could each accommodate five stacked modules, each enclosing containers of cargo up to 50 tons.

This trip, the modules enclosed three containers with peculiar contents: liquid methane. They had been loaded with little advance warning at Caracas, Venezuela. The expected cargo had been withheld. An emergency had demanded that the methane be taken posthaste—*hang the expense*—to Minerva. This independent island-nation of the south Indian Ocean needed it as soon as possible.

On top of one stack was another unusual item. This was an irradiated plastic container in which, under the label "HEAVY METALS," was a quarter-ton of platinum and iridium. Silver did not know why the tiny state needed such a large quantity of these metals, but it was not his place to ask questions. However, he alone had been told the true contents of the container. He understood why this was necessary. The metals must be worth at least $60 million.

Among the passengers, the most distinguished was Dr. Pierre de Rioux, a very wealthy industrialist who could be France's next premier.

With him were his blonde secretary and two tough-looking bodyguards. Though it was normally forbidden to bring arms abroad, the guards carried automatic pistols and knives. The Acme executive office in New York had authorized this. De Rioux was traveling incognito, another secret which Silver was not to transmit even to his wife.

The rest of the passengers consisted of eleven Americans, nine Frenchmen, and ten South American businessmen and their mistresses. None, as far as he knew, were going to Minerva to apply for naturalization papers. You couldn't get citizenship there unless you owned more than $3 million.

Silver made a final check of all stations. Now he was free to go to Jill's cabin, allotted her as the chief steward-person. After spending some time with her, he would go to the captain's quarters, a cabin just above the control rooms. According to regulations, the captain must sleep there alone, even if he were married. Old Micawber had some strange ideas, but he was one who could enforce them.

3.

Before leaving, he checked the navigational bridge. Third Mate Siskatoo, an Alaskan Indian, was standing his watch. The pilot was at the control panel, though the controls were on automatic. The radar man was intent on his scopes. Sparks, sitting in a corner, was busy monitoring his communications set.

"I'll turn in now," Greatheart said to Siskatoo.

"Have a good sleep, Captain." The Indian's dark face split into an ivory grin. Silver had once remarked that the marriage was six months old, but the honeymoon was still going on.

"Watch out for blonde line-squalls," Siskatoo added.

Silver mock-winced. A passenger, Mrs. Katharine Hooward, a tall, willowy, busty, blonde about thirty-five, had given him some trouble. If he hadn't married, he wouldn't have called it trouble. (However, a company regulation did limit the zeppelin personnel in the degree of social intercourse permitted with passengers.)

Jill had commented, laughingly, on Mrs. Hooward's too-obvious passion for him. Mr. Hooward, though he had said nothing, was very cold to Silver. Greatheart found the situation embarrassing.

Silver said goodnight-all and started for the navigation room when Sparks said, "Just a moment, sir. A message from the head office. It says that the navigational satellite is malfunctioning. There's no telling how long it will be down."

Silver looked at the screen in front of Sparks. The message was in large white letters with some alphanumerical codes in the margin.

"That means we'll have to switch the navigation to the computer," he said to Siskatoo, who already knew it. It also meant that if, by some unlikely chance, the zeppelin went down and couldn't transmit messages, its locations would be unknown. Other satellites could pick it up, but only if they were told to do so.

"We can make it on our own. No sweat," he said. "Siskatoo, you'll take care of the computer feed-in."

He left the bridge and went through the navigational and smoking rooms. Beyond was the main passageway, which ran along the main keel from nose to stern. The only one visible was Albert Agocelli, a steward. He was carrying a covered tray, probably a snack for the bridge crew.

Forty yards away, the cabins began. The passengers, officers, and stewards were quartered there. De Rioux, or Corday, as he was listed, was in the first cabin on the left. His two bodyguards slept with him. In the next cabin was his secretary. Jill's small cabin came next and then two cabins down was a large room where the Hoowards were now sleeping. At least, he hoped they would be. At this late hour, Mrs. Hooward wouldn't be waiting to grab him and exercise her not inconsiderable charms upon him.

Whistling softly, he strode down along the passageway, which curved downward gently at this point. His bionic left leg moved slowly. Its neutral wires received and transmitted messages through the connections to the protein nerves of his upper leg. The electromechanical devices within the irradiated plastic limb seemed to work as well as, and sometimes better than, his wholly flesh right leg. Some of the women he'd known, in the biblical sense, had been disconcerted by the hard, shiny artificial member, but Jill had not been upset in the least. She really loved him. Idly, he wondered how Mrs. Hooward would react if she were confronted with it. Well, he'd never know, not if he could help it.

Silver was somewhat vain, and he could not help thinking what a fine figure of a man he made. His uniform was a tight but crinkly silver-gray plastic. His black knee-length boots were shiny. The only thing he didn't like about his dress was the black silver-banded plug hat. That was Micawber's idea—the silly old ass.

However, his physical attributes more than made up for the hat. He was six feet, six inches high, weighing 245 pounds, broad-shouldered, slim-waisted, and long-legged. His face was, he might as well admit it, handsome, though his nose was perhaps a little too long and curved. The long, shoulder-length, wavy hair, once yellow but now, at the age of thirty-three, a dark brown, and his long moustache made him resemble the late but not necessarily lamented General Custer.

No wonder that Mrs. Hooward had the hots for him.

He forgot about her when he reminded himself to cover the cage containing his two pet ravens. These were in Jill's cabin, since regulations forbade pets in the captain's quarters. Last night, he had forgotten to throw the cover over the cage. He'd been forced to get out of bed when they had made some raucous and deflating remarks. Jill had howled with laughter. Of course, the ravens weren't capable of originating such bawdy language on their own. Jill had coached them.

Recently, he had spent some time with Jill in training

the two big birds to attack people if given a codeword. So many dangerous situations occurred to both himself and Jill that he thought this was a good idea. You never knew when they could come in handy. But he hoped that it wouldn't be necessary.

Agocelli passed him. "Good evening, sir."

Silver said, "Isn't it, though!"

At that moment, he saw a figure emerge from the dim light of the passageway. It was about a hundred feet away, and it seemed to have formed from the air, like ectoplasm shaping itself into a ghostly figure.

Silver froze. It was one of those apparitions that appeared whenever he was in danger. Always they were one of his ancestors, Thomas Jefferson, Sally Hemmings, Crazy Horse, Arizona Jim Silver, Long John Silver, all of whom had long been dead. Sometimes, it was his living grandmother, a Sioux named White Spots. This time, it was Crazy Horse, a tall, good-looking, but ferocious-faced warrior. He held a lance in his hand and he shook it at Silver.

Refusing to believe that there were ghosts in this world or any other, Silver had formed a theory to explain the figures. He was especially sensitive to danger, though he didn't know why. When his subconscious scented peril, it warned him through the exteriorly projected images. Usually, on seeing these phantoms of the mind, Greatheart reacted swiftly. But this situation had been so peaceful, so free of any intimations of danger, that the warning caught him off guard.

A snake hissed behind him.

He broke out of the cocoon of astonishment. Whirling, Silver lifted up a hand to ward off whatever attacker was behind him. If it really was a snake—*but how could a snake be aboard?*—it would break its fangs if it bit the bionic leg . . .

Suddenly a biting odor filled his nostrils.

Silver's senses flew away like fireflies escaping a spray of bug-killer.

4.

Greatheart awoke with a scream in his ears and confusion and a pain in his head.

He sat up, groaning, as the pain burst and caught fire, like the *Hindenburg* exploding. He was sitting naked in a strange bed in a strange room. Not so strange now that he looked around. It looked much like his cabin except that the photographs of himself in the graduating class at Friedrichschafen and of Jill and himself just after their marriage were missing.

That was not really so, he told himself. What business did an unclothed Mrs. Hooward have in his room? Why was she standing at the foot of the bed screaming? What was Mr. Hooward doing? He was clothed; he was, in fact, dressed to kill. His right hand held a big cane above his head. It seemed to Silver's whirling senses that Mr. Hooward intended to hit him over the head with it.

Ah, he was right. Hooward's thin face was as red as a face could get without exploding its blood vessels. His brown eyes, usually so little and heavy-lidded, were as wide as the gape of a feeding baby vulture. Red veins in his eyeballs seemed to squirm like snakes. His thin lips were even thinner, like the edges of a bloody knife.

Mr. Hooward was going to break his skull.

Mrs. Hooward stopped screaming, and cried, "Jeffrey! Don't do it! You'll go to jail for life!"

Mr. Hooward stopped. The only sound now was his breathing, like the burbling of a steer drowning in quicksand.

"You shut up!" Mr. Hooward yelled. "I'll give you the same thing in a minute! You put knockout drops in my drink! My own wife!"

Greatheart, croaking like one of his ravens, said, "Take it easy, fellows. I don't know what's going on, but I'm sure there's a reasonable explanation."

There had to be one, but he doubted that he could come up with it.

"Yes, and I know what it is!" Mr. Hooward shouted.

Greatheart rolled swiftly away from the bed and bumped against the bulkhead. No escape that way.

Mr. Hooward yelled, "Die, you filthy animal!"

Silver lunged upward and caught Hooward's wrist in his hand. Hooward struggled, then went limp as somebody banged on the door. Muffled voices sounded.

"You'll pay for this, you sneaking bastard!" Hooward said. Silver released the wrist. Hooward whirled, ran to the door, unlocked it, and snatched it open.

"Come on in, everybody! Take a good look! What do you think of that?"

Dramatically, he turned and pointed a long thin finger at his wife and Silver. Scorn had replaced anger.

Silver groaned and pulled the sheet up over his waist. First came the second mate, James Flaherty. After him—Lord preserve Greatheart Silver—Jill! She pushed forward toward her husband, who cowered in geometric progression according to the inverse cube of her proximity to him. Behind Jill were several crewmen. Then Monsieur Pierre de Rioux, the great French statesman and financier, his secretary, and his two bodyguards. Urging them on in were four of the passengers from Brittany, two Americans, another stewardess, six men who were usually found playing poker in the smoking room, and three cigar-smoking men who only came out of their cabins for meals. Half of the crowd was in pajamas.

"No smoking!" Silver cried. Had that thin, ragged voice come from him?

By then others had jammed themselves in. Jill was propelled forward until her knees were pressed against the edge of the bed.

He did not want to look at her face, but he had to. Silver wondered if he looked as stricken as she did.

"It isn't what you think, Jill."

Mr. Hooward was bellowing then. He'd been forced by the crowd into a corner but had battled his way to the bathroom. Now his head stuck out of its entrance, and he yelled, "Let me at that creep! I'll kill him!"

More people squeezed in. Mr. Hooward was forced out of sight, shoved into the toilet. His voice, calling for vengeance, threatening to tear Silver apart, sounded like a banshee's. It mingled with the gurgling roar of an advertently tripped flush lever.

Mrs. Hooward started shouting, "My clothes! My clothes! Where are my clothes?"

Silver wondered where his own clothes were. Probably on the floor along with hers.

Giving up the futile request, Mrs. Hooward crawled into his bed. "What are you doing?" Greatheart said, his voice ascending toward a screech.

"I won't be naked in front of all these people," she said. She pulled the sheet over her, leaving Silver exposed. He yanked it back savagely.

"It's a little late for that," Jill said dully.

More people had shoehorned themselves in. Jill was pushed onto the bed. She stood up and bumped her head on the overhead.

"For God's sake!" Silver yelled. "Flaherty! Get these people out of here!"

5.

Flaherty managed to hear him above the babbling and bellowing. Though a short man, he was thick-necked and

deep-chested. His Irish brogue rose above the clamor, like the roar of the Bull of O'Bashan. "Ivrybody out a here ixcept the guilty parties, the intimately concarned, and officers of the ship!"

"What do you mean, guilty parties?" Silver shouted.

He looked up at Jill. She seemed to be thinking about a choice. Either she was going to kick him or she was going to weep. Her dilemma was solved by doing both.

Silver said, "Ouch!" and then felt tears falling on his stomach. Though he was absolutely innocent—unless a few fantasies concerning Mrs. Hooward were counted—he still felt guilt. Shame, too. They pulsed through him like alternating currents.

"Damn it, this is a frameup, Jill!"

"I know whose frame you were up!"

"Please, Jill. It *is* a frameup ... and guess who's behind it all?"

She stopped crying, and her angry expression softened a little. "You mean my father?"

"Who else?"

"You can't blame everything on him."

"Please let me explain."

"I intend to! It had better be good. *Better than* good."

Silver groaned. "I don't *know* what happened!"

"Don't *tell* me you *blacked out* and woke up in here!"

He groaned again.

"We just got caught, that's all," Mrs. Hooward said.

"Don't listen to her!" Silver cried. "She must be in on it!"

"I don't know how she could be an innocent bystander," Jill said coldly, but her voice trembled.

"I am sorry, so sorry," Mrs. Hooward said. "I was just mad about your husband! It was one of those things. He couldn't help himself either. Everything would've been all right, no one the wiser or hurt, either, if only my husband hadn't waken up sooner than he should have. I should've put another drop in his drink."

"You're pretty cool about this, sister," Jill said.

Silver's heart rallied. Maybe Jill might believe him. He was glad he'd resisted the impulse to sock Mrs. Hooward after her last remark. She might say too much, and if she did, she'd be caught in a lie. Jill was upset, but she would be wondering if perhaps her father hadn't arranged this setup. True, Jill had told her father that she'd never see him again if he tried any more shenanigans. Old Micawber had sworn on a stack of financial records that he would never interfere again.

But conniving, cheating, and double-crossing were among his major genetic features. He had to have been born with them. Otherwise, how account for his head start in crookery? At the age of twelve he'd stripped his own father of the chairmanship of Acme Industries, though through adult collaborators, of course.

"We were swept off our feet," Mrs. Hooward said. "Carried off by a tidal wave of passionate vibrations."

"Shut up or I'll kick you, too," Jill said. "Much harder."

By then Flaherty had managed to bulldoze most of the crowd out. There was a brief interruption when one of the women passengers shrieked out that the man behind her had pinched her fanny. The woman's husband scuffled with the alleged molester until Flaherty and a crewman threw them out. All three complained about the violent treatment and threatened to sue Acme.

One more problem, thought Silver. But it was minor compared to the other.

The first mate, Reynold White, entered, yawning. His black face sagged at the spectacle, and his brown eyes widened. Then he assumed his official expression, inscrutability.

Perhaps he was having some trouble trying to keep from laughing. Silver glanced at him while, wrapped in the sheet and carrying his clothes retrieved from the deck, he headed for the toilet. White's stony face seemed to be breaking up. Mrs. Hooward diverted him. She was protesting at being left uncovered.

"You're no gentleman, you swine!" she shouted after Silver.

"You're no lady," he said, and closed the door. Within two minutes he emerged, fully dressed except for one sock, which he had been unable to find. His artificial leg was unshielded beneath the boot. The other sock had gone on his living leg, but since his artificial leg was equipped with delicate sensors, he felt its contact with the interior of the boots. Well, he didn't have to worry about developing a blister.

Mrs. Hooward was just finishing dressing. Judging from the expressions of the men, the process had been stimulating. Whatever her character, she was lavishly endowed.

The stateroom door had been closed. The occupants included the first and second mates, the Hoowards, and the Silvers. White was telling the Hoowards to put out their cigarettes.

"I'm too nervous not to smoke," Mrs. Hooward said. "Besides, that's a silly rule. Helium can't burn. This isn't the *Hindenburg*, you know."

"It's the rule, anyway, ma'am," White said.

"And what if we don't?" Mr. Hooward said.

"I'll take all your tobacco away from you and forbid you to go to the smoking room," White said.

"Who's the commanding officer here, anyway?" Mr. Hooward said. "Isn't Silver the one who gives the orders?"

There was a silence. White looked at Silver, who knew

what he was thinking. Regulations covered just such a situation as this. Silver's status depended now on what the Hoowards said.

White cleared his throat. "We-e-e-ll, I don't know what happened. Maybe you'd better explain. Captain, do you want to speak up first?"

Mr. Hooward savagely threw his cigarette on the deck, where it continued burning. "To hell with it! I'll tell you what happened! My wife, my future ex-wife, I should say, put a Mickey Finn in my drink. She did that so I'd pass out and then your captain—some captain!—sneaked in. I woke up quicker than she thought and caught them in bed."

White looked at Silver. "Is that true, Captain?"

Greatheart looked at Jill. She was leaning forward in a chair. Her face was set and pale, she was trembling, and her gaze was beamed in on his face.

"Partly true," he said. "I don't know whether or not Mrs. Hooward put knockout drops in her husband's booze."

Jill spoke in a shaky voice. "What booze? I don't see any empty glasses."

The others looked around. Mrs. Hooward looked stunned. Then she said, quickly, "I washed them out and put them away."

"You're not the type," Jill said flatly. "You'd leave them for the stewardess to pick up."

"Prove it," Mrs. Hooward said.

"We'll search the cabin and see if you even have any liquor," Greatheart said. He felt better, and Jill looked as if she had been relieved of some doubt.

Mr. Hooward spoke up. "There wasn't any booze. I don't drink because I'm diabetic. Katharine seldom drinks; she prefers pot. I drank a can of sugarless root beer. I don't see it. What'd you do with it, Katharine?"

"Put it in the wastebasket. Look for yourself."

Flaherty reached into the container and drew out an aluminum can. He held it up so that everybody could see the label.

"Slim's Root Beer," Flaherty read out loud. "Sugarless. An Acme Canning Company Product."

"My father owns that, too," Jill said.

She looked at the Hoowards. "I wonder if he owns you two, too?"

"I'll sue for defamation of character and libel!" Mr. Hooward shouted.

"That's enough of that!" White snapped. He turned to Silver. "You were saying . . ."

"The only other statement of Hooward's that is even partly true is that I was in bed. But I don't know how I got there."

He paused and then described exactly what had happened to him. A silence pregnant with disbelief followed.

Greatheart said, "White, call in Agocelli. Flaherty, you get two crewmen and search Agocelli before you bring him here. Put a guard over his quarters. Make sure no one leaves it without being searched. Put two more crewmen on a search of his bunk and effects."

"Yes sir," White said. "What are we looking for?"

"I was coming to that. Based on the hissing sound I heard and the burning odor I smelled just before I passed out, and the headache I woke up with, you'll be looking for a small spray-can. I must've been rendered unconscious by some kind of gas."

Mrs. Hooward said, "That's ridiculous! You're lying to save your own skin!"

White stepped close to Silver and spoke softly. "If Agocelli is involved, sir, he wouldn't be stupid enough to hide the can where it could be found easily. He'd get rid of it."

"I know. But he may not have had a chance to hide it yet. And if it isn't found on him or in his quarters, then it may be somewhere inside the ship. You'll ransack the entire ship if you have to."

From the mate's expression, he knew that would take the entire crew a very long time.

Greatheart said, "You'll look in the garbage disposals, too, of course. And check if any of them have been used recently. The computer will register if any hatch opening to the exterior of the hull has been used."

White, still speaking in a low voice, said, "You know that if the captain is accused of a crime by a passenger, he's to be relieved of command until he's proven his innocence. That's a company regulation, sir."

"I heard that!" Mr. Hooward shouted. "I demand that he be relieved of duty according to regulation!"

White shrugged. He said, "I'm sorry, sir. I had meant to give you a break. Maybe . . ."

"Then you should've spoken to me in the passageway," Greatheart said. "Okay. I won't burden you with any trouble from me. I relieve myself. As of this moment, you're acting captain."

"Thank you, sir. Your suggestions will still be carried out."

Jill said, "Could I see you in my cabin for a moment, Greatheart?"

"I'll be along after Agocelli has been questioned."

"I have some questions of my own. For you," she said, and she walked out. Mr. Hooward snickered.

Flaherty left. White used the cabin telephone to inform Third Mate Siskatoo of the situation. Then he gave orders to rouse the entire crew for the search.

Silver waited until White had hung up the phone. He said, "There's the possibility that Agocelli could have

slipped the can to a passenger."

"They'd raise a big stink. Micawber would have your head, not to mention other parts. Look, Captain, your suggestion, if you'll pardon me, sounds a little paranoid. I can see how the Hoowards could be in the plot—and it's possible they could bring a third person into the plot. But surely not a fourth!

"We'll look for this alleged can, but we won't disturb the other passengers any more than we have to."

A knock sounded at the door. White opened it and admitted Flaherty, a crewman, and Agocelli."

"I'll sue the company!" Agocelli cried. "I'll sue you, Silver! And I'll register a complaint with the union!"

"That's up to you," White said. "Flaherty, did you find anything?"

"Nothing except Agocelli. He was in the galley eating a sandwich."

White looked hard at the steward, a little man with a weasel face, a thin body, a big belly, and skinny arms and legs.

"Agocelli, I have some questions, and I want the truth."

He paused.

At that moment, men yelled outside in the passageway. Explosions followed. White and Silver raced to the door. The first mate got there first and opened the door. Silver pressed his big body against White's back to urge him out so he could get a look. Something whined; something else went thud. White gave a small cry and fell face down upon the passageway deck.

6.

While pistols and automatic rifles filled the passageway with hellish noise and the Hoowards screamed, two men forced their way into the cabin. Silver backed up with his hands above his head. One of the men closed the door and stood by it, crouching warily. The other man held his GK-3 automatic rifle upon the occupants. He spoke English with a French accent.

"Hands behind your neck. Okay. Now back up to the wall."

"It's not a wall," Flaherty said. "It's a bulkhead."

"For God's sake!" Silver said. "This is no time to worry about terminology!"

The two men were French passengers, ticketed to get off at the island-nation of Minerva. The tall, thin, redheaded man by the door was Jacques-Pierre Mellezour; the other, Robert Calloc'h, was short, massive-shouldered, and big-bellied.

Mellezour turned his head and spoke loudly to make himself heard above the gunfire. "I am Captain Mellezour of the First Corps of the Children of Breiz. Now, Captain Silver, how did you find out about us?"

"Sure, and he's not the captain," Flaherty said. "He's been suspended from his duties. First Officer White—that poor divil of a black lying on the deck outside—he's captain now. Unless he's dead. In which case, me good man, I'm captain."

Mellezour looked confused.

Greatheart said, "No, Captain Mellezour, I'm captain again. Actually, no formal complaint has been lodged against me. The Hoowards have to sign a statement charging me with something illegal and/or irregulatory. Besides, this is an emergency which threatens the ship and its passengers. I'm captain."

"Actually," Flaherty said, "Third Mate Siskatoo is captain. He's on duty in the control room, and the captain is incapacitated. Namely, by you. You'd have to speak to Siskatoo."

Mellezour waved his rifle wildly. "I don't give a damn

just now who's captain of this ship! What I want to know is, how did you find out about us? Who set up this ambush?''

"I don't know anything about an ambush," Greatheart said. "I don't even know what you're doing with those guns."

Calloc'h said something in a language wholly unintelligible to Silver. He supposed it was Breton. Mellezour spoke in French. "Traitors?"

The gunfire cut off suddenly.

Mellezour spoke to Calloc'h. Calloc'h gingerly opened the door and peered down the passageway toward the control room. A shot. Calloc'h, apparently cursing, jumped back and slammed the door.

"You are not lying?" Mellezour said to Silver.

"No. What's your game? Hijacking?"

"It is no game, my captain," Mellezour said. "It is the highest patriotism. We are members of the Children of Breiz. Breiz, that means Brittany. Originally, it was the Sons of Breiz, but certain feminist militants threatened to form a splinter organization unless we called ourselves the Persons of Breiz. We compromised on Children.

"Anyway, we have been demanding independence for Brittany, which is presently an oppressed department—province—of France. No doubt even you Americans, who read nothing but the sports section of your newspaper and the comic books, have heard of us?"

"Last time I read about you," Greatheart said, "you had blown up a mailbox in Paris. You killed ten adults and six children."

"That was too bad about the children," Mellezour said. "But you can't make an omelet without breaking eggs.

"We patriots boarded this dirigible at Caracas in order to seize the reactionary financier and potential premier of

France, M. de Rioux. We intend to hold him as hostage, to demand the release of six of our comrades now awaiting the guillotine."

"And where were we to be taken after your demands were met, if they were?"

"Ah, the captain anticipates? That is good. You are cooperative, is it not? If our demands are not met, we will throw de Rioux, his secretary, and his two bodyguards into what you Americans call the big drink. Then we will disembark at a certain port of a certain nation of Africa. Where your airship will be confiscated because it has illegally entered. No doubt it can be freed for a certain sum."

"No doubt," Silver said. He was trembling with rage.

Mellezour said, "Two of my brave ones are lying dead upon the floor."

"Not floor. Deck," Flaherty said.

"How would you like to join them?" Mellezour said. "Do not interrupt me for trifles. We were on our way to seize M. de Rioux in his cabin, when people in the control room shot at us. De Rioux's bodyguards also joined in, but they were gunned down. Not only that, somebody fired upon us from the door of the cabin near this one. Two doors down, I believe."

"That's Jill's cabin!" Greatheart said.

"Jill?"

"She is the wife of the captain," said Flaherty, "I mean, he *was* the captain. That still has to be . . ."

The telephone rang. Mellezour and Calloc'h jumped. Mellezour's rifle stuttered, the explosions half-deafening everybody. Though his ears rang, Silver could hear Mrs. Hooward yelling.

"Shut up!" Mellezour cried. "'That was an accident. I was so startled, I squeezed the trigger. Nobody is hurt, though, alas!"—he waved at the row of bullet holes in the bulkhead—"there has been some damage."

Calloc'h answered the phone. After listening a moment, he said, "It's the officer of the control room. He asks for the captain."

"I'll talk to him," Mellezour said. Standing sideways, his rifle pointed outward, he talked to Siskatoo. As the conversation progressed, it became evident that Siskatoo was a prisoner. Five armed passengers had invaded the control room a minute before the Bretons had come into the passageway.

"What do they want, these criminals?" Mellezour said. He looked at the others. "The bandit chief himself will speak to me."

The conversation progressed from an icy politeness to furious screaming. Then Mellezour put his hand over the receiver.

"They are American gangsters, Captain," he said. "They have taken over the control room. They intended to hijack your ship for the platinum and iridium, which they say is more valuable than gold. They offer to share part of it with us if we will cooperate with them."

Calloc'h spoke in Breton.

Mellezour said, "Do not be stupid, my compatriot. Of course we will get vengeance for the blood of our comrades. But we will appear to cooperate. And once they are within range of our guns, we will massacre them."

He removed his hand from the phone.

"Your offer sounds tempting, Hooke. I think we can come to terms agreeable to both parties. How will we arrange a meeting where—I hesitate to say this but you understand, is it not?—we will be safe from, forgive me, treachery?

"Also, how would you like to exchange hostages? One of your men for one of mine? You will have to confer with your colleagues first? I also must have a conference with my colleagues. After all, one of them must volunteer to be a hostage."

His face became even redder. "What? I be a hostage? Name of a pig! I am the leader! The heart! The brains! The intestines! My men would fall apart without me. Would you be a hostage? Ah, I thought not!"

A minute passed while he listened again. Then he said, "Very well. I will call my men and I will put forward your so interesting proposal."

He hung up. "Difficulties arise only to be overcome. Now I will call . . ."

His outstretched hand stopped. The phone was ringing. "Name of a thousand devils! Hello!"

He turned once more. "Captain, it's your third mate. Hooke has given him permission to speak to you. But hold your phone out so I can hear also."

Silver walked across the cabin and unclasped his hands slowly from his neck. Calloc'h backed away. Mellezour put his ear close to the receiver.

"Captain? Siskatoo. We're in a hell of a fix, Captain. The robber chief didn't say anything about it, mainly because I hadn't said anything about it. But when these thugs burst in here, the pilot tried to jump them. He laid one of them out, but they gunned him down. He's still alive, though. They also shot up the computer and the teleset. The electrical lighting system, air-conditioning, and telephone systems still are working. So's the radar.

"But, Captain, we don't have any control! The engines have stopped operating, and there's no rudder or elevator response!

"We're drifting, Captain!"

7.

Silver asked to talk to the chief of the robbers.

Hooke's voice was like gravel sliding down a chute.

"Yeah, what is it?"

"Captain Silver here. Did Siskatoo tell you about the hurricane coming our way?"

"Yeah, he did. What can I do about it?"

"Without aerial control, we won't be able to get away from the hurricane. Also, there may be line-squalls preceding it. They could break up this airship in a short time. The control equipment must be fixed."

"That sounds reasonable," Hooke said. "If this ain't just a trick. So what do you want to do?"

"Arrangements must be made to get some engineers and repair equipment into the control room. At once. We may not have much time."

"You wouldn't be trying to scare me, would you?"

Mellezour snatched the phone away. "Hooke? I don't think he's trying anything underhanded. The danger sounds very real to me."

He listened, then nodded and said, "I comprehend. First we must arrange for hostages? Very well. I will call my men, and when we have decided what to do, I will call you back, is it not so?"

He replaced the phone on its hook.

"First, though, how many men will be needed? And where is the repair equipment stored?"

"The chief electronics officer, Moon, and the mate—in both senses, since he's her husband—are enough. I think. Ask her. Maybe she'll need another man. The storage room is off this passageway, near the aft section."

"This had better not be a trick," Mellezour said. "Remember, if these repair people do anything suspicious, we can always knock you off. Or some of the passengers."

Mrs. Hooward gasped; her husband whimpered.

Mellezour reached for the phone. It rang before he touched it, and he jumped. Calloc'h grinned. Mellezour scowled. Calloc'h's grin collapsed.

Mellezour's face turned from red to gray. Muttering something in his native Celtic language, he handed the phone to Greatheart.

Moon's voice crackled in his ear. "Captain? I'm being held prisoner here, in the aft observation room, by four of these Children of Breiz. There are twenty of the crew here, including my husband. Three crewmen got away. These terrorists shot at them, but I think our men got away into the upper structure. One of them knocked down a Breizist and took his rifle.

"But their wild firing tore some big holes in Gas Cells Three and Four. They also punctured some of the containers holding the liquid methane. The helium's coming out of the cells, and the methane's boiling out of the containers."

Silver took a deep breath. He wondered if his color was the same as Mellezour's.

"Okay, Moon. Is anyone wounded? Or . . . dead?"

"No, sir. We're all right, though I did wet my pants when these bandits stormed in."

"I doubt you're the only one who did that," Silver said. "Now, have you warned the Breizists not to smoke?"

"Yes, sir, but they're smoking anyway."

Silver told Mellezour what she had said. The Breton grabbed the phone and launched into a high-pitched gabble. His face turned from gray to red once more. When he handed the phone to Silver, he said, "That's taken care of. I promised to shoot the first man who lights up."

"A gunshot'll set off the methane, too," Silver said. He did not explain that methane was lighter than air. It, like helium, would be rising. But in a short time, the gas might fill the lower levels of the hull. Maybe he could use that grace period.

"Mellezour, those leaks have to be fixed. If the cells

continue to lose helium, the ship will become heavy. Also, unbalanced. Eventually, the ship'll fall. The methane will asphyxiate everybody aboard, if it doesn't blow up first."

Mellezour, like a human chameleon, turned from red to gray again.

"My God, what kind of mess have you gotten us into?"

Greatheart was too outraged to be able to protest.

The Breizist got on the horn once more and talked rapidly to Hooke. A sound like an angry Donald Duck came from the transmitter.

Mellezour put his hand over the mouthpiece. "He says he isn't sure this isn't a trick on my part."

"What do you care?" Silver said. "You control the aft section. Get the repairs on the gas cell and the methane containers going at once. Oh, yes, some of the crewmen must go aloft and open all the hatches. That's so the methane can escape. The hatches can no longer be opened by remote control from the bridge. They'll be the smaller hatches. The big hatch, used for loading freight, is too heavy to be moved manually."

"Which means my men will have to go along and watch them," Mellezour said. "What are you trying to do, divide and conquer?"

"Mr. Mellezour," Silver said dignifiedly, "my foremost duty is to ensure the safety of the ship and the passengers. I will do nothing to endanger them. I have sworn an oath to put that above everything else."

Mellezour called the aft observation room. In a few words he told Glanndour, his lieutenant, to start the repair work. Some crewmen should be locked in a room as hostages to ensure good behavior on the part of the workers.

Glanndour was a loud talker, too. Silver heard him protest. He could spare only one man to watch the prisoners. That left four, including himself, to go into the hull to watch the repairmen,

"That can't be helped," Mellezour said, "Oh, watch out for those crewmen that got away. They might try something."

"I doubt it," Silver said. "If they don't give themselves up soon, they might be overcome by methane. Of course, they might not know that the containers have been punctured." He paused. "Listen. They're in real danger. Why don't you let me talk them out of hiding? I can use a bullhorn."

"No," Mellezour said loudly. "You stay right here. They'll just have to take their chances."

"But we need every hand we can get for the repairs."

"No. As you say, they'd be overcome by the gas. They'd be three fewer problems."

"But they'll fall through the hull covering. The skin is a tough aluminum-titanium alloy, but it's only twenty-six millimeters thick."

Mellezour shrugged, and said, "That's what they deserve. And if they do fall, it'll mean just that much less weight for the ship."

The Breton and Hooke held another conference. It was both brief and inconclusive.

Mellezour spoke to Calloc'h. "If only one of us could get to the cabin opposite the captain's wife's cabin, and do it swiftly enough, he might not get shot. Then he could shoot through the walls . . ."

"Bulkheads, damn it!" Flaherty said.

Mellezour paused, glared at Flaherty, and said, "You could spray the walls of her cabin and liquidate Hooke's men."

Calloc'h said, "You started out by saying, 'us,' and now it's 'you,' meaning me. It would be suicidal."

"I don't really think so. The men in the woman's cabin

would be taken by surprise. However, perhaps you could just get across the passageway to the cabin opposite this. Then you'd have the correct angle at which to empty a clip into the cabin. If we got rid of those men, we'd be in a better position to bargain. As it is . . ."

"That's my wife in there!" Silver cried. "You'd kill her, too!"

Mellezour said, "I am a humanitarian, Captain Silver. I regret very much spilling the blood of uninvolved people. Not innocent, I say. Just uninvolved. Though, in actuality, there is no such thing as an innocent or an uninvolved person in this complex world. Everybody is either for or against one. One must, even though with deep sorrow, break some eggs . . ."

Greatheart roared, and swung his left fist. It sank into Mellezour's stomach. The Breton said, "Ouf!" and he folded in the middle. His red face became gray again. The rifle clattered on the deck. Something struck Silver on the head.

8.

The overhead lights were in his eyes. The headache from the spray was now replaced by a bigger and more painful one. Groaning, he sat up. He was by the far bulkhead, in the corner near the toilet. The other prisoners were all sitting with their backs against the bulkhead. The two Bretons, by the telephone, were eyeing him.

Mellezour said, "I should have shot you, as Calloc'h urged me to do. But I am a kindly man, Captain Silver, and an understanding one. I appreciate your concern for your wife. Your reaction was laudable in one sense, though blameful in another. As captain, you should have exercised an iron control.

"Since you have demonstrated that you're not fully in

charge of your emotions, you'll have to be watched more carefully. One more reprehensible move like that, and you'll be shot."

He smiled. "Or perhaps you'll restrain yourself if you know that your wife will be shot."

He picked up the phone and called the aft section.

"Glanndour? Oh, it's you, Luzel. Where's Glanndour? Out with the workers? Well, call Glanndour. What? He isn't near a phone? The incompetent fool! Very well. But if he comes back, have him call me at the captain's cabin. No, you idiot. That's not the number. I meant the cabin where I am. The captain's here, too. Don't call his own cabin. It's held by the criminals."

Silver had by then gotten to a sitting position and moved slowly backward until he was stopped by the bulkhead.

Flaherty whispered, "How's your head, Captain?"

"It feels like the inside of a bell that's been rung once too often."

"Sure, and that's a pity. You didn't even have the fun of getting it. Hangovers and the clap you don't mind . . ."

"No talking there!" Mellezour shouted.

He phoned the control room. "Hooke. This . . . What do you mean, address you properly? You're the captain now?"

He put his hand over the receiver. "What kind of madness have I gotten into? Now he wants to be called Captain Hooke!"

Though it hurt his head, Greatheart leaned over and began removing his right boot. The Breton stopped talking and frowned at him.

Greatheart said, "My feet are sweaty. They itch. Is it okay if I scratch them?"

"Watch him, Calloc'h."

The boot off, Silver removed his sock and began to

work his foot over with his fingernails. His face assumed a relieved expression.

"Just to make sure, *Captain* Hooke," Mellezour said, "Have you informed all your men of the exchange of hostages? There will be no gunfire?"

Mellezour nodded, then said, "Very well. My men have the same orders. Actually, nobody can shoot anyway unless he wishes to sacrifice his own hostage. And it is absolutely vital that the control equipment be repaired as quickly as possible. Almost all of my own men are busy with the repair work on the gas cell and the methane containers. So, you see, we must trust each other. Otherwise, we will all die."

His face glowed with a rush of blood. "What? What is that? I assure you that I am not full of what-do-you-call-it? *La merde du taureau* would be the correct translation in French. I do not sully my lips with its American translation, and we will get along better if you refrain from such vulgar phrases."

"Very well. We comprehend each other, is it not so?"

He put the phone on the hook and peered around the corner of the half-opened door. Calloc'h, reluctantly prepared to play the role of hostage, moved by him and out into the passageway.

Cursing under his breath, Greatheart began to take his other boot off. One glance from Mellezour would tell him that the foot was artificial. If only he had been able to find all his clothes. For want of a sock . . .

The Breton was alternating glances down the passageway and at his captives. He took a quick look out of the door, then turned his head to Silver.

"Throw your boots over to me," he said. "Gently. And then roll up the cuffs of your pants."

"Okay," Silver said.

He slid the right-foot boot on its side across the deck

and resumed pulling off the other boot. Now he was glad that he didn't have a sock on his plastic foot. He would have to act swiftly, and taking the sock off would have given Mellezour time to shoot. When it was halfway off, he pressed on a button on the inside of the cuff. There was a click, but it would be inaudible to Mellezour.

Flaherty said, softly, "What the divil was that?"

"Don't say any more," Silver said.

He leaned back. He had only one shot, and if he failed he'd be blasted by Mellezour. Maybe he shouldn't be trying this, since his first duty was to the passengers. But he was tired of inaction and of being ordered around.

As the boot slid off, he held it so it would, hopefully, conceal the brown, hard plastic.

It would have to be done very swiftly. And aiming a foot at a target, even at this close range, wasn't easy. However, he had practiced shooting in just such a posture.

His finger poised above the button. One press readied the mechanism within the artificial member, just as the cocking of a six-shooter pistol hammer turned a loaded chamber and brought its load within the radius of the hammer. A second pressing of the button fired the small missile-shaped syringe.

Mellezour had turned his head. Silver released his two-fingered hold on the boot. As it dropped to the floor, he pressed the button on the side of the leg.

Two explosions resulted. Not from his leg. They came from the passageway. Rifles.

So startled was he, he almost missed. But the gray cylindrical missile streaked out with a slight hiss from its muzzle in the bottom of the plastic foot. Instead of hitting its target, the side of Mellezour's hip, it rammed into his neck.

The Breton grunted and dropped his rifle. He grabbed

the side of the doorway, grunted again, and pitched forward, his face landing on the passageway deck.

Silver was up and running. After snatching up the rifle, he whirled and threw it to Flaherty. He grabbed Mellezour's ankles and started to drag him inside. Guns blanged in the passageway. A bullet struck the door and slammed it against the Breton's legs. Silver dropped them and jumped back. He waited a moment, then, hearing no more shots, cautiously looked out.

Mellezour was full of holes.

Silver pulled the body in and shut the door. With more pleasure than he should have had he slapped Mrs. Hooward's face. She stopped screaming.

Flaherty said, "Here. You better take this." He handed him the automatic rifle. "I don't know how to operate it."

The phone rang. Silver answered it. A gravelly voice cursed him for a full minute.

Silver yelled, "What's the matter?"

"You *$%¼&.!" Hooke said. "You double-crossed me! But your own man got it, too, though that ain't much satisfaction to me! I'll kill you, you weasely frog, you!"

"I don't know what you're talking about."

A silence. Then Hooke said, "Say, you ain't the frog! Who are you?"

"Captain Greatheart Silver. Mellezour's dead, killed by your men! It was your men that fired. Wasn't it?"

"Are you kidding? It was *your* men. From the cabin between you and us!"

Silver was astonished. Hooke said, "You still there?"

"No, it wasn't one of us. We thought the men in that cabin were yours. We thought you'd called them and told them to hold their fire while the hostages were exchanged."

"Some exchange!" Hooke said. "They're both dead,

leaking all over the floor."

Silver checked himself. He'd almost said, "Deck, not floor." Flaherty was a bad influence.

"Then who are those men in the cabin?"

"Hell, I don't know! What's going on here, anyway?"

"I'll call them and find out," Silver said. "I'll call you back."

He hung up. Flaherty had removed the needle from the still unconscious Breton and was binding him with belts. Hooward was complaining that he couldn't keep his pants up.

"Is that what they was?" the man said. "We wondered why they was coming down the hall. They didn't have no guns on them, none showing, that is. We figured it was a trick so we shot them. Say, just what's going on?"

Silver explained. After a considerable pause, the man said, "So that's how it is? What a mess! Well, it don't make no difference to us. We're still holding Jill Micawber for ransom!"

9.

Silver was too stunned to say anything for a moment.

"Hello! Are you still there?"

"Yeah," Silver said. "So that's why you fired on us."

"Yeah. After we grabbed the Micawber chick, we was going to take over the control room. We was going to demand forty million smackolas from her old man. Cheap at the price. And we was going to have the money delivered by chopper while the ship was still in the air over Minerva. Then we was going to have you drop us off at a place it wouldn't be smart to tell you about now."

"How is my wife?" Greatheart said. "Can I speak to her?"

"No, you can't. She's okay. But if you try anything, we'll sieve her."

"Look," Silver said, "if you don't let my engineers by, they can't repair the control computer. This dirigible is going to fall into the sea soon unless all repairs can be made quickly. Of course, before then, we may be smothered by methane. By the way, if anyone's smoking in there, make them stop. Methane is highly explosive."

There was a curse, followed by shouts at somebody named Smith. At the same time, the ravens, Huggin and Muggin, yelled obscenities and Jill's voice came faintly to him.

When quiet came, Silver said, "What's your name?"

"Captain."

"Captain who?" Silver said.

"William Captain. Spelled K-a-p-t-e-n. And don't make no jokes about it. So, what're we supposed to do? One thing, though, we ain't letting loose of Micawber's kid whatever happens. She's our ticket to Paradise."

Silver wanted to yell at him. Instead, he spoke quietly. "That's okay. The main thing right now is to save the ship. We can talk terms later. I'll call Hooke and tell him what's going on. Speak to you later."

"Real bad news?" Flaherty said. "You look pale."

Silver told him. To his surprise, the Irishman burst out laughing.

"Three gangs of crooks all trying for different things but at the same time? Captain, this ship is jinxed!"

"It isn't funny," Silver said. He was wondering if perhaps the jinx wasn't on the ship but on him. He'd been in command of the AZ-8 after its captain was killed, and the ship had been wrecked. It had not been his fault, but he had gotten blamed anyway. Then he was in poverty and trouble up to his ears for a couple of years. That was old man Micawber's doing, but, nevertheless, he had been touched with extraordinarily bad luck. Now he was captain of the AZ-49, on his first voyage as captain, and he couldn't be in a worse pickle. Well, yes, he could. He could be dead. Outside of that, however, he was in a mess. And if he lost this ship, he would be under a cloud. Though this was the late twentieth century, people, especially airship people, were superstitious. Word might get around that he was truly jinxed.

He shrugged, and called the station just aft of Cell No. 1. Luzel was very angry about the death of Mellezour and the capture of Calloc'h. Silver said nothing until Luzel had cooled off.

"As your leader said, you can't cook an omelet without breaking some eggs. However, we're dealing with human lives, not eggs. Now, Luzel . . ."

"It is now Captain Luzel, if you please."

"All right, Captain Luzel," Silver said. "Here's the situation."

After he had finished speaking, he hung up to let Luzel phone Kapten and Hooke. Occasionally, he tried Hooke, and, when he no longer got a busy signal, he phoned the bridge.

The gravelly voice said, "Captain Hooke! You made up your mind yet?"

"This is Captain Silver. I'm waiting for all of you to get together. Meanwhile, could I speak to Siskatoo? I want a weather report."

"Yeah. I guess it's okay."

Siskatoo said, "According to radar, we're being pushed by the wind at eighty mph on a southeasterly course. My calculations are that we'll be over, or in the vicinity of, Easter Island, I mean Rapa Nui, in about eight hours. The main force of the typhoon hasn't caught up with us yet. But when it does, it'll be bad. There are some very violent air currents preceding the front."

Siskatoo drew in a deep breath, then said, "Captain, when the hell're we going to get things fixed up? The

ship's getting heavier. You noticed the deviation of the horizontal? It's about ten degrees now."

"Yes, I noticed," Silver said. "But Luzel says the damage to the gas cells and the containers was worse than first estimated. And the repair crew only have ten oxygen masks. Luzel insists that three of his men wear masks so they can keep an eye on the crew. That leaves only seven men working. It isn't nearly enough. Meanwhile . . ."

"Yes. I know. The methane's filling up the top of the hull faster than the top hatches let it escape. Captain, can't you convince those dummies how desperate the situation is?"

"Who you calling a dummy?" Hooke roared. There was a click.

Silver had wanted to ask how much altitude had been lost. However, though methane did not have the lift of helium, it was lighter than air. Thus, it was giving some bouyancy to the hull.

The phone rang.

"Captain Luzel here. How many parachutes are there on this tub? This female engineer says we don't have any. She's lying, is she not?"

"No, she's telling the truth. Why did you want to know?"

"You mean we got to go down with the ship?" Luzel said. Silver couldn't see his face, but the man's voice was pale.

"All the way," Silver said. "Anyway, if you chuted, you'd just land in the ocean and drown."

He added, "Let me talk to Moon."

"Okay. I'll get her . . . what the . . .?"

Faint gunfire and shouts sounded. Silver yelled questions, but Luzel had evidently deserted the phone. More shots came. He held the phone to his ear and cursed.

What was going on?

Ten minutes by his wristwatch passed. Ten minutes during which the punctured cells were losing who-knew-how-much helium. Ten more minutes for the storm to reach them. Then Luzel, breathing hard, came back on.

"Those sons of pigs, your escaped crewmen, tried to jump some of my men! One of them grabbed Emgann, and they both fell off a catwalk and went through the hull! Another got a rifle and wounded another of my men. Three of your men, including the one with the rifle, got away. They're somewhere in the hull down at the other end. I think. Listen . . ."

"I am not responsible for their actions," Silver said. "I am not in a position to give them orders, as you well know."

"Yes? That doesn't matter. What does is that more holes have been shot in the cells and in the containers. I would say that all the containers are leaking. I am not letting any repair work be done as long as your men are out there. We'd be easy targets."

"I could call them in with a bullhorn," Silver said. "But, as you well know, I can't leave the cabin. Have you asked Moon to call them in?"

"Of course, I did. And she did. But they refuse to come in. I threatened to shoot some of their crewmates, and one of them shouted back that that was too bad. But they weren't giving up.

"What's more, they threatened to release the valves on top of the gas cells and force the ship down if *we* didn't give up. They wouldn't do that, would they, Silver?"

"I hope not," Greatheart said. "Our only hope is to come to an agreement on getting the repairs, fore and aft, done as quickly as possible. You've got to strike an agreement with Kapten and Hooke. And quickly! It may be too late already!"

10.

Silver said a few more words, then called the kidnappers and the robbers. After more precious minutes passed, he hung up. He would have to wait until they had discussed the matter with Luzel. Meanwhile, the AZ-49's tail was dragging, getting near a stall condition. Airships, like airplanes, could stall. And it was dropping toward the storm-whipped waves of the Pacific. Once the full fury of the typhoon struck, it would be subjected to violent updrafts and downdrafts. Though the dirigible was better constructed to take punishment than the pre-1989s, it could break up under such sudden alterations in altitude.

A working agreement could have been reached by the three gangs long ago if it were not for distrust and greed. The exchange of hostages had been agreeable to the Breizists and the robbers. The kidnappers, however, had refused. Kapten wouldn't say why, but Silver guessed the reason. There were too few of them. To lose two of their party as hostages might, for all he knew, reduce the number holding Jill to one. They had already lost a man; he lay in the passageway, cut down in that first furious burst of gunfire.

"Captain? Siskatoo. Radar shows we're a thousand feet from the surface. Losing altitude at the rate of a foot of a second."

Silver pulled his electronic calculator from his pocket. He worked it, then said, "We now have less than sixteen minutes!"

"Yeah, I know."

Siskatoo did not sound perturbed. Perhaps he was playing the role of the stoic, imperturbable Indian.

Silver called Hooke and told him what must be done. Hooke's voice seemed to break into a sweat.

"Okay. But I sure hope this ain't another trick you've

pulled out of your sleeve."

Silver wanted to ask him what tricks he had played, but there wasn't time.

"You call Kapten and I'll call Luzel."

"Captain who? Oh!"

Silver called Luzel. The Breton said, "Whaaat? We're doomed! Fifteen minutes, you say?"

"Less than that now," Silver said with all the calm he could muster. "Relay my orders to Moon. Tell her everything except the cutting lasers, the extra ropes, and the tools must go overboard. She knows why. First, though, the ballast breeches . . ."

"Breeches?"

"The forked bags of water hanging alongside the cat-walk above the keel passageway. Ordinarily, in case of emergency, they could be dumped by remote control from the control room. But they'll have to be discharged manually now. We might have to discharge the big tanks of ballast water, too."

Luzel almost wailed. "But we can't! Three of your men, one armed, are out in the hull!"

"I'll get them to give up. They won't ignore me. After all, I am the captain, whatever anyone else says."

More precious minutes were lost while the three parties talked to each other. Then Hooke rang Silver.

"Okay! Those clowns holding your wife say they won't come out. But the won't shoot anybody going by their cabin—as long as nobody's carrying weapons. And we can only go by one at a time."

Silver said, "Have you gone up the ladder to the cabin above? My cabin?"

"Do you think I'm a dummy?" Hooke said. "Of course I have. I got a man stationed there so them Frenchies won't sneak up on us from that way."

"Then I'll tell Luzel your hostage will leave by that

cabin. He can walk to the stern on the catwalk above the main passageway. But you better call Kapten and tell him your man will be walking overhead. If he hears him, he might shoot up through the overhead. Kapten's very nervous."

Hooke called Kapten and told him what they'd be doing. Kapten objected. He thought that the robbers, once on the catwalk, could easily shoot down through the cabin's overhead. Hooke called Silver back to tell him this.

Silver said, "Oh, my God! Jill'd be killed!"

11.

"Yeah. That Kapten's right, though. It's a great idea. But I ain't going to shoot if there's methane around. Besides, I got my own life to think about. Listen. You'll be on your own for a while. Don't think even once about ducking out and trying something dirty, see?"

"Where would I go?" Silver said, and hung up.

A moment later he and Flaherty left the cabin. Mr. and Mrs. Hooward were moaning in the corner, holding on to each other. In the passageway, Silver stopped briefly to determine if White was dead. He was. He ran down the passageway. Doors opened behind him, and voices called. He looked back. A number of passengers were cautiously opening doors to see what was going on.

Once in the tail section, he talked quickly to the electronics people. Moon left with a party of four, headed for the storage room. Luzel, an unlit cigar in his mouth and a rifle cradled in one arm, greeted him from the top of a ladder. He looked like the twin brother of Mellezour. Silver climbed up. A Breton handed him a bullhorn.

He opened a hatch and stepped out onto a platform. Its ladder led down to the port catwalk, which ran all the way from the platform to the nose. To his left the visibility was comparatively unrestricted, though there were plenty of crosswires and transverse girders. On his right the massive deep-ring main frames, bracing wires, and the bulging cells obstructed the gaze. The whole was shrouded in a deep twilight; the scattered lights were brave but weak candles in the gloom.

Holding the bullhorn, he went down the ladder and advanced on the catwalk until he was near the port cargo hold. This was a towering structure of girder latticework and shear wires. The bottom girders of the hold were twenty feet above his head. Craning his neck, he could see the rectangular modules stacked within the hold.

Smoke roiled from some of them, the bullets having penetrated both the module sides and the sides of the containers within the modules. The liquid methane within the containers was boiling out through the holes, turning into an invisible gas a short distance from the jets. Not only was it invisible, it was odorless. The natural gas used commercially was provided with a smellable additive in order to warn its users.

A sudden cutting off of oxygen if a man were surrounded by it, or an explosion if a spark were present, would be the first—and last—notice of its presence.

Two of the cells were alarmingly deflated. A landsman wouldn't have thought much of their shrinkage, would scarcely have noticed it. But he saw that the situation was indeed desperate.

His bullhorn bellowed, echoing in the vast hollow between the cell bays and the port hull.

"Williams, Carszinski, Chong! This is your captain. Can you hear me?"

A faraway voice answered, seeming to come from above and to his right. If so, the three were in grave danger of suffocation. They must be far forward, however, since a more central location would have caught them in the upward- and outward-spreading gas. Perhaps a top forward hatch was giving them ventilation.

"Give yourselves up! Come on in! There'll be no retribution! The ship's in a bad case! We have to start repair work at once, and it can't be done until you surrender! Otherwise, we'll be in the ocean in a few minutes!"

"Is that straight stuff, Captain!" Chong's voice rang. "You aren't just saying that under duress?"

"No! This is a number-one emergency!"

"Okay! Tell those %$*@+!s not to shoot!"

"They've promised they won't!"

Luzel came out onto the platform, a rifle held ready.

"They're surrendering?"

"Yes. They should be visible in a few moments."

He pointed toward the fore section. Far off, a small figure was moving on the catwalk toward them.

"Hooke's man, coming for the hostage exchange."

Luzel said, "Ah, there they are!"

He pointed at three shadowy forms that had emerged from behind the second nearest main cell to the nose. They were climbing a perpendicular ladder used mainly by inspectors and sailmakers.

"Hooke's man doesn't seem to be armed," Luzel said.

He turned and said, "Keriverc'hez!" A tall muscular man stepped from behind the door. Luzel spoke a few words. The man went down the ladder and began walking slowly. Hooke's man had reached the central part of the catwalk and now was waiting for the Breton.

Silver said, "We don't have nearly enough sailmakers to patch the holes in the time we need. The sailmakers will have to use every hand available, supervise them. But we'll need all the gas masks. At that, the patching will have to be done from the bottom up. Helium can asphyxiate a man, too.

"Also I don't want to do this since it increases the danger, but there's no other way—holes will have to be drilled through the module sides and the container sides. The release of the liquid methane will lighten the cargo considerably. That'll keep us aloft much longer.

"Unfortunately, that can't be started until after the lower holes in the cells have been patched.

"Meantime, the laser cutter can begin work on the girders at the bottom of the cargo holds. We only have one laser, which means the work will be slow. The bottom girders will be removed so the modules will drop through. That'll mean a tremendous loss of weight."

Luzel paled. "You can't do that!" he cried. "The laser's heat will ignite the methane!"

"No, the hydrogen and methane will rise. The laser'll be below the leakage."

He added, "Also, I'll have to release some helium from various cells. That's necessary to trim the ship, that is, put it into equilibrium. Normally, I could do that by remote control from the bridge. But the computer isn't working, so the valves must be operated manually. It's a ticklish job, since it's guesswork, and I'll have to run the operation by phone. I can't take the time to run back and forth from cell to cell. Besides, I'm not a long-distance runner.

"The trouble with trimming the ship is that we'll be losing helium we can't afford to lose."

Luzel looked as if he'd like to object. Instead, he suddenly pointed his finger at the three crewmen. These had almost reached the catwalk.

"Your man still has the rifle!"

Silver swore. He should have ordered that the weapon be dropped overboard. That would lighten the weight and also prevent the trigger-itchy fingers of Hooke's or Luzel's gang from shooting. But he had his mind so overloaded with problems that he had forgotten. There was no excuse for it; a captain shouldn't forget anything.

He quickly put the bullhorn before his lips.

"Williams! Carszinski! Chong! Whichever one has the rifle! Drop it! Right now!"

Too late. The two hostages were yelling and dropping onto the catwalk. Flashes of gunfire stabbed from the dim light at the fore approach to the catwalk. One of Hooke's men must have been stationed there to watch, and now he was firing at the crewmen.

All three fell, one landing across the catwalk, the other two bouncing off of it and over the side. With one went his rifle.

Silver remained standing. Luzel dived to the platform deck. Suddenly, bullets were screaming by him and ricocheting off the girders. Silver decided to dive, too.

His face pressed against the metal deck, he cursed and raved. The murders of his men had filled him almost past the bursting point. Hooke's man was out of reach. He grabbed Luzel. Silver could have taken the man's rifle away from him then and shot him. Into the aft section he would go, rifle blazing. Wipe them out.

Sanity cooled off his white-hot fantasy. He let loose of Luzel's throat.

"Sorry," he said, though the word choked him. "I just grabbed the first thing that came in reach."

Luzel coughed, then said, "One of us has to get to a phone and explain to Hooke."

However, there was a safer way to communicate. Luzel called out instructions to a man behind the door, and in a few minutes he returned. Hooke had said that the exchange of hostages could now proceed. He did not offer an apology.

The two got up. Luzel was actually smiling. Silver restrained the impulse to knock his teeth out.

"I suggest," Silver said, "that all the corpses be thrown overboard as quickly as possible. That'll lighten the load."

Luzel's smile became even broader. "Perhaps we should also throw the passengers out? They are useless, and their total weight must be considerable."

"That is a logical step," Silver said, briefly amused by the ludicrousness of the suggestion. "But it isn't humane."

They stepped aside as riggers, carrying a laser cutter and associated equipment, crowded past them. Fortunately, the electrical generators in the tail cone had not been damaged. Otherwise, the ship would be in even greater danger.

The sailmakers and their assistants went by. Some wore oxygen masks, and all carried rolls of patching material and patching "guns." A minute later, the hostage from Hooke came up the ladder. Luzel's man had disappeared into the gangway at the other end.

The hostage was a tall, thin man with a wart on his nose. His face was a pale green.

"I'm Miggleton," he said. "And I'm sick." He rubbed his stomach. "I think I got appendicitis. That's why she picked me to be a hostage."

"She?" Silver and Luzel said simultaneously.

"Yeah, she. Hooke. Why, didn't you know she's a woman? Hooke the Hooker they used to call her in Chicago. Now she's fat and fifty, she's turned her hand to robbing banks. She shoulda stayed in that profession. Hijacking airships ain't turning out so hot."

"Yeah, but that voice . . ." Silver said.

"Ain't that something? She sounds like a truck driver. She was one, too, for a while."

Four of Luzel's men, armed, had gone down to the catwalk to guard the repair crews. Silver wondered if there were any more in the tail section. If so, they were greatly outnumbered. It should be possible to overwhelm them.

But some of his crew were bound to be killed or badly wounded. Besides, for the moment, all energies had to be concentrated on keeping the airships buoyant and on regaining aerial control.

Nevertheless . . . he struggled with his wrath, and he won. A captain must be cool at all times.

"Ain't you going to get the doctor for me?" Miggleton whined.

"You can go to sick bay," Silver said. He gave him directions while Luzel, frowning, listened in. "I don't know where the doctor is. If he's in his cabin, which is within shooting range of Kapten's cabin, you're out of luck. It's up to you to phone him; I don't have time. The doctor's name and cabin number are on the ship's directory on his desk."

"I don't know about letting him roam around unguarded," Luzel said. "I'll take him down there."

Miggleton was not so sick that he wasn't curious. "What're all those men doing?"

Silver told him, although Luzel had lifted his finger to his lips to indicate he should not do so.

Miggleton's eyes bugged. "You mean, you're going to throw out the platinum and iridium? You can't do that! They must be worth millions!"

"Yes, and it weighs a quarter of a ton," Silver said. "It has to go."

"You can't *mean* that," Miggleton said. Even more sweat formed on his forehead and upper lip. "Man, that's why we're holding up this ship!"

"Would you rather *swim* for it?" Silver said.

"Hooke ain't going to like this," Miggleton said. "She won't allow the repairs to the controls if you dump those precious metals."

"Tell her it's the metals or her life."

"No, *wait!*" Luzel cried. "That's a fortune! It could be

used to finance the operations of the Children of Breiz!"

"You ain't thinking of taking it all, are you?" Miggleton said.

Luzel drew himself up. "Of course not! I am a man of honor, a patriot, not a common criminal such as yourself. I agreed to split the metals with your party, and my word is iron. It is true that it may be necessary to sacrifice it to save our lives. But for the present, we will hang on to it as long as possible."

"That can't be done," Silver said. "The methane containers are all on the bottom. The metals container is on top. It's too heavy to move, so it goes with the rest of the cargo."

"How'd you get it in the freight container structure?" asked Miggleton. "Didn't you use a crane?"

Silver rolled his eyes at such ignorance. "The cargo's lowered into the hold through a big hatchway by a helimp while the freighter is in the air."

"What's a *helimp*?"

"A blimp with helicopter motors."

Miggleton's brow went up. "Hooke's going to kill everybody in sight if you dump those metals."

Silver was unswervable. "If we *don't*, this ship's going to crash. As it is, cutting the holds' bottom girders will weaken the ship's structure. If it's hit by any violent drafts, it may buckle. Or break."

Silver was exaggerating for effect, though not by much.

Luzel turned gray. Miggleton looked even sicker. Luzel, apparently deciding he didn't want to leave the scene, called one of his men to conduct the hostage to sick bay. This made Silver certain that there were only five Breizists. Luzel, however, gave some additional instructions in Breton to his man.

Silver went into action at once. Using the platform

phone to give directions to the crew, he readjusted the helium contents of the bags. The ship resumed a near-horizontal attitude. For a while, there would be no tail-heaviness.

In the meantime, however, the air had become bumpier, forcing the men on the catwalk to hang on for safety. The sailmakers and riggers relied on their belts.

Silver told Luzel, "Since we're without propulsive power, we're drifting. We don't have dynamic stability. We could stall if we get tail- or nose-heavy. Releasing the gas makes the ship even heavier. We *did* gain some buoyancy when we released the water ballast. Now we have to discharge the big water ballast tanks, the fuel, and the slip tanks. The big fuel tanks will have to be emptied, too, and then the tanks'll be cut loose. But first, the cargo must go."

By then, the rigger C.P.O. had plugged in the cord of the laser cutter into a girder connection. His safety belt fastened around a girder, his feet on another, he was moving the tip of the cutter across the girder on the deck of the port hold.

"Hopefully," Silver said, "cutting the bottom girders on three sides will weaken the deck so much that the weight of the containers will bend the girders on the un-cut side. And the modules will drop through. If they don't, then the cutter has to get underneath and cut the inside ends of the girders.

"Another problem is that we only have one cutter and so we can't cut the decks of both holds at the same time. When the port cargo modules drop, the starboard modules will remain. Their weight will roll the ship so many degrees—I don't know how many—to starboard. Everybody will have to be warned of that. Otherwise, they might be pitched overboard."

He added, "We have to cut some bracing wires, too.

That will weaken the ship's framework some. On the other hand, the loss of liquid methane has lightened the load. Still, the modules and the empty containers weigh many tons."

Luzel said, "Is that why you sent men to the starboard hold to drill holes in the containers?"

"Yes. The less weight there, the smaller the degree of roll to starboard. Let's hope the containers don't jam when the bottom goes out. It'll be a hell of a job man-handling the modules. We'd have to cut the vertical girders and more bracing wires, and that'd put an additional burden on the framework."

The man whom Luzel had sent with Miggleton reported.

"My captain, the hostage is with the doctor. But the doctor complains that, in accordance with orders, he had thrown practically all his medical equipment overboard. He says the company will have to reimburse him for the loss. I told him that was no concern of ours.

"He is going to conduct an operation, however. But he disclaims any responsibility for fatal results.

"Also, as you ordered. I forced all passengers out, except for the reactionary de Rioux, who refused to leave his cabin. I set the passengers to work throwing the dead men overboard."

Luzel said, "Kapten gave you no trouble?"

"No, he lived up to his agreement. He kept his weapons trained on the passengers, who are, of course, scared to death. The corpses were carried to the observation deck, where they were cast out through the open space left by the removal of a window."

The man grinned.

"One of the corpses was a kidnapper, one of Kapten's men, who had been shot by Hooke's men in the passageway. Only it seems that he still had some life. Just before he was swung out of the window, he opened his eyes and he protested. 'I am not dead yet,' he said.

"'Who would take a criminal's word for that?' I said. The passengers holding his shoulders and his feet also protested. I told them that they would eject the kidnapper or I would see to it that they too went out the window. And so he went out. He was doomed to die soon, anyway, and the sooner we got rid of his weight, the better."

"Well done," Luzel said.

Silver felt sick. He had no sympathy for the kidnapper, but the callousness of the Breizists showed what they could do if pressed hard enough. The time might come when they would feel it necessary to pitch the passengers out. And then . . . the crew?

Silver called Siskatoo.

The third mate said, "Out altitude is now fifteen hundred feet. Unless we lost a lot more weight, we'll strike the surface in about fifty minutes."

"How's the computer repair coming along?"

"Moon says it'll take at least two hours to fix it."

Silver ordered three crewmen to go into the main passageway and set the passengers to stripping the cabins. Everything removable, including their baggage, was to go.

The cooks and stewards were to detach the stove, refrigerators, and sinks and get rid of them. All galleyware except trays and glasses was to be cast out. All food except a twenty-four-hour supply would also go out.

During this time, the zeppelin was hit by ever stronger gusts. Silver had to cling with one hand to the phone box to steady himself. Though the air was bumpy, its effect was smooth compared to that an airplane would have experienced. The ship was not moving against the wind; it was moving *with* the wind. Its troubles would come when it encountered violent up- or downdrafts.

Just after Silver hung up, Luzel got a call from Hooke. When he turned from the phone, he was pale. If Luzel suffered any more color changes, Silver thought, he would become a permanent human chameleon. If he didn't die from shock first.

"Hooke insists that we save the platinum and iridium, no matter what happens. Otherwise, she'll stop the control repair work. And she just might shoot some of your men."

"She's out of her mind!" Silver yelled. "Doesn't she realize that if we don't get the motors, rudders, and elevators working, we're helpless? Even if we made the coast of South America, we'll be able to land only by crashing. And we might not be able to pick a good, smooth landing site. How'd she like to end up on top of a mountain with its peak up her . . . ?"

Luzel interrupted. "I told her that. She says she doesn't care. This is her chance to make a fortune, and she isn't going to give it up. She'll throw out the passengers first."

"That means a long delay in the cutting operation! Okay, then, I guess I can't do a thing about it! Tell her we'll save her precious metals!"

"Perhaps," Luzel said, "I could storm the control room?"

"No! The electronics men might be killed. Then where would we be?"

He stopped. A machinist mate had halted before him. "Captain, the chief sent me to tell you that all the methane containers have had holes drilled in them."

"Very well," he said. "Get back to your duty."

He turned to speak to Luzel. "I won't ask for volunteers to unpack the metals. I'll do it myself."

"Why you?" Luzel said suspiciously.

"Because we're shorthanded. Because it's too dangerous."

Luzel narrowed his eyes even more. "But you will have to station men on the ladder to hand the metals down to each other?"

"No. I'll lower each ingot by rope. That'll only require two men. Me and another."

"Go ahead, then," Luzel said, smiling. "To tell the truth, much as I acknowledge the necessity of getting rid of weight, I profoundly regret losing all the money those metals represent. Perhaps we can salvage them and the ship, too."

A few minutes later, Silver, wearing an oxygen mask borrowed from a rigger, climbed up a ladder alongside the starboard cargo hold. Coiled over one shoulder was a long light rope. On his head was a metal helmet to which was affixed an electric lamp. A safety belt was attached to the broad leather belt around his waist. Clips on this held a pair of wirecutters and stuck under the belt was a short crowbar.

As he passed the holes which had been drilled through the module sides and the containers, he heard the hiss of liquid methane evaporating and saw the almost foot-long jets of semiliquid gas. He was surrounded by a deadly invisible explosive. But as long as his mask operated and he made no sparks, he was safe.

Once, halfway up the 150-foot ascent, he looked down. The men on the catwalk were not exactly lilliputian figures, but they certainly looked a long way off. Like him, they were being raised up now and then by the gusts of wind.

Toward the nose the chief rigger, Salmons, was using his laser to cut the bottom out of the elevator shaft. This led from the catwalk to the top of the zeppelin and was

used to carry personnel and equipment. Silver had decided that the elevator itself should be dropped before cutting proceeded on the hold decks. Getting rid of it would add to the ship's lift, and the work could be done quickly.

Just below the ladder were Luzel and a crewman with a plastic bucket.

Silver resumed climbing. After what seemed like a long time, he reached the top of the hold. Above was the dark surface of the huge hatch through which the helimps loaded supplies and cargo. At regular intervals, the helimps also picked up crewmen and deposited their reliefs.

There were a few overhead lights, but they were inadequate for his purpose.

He climbed over the top and got onto the top cargo module, which was open on top. He removed the rope from around his shoulder and lowered it over the edge. The crewman at the bottom tied its end to the bucket, which held an electric drill and a long extension cord. Silver hauled it up and then tied the one end of the rope to the horizontal girder forming the top of the hold.

The plastic container stamped "HEAVY METALS" was against the far side of the hold, resting on top of a methane container. Brace wires secured it, preventing it from sliding. Standing well back so the suddenly severed wires wouldn't strike him, Silver used his cutters on them. Then he forced open the lock and raised the lid. It would have been easier to have used a key, but that was in the possession of a man in Minerva.

His helmet light showed rows of forty-pound dull-gray brick-shaped ingots.

After gazing at them for a few seconds, he muttered, "Maybe I can fool Hooke and Luzel. It's worth it to get rid of over 1,100 pounds. More, counting the container's weight."

Using the crowbar, he forced up one end of the tightly packed ingot. Then he lifted it out and carried it to the fore part of the hold. Straight below him there were no girders or wires to deflect the ingot. And he was hidden from the view of those below by the vast, bulging gas cell in the next bay.

Over the ingot went, disappearing into the darkness. It would pierce the hull-covering and hurtle into the storm-torn Pacific.

The next ingot he sent down in the bucket. The third he dropped after the first one.

Neither Luzel nor Hooke knew exactly how many ingots there were. And they wouldn't have time or the means to weigh them. The only scales on the ship had been thrown out during the lightening procedure. Silver had made sure of that.

Working swiftly, he walked back and forth. There was no time to stop and rest, to catch his breath. Back and forth. Up and down. Sweat, pant, gasp, groan. It was just like his honeymoon—minus the pleasure. If it hadn't been for his gloves, his hands would have been burned by the speed with which he lowered the bucket.

In exactly an hour, he had cleaned out the container. Twenty-eight ingots had been disposed of, averaging two minutes and eight seconds for each ingot. That was twice as fast as union regulations permitted.

Sweat running into his eyes, his mask-enclosed face feeling as if he were in a turkish bath using salty water, he dragged the empty container across the top and heaved it over the side. An end struck a wire as it rotated, causing a faint hum.

12.

Silver plugged the extension cord of the drill into one of the receptacles along the top girder of the hold. He

drilled three holes in the top of each container in the star-board hold, then disconnected the cord and climbed over a girder to the port hold. Once, a bump almost dislodged him. Here he repeated the procedure. It wasn't absolutely necessary for him to make additional holes, but the more there were the faster the top containers would lose their contents.

The drilling was disconcerting. The moment the point broke through, it was blown back out by the enormous pressure of the escaping methane. He had to hang on to the drill to keep it from being jerked out of his grip and into the air. Moreover, he had to be careful not to let any of the jet touch him. It would have frozen his skin, at the same time giving him a terrible burn.

By the time he climbed back down, he found that the ingots had been laid end to end along the catwalk. There was no time for men to lug them to a safer place. Moreover, the elevator and its cables had dropped through, and Salmons was busy cutting along the girders of the starboard hold's deck. Despite the frequent jarrings from the rough air, Salmons had worked swiftly. The girders had been severed on three sides of the hold, and he was working on the port hold.

Silver was disappointed in that the weight of the almost-empty containers had not been enough to bend down the girders and let the containers fall through. It would be necessary for Salmons to go between the cargo structures and cut the girders on the inside. If the containers jammed, the horizontal girders outside the hold and perhaps the vertical girders at the bottom of the hold would have to be cut.

That was a very dangerous procedure. If the bracing wires did not hold, the cargo structures could topple over with the containers still in them. Should they fall sidewise, they could—and probably would—tear through

the network cording around the neighboring cells and make huge holes. If they fell sidewise, they would wreck the hull framework. In the first case, that of cell damage, the ship would become so heavy it would plunge into the sea. In the second case, the framework might be completely broken and the ship would break in two. If it held together, there would be no way to get the containers out. And Silver was depending upon jettisoning them to keep the AZ-49 aloft.

However, there was some good news. Despite the difficulty in working in the rough air, the sailmakers had patched all the holes in the cells. They had done an admirable, almost miraculous job in such a short time.

Heading aft, Silver saw a man running down the catwalk. It was Agocelli.

Agocelli stopped. A Breizist at the far end yelled at him, asking what he thought he was doing. Agocelli shouted back that he was delivering a message from the control room. The third mate had phoned Silver, but he wasn't in sight. So the guard at the hatch, seeing Silver, had told Siskatoo. And he'd sent Agocelli.

Silver, impatient, yelled *"What is it, Agocelli?"*

"Officer Siskatoo says to tell you that we're about to hit really rough air! Everybody should tie themselves down, if they can, and if they can't, hang on!"

"Is everybody notified?"

"Yes, sir. I gotta go, Captain."

"Before I hit you?" asked Silver. At that moment he was hurled down onto the platform deck. An invisible force, pressing him downward and also to port, perhaps 35 degrees, made it impossible for him to rise. For a moment, the unexpected and violent change of situation scattered his senses. Then they decided to come home. Now he knew what was happening. A terrible updraft was carrying the giant airship toward the skies as if it were a stone ejected by an erupting volcano.

Metal groaned all around him. Behind was a screech that tore at his nerves. Girders were coming apart . . . and then came the twang of shear wires snapping.

The pressure increased. Turning over, holding on with one hand to an upright, he looked back. The electric lights were flickering, but he could see between the girders of the starboard cargo hold.

It was empty.

The bottom girders had broken under the load, precipitating 560 pounds if the containers were completely empty. *More* if the liquid methane had not completely evaporated.

The sudden loss of weight had made the ship rise even faster in the updraft. And the containers in the port hold must not have fallen. It was their weight which was causing the list to port. This was not so much now, perhaps 15 degrees, but that was far too much.

Slowly, the pressure on him eased. The updraft was losing its hold on the vessel. The gas cells nearest him had swelled. As the altitude increased, the lessening atmospheric pressure allowed the helium in the bags to expand.

He did not know whether or not the ship had been carried above its pressure height. The air seemed thin but it did not seem as oxygen-poor as it would have been if the altitude were 20,000 feet. In fact, it had to be much lower. If the pressure height had been exceeded, he'd have been unconscious by now. And the automatic valves on the bottom of the cells might not have opened swiftly enough to relieve the pressure. In which case, the cells would have burst.

He noticed that the ingots lining the catwalk were gone. Of course. They would have slid overboard when the ship had leaned to port.

So much the better. That meant less weight. But Hooke was going to be furious. Maybe she'd be too scared to even think of her loss.

He stood up and started walking forward to check on the damage. Suddenly, he was floating a few inches off the catwalk. Terrified, he grabbed for something to hold onto. There was nothing to reach, though a wire was only a few inches from his hand.

Once more, he was bewildered. As his feet slowly regained the catwalk, he realized that the ship was now in a terrific downdraft.

His hands gripped the side of the walk. It was well he did, for his grip was almost torn away by a sudden violent jerk to starboard. More yells. A crack of something large breaking. Screams of torn metal.

What else could happen?

That question was answered at once. Something struck the deck in front of him. Something else hit him in the back, causing him to cry out with surprise and pain. Other objects splattered onto the metal in front of him, and his leg felt another blow.

He was so confused that it took several seconds to recognize the orange-sized grayish-white objects, some of which were spread out by their impact.

Hailstones!

He said, "Ooof!" as another hit him between the shoulder blades. One smashed just before his eyes, spraying icy particles on his forehead and nose.

Then it was over. He lay for a few seconds, waiting to be hit again. Quivering, he got to his feet, his hand squeezing an upright.

Agocelli, moaning, ran by him.

Vaguely, he noted that the zeppelin had almost regained its proper horizontal attitude. At least, it felt as if it had.

The catwalk was twisted, curving in two places. Shear wires hung loose here and there, and a transverse ring was definitely out of line with the rest.

Moreover, there were holes in the gas cells again. Ordinarily, the hull and the bags would hold out against any normal-size, normal-velocity hail. But these monsters had come plunging through like meteors of ice. What made the phenomenon so strange, however, was the fact that the ship had been falling when the hail struck. The pellets must have been hurled by a different draft than the one which had pressed down on the ship. Or was that possible?

By then his mental numbness had lifted. Now he knew that the restored lateral attitude of the vessel had to be due to the loss of the modules and containers in the port hold. The bottom girders had snapped.

He continued on the crosswalk to the port catwalk. From the platform, he looked down the length of the hull. The nearest cells displayed some holes; shear wires were dangling; but the port hold indeed was empty.

However, one of the containers, undoubtedly from the topmost module, had somehow been tossed out before the cargo had fallen. The brown plastic cube was on its side, resting against a girder, kept from falling by some wires.

He staggered to the phone, noting on the way that the ship now seemed to be nose-heavy. There were no outside references to determine this, of course, but gravity was definitely pulling him forward.

Siskatoo answered the phone. Frightened voices almost drowned out his. But he spoke calmly, as calmly as if he were ordering dinner.

"We came close that time," Siskatoo said. "Another twenty feet, and we'd have crashed. We're rising now, but we are nose-heavy."

"I'll get the sailmakers on the bags," Silver said, "if they weren't all pitched overboard. Now, Siskatoo, everything in the control room goes out. The control computer, the chairs, the radar."

"The radar?" Siskatoo said, shaken.

"Yes! We can't afford its weight, and it won't make any difference if we know how fast we're falling if we can't do anything about it. I'll also send riggers to cut out the equipment in the radome.

"And tell Hooke that her weapons have to go, too."

"She won't go for that."

"Make clear what might happen if she hangs onto them. Exaggerate the case, though God knows every ounce less is really going to help."

He called Luzel, who sounded scared. In as few words as possible, Silver told him the situation. Then he asked for the rigger and sailmaker C.P.O.'s.

Salmons, who answered first, was breathing heavily. Silver ordered him to dump all the oil in the fuel tanks and then cut them loose. After that, he was to cut loose the nose- and tail-engine gondolas. Then the housings and struts for the gear transmission and propellers.

"After which you will remove the mooring bolts of the inboard diesels and all their connections. Then you will muscle the engines overboard.

"Shove them over on alternate sides. The fore starboard engine first. The aft port engine next, and so on. We don't want to unbalance the ship any more than we have to."

"Yes, sir. Only we don't have near the tools we need. Most of the heavy crowbars went into the drink to lighten the ship, or lost during the drafts. Not only that, we'll have to run back and forth like madmen! My crew is pooped out!"

"Do the impossible," Silver said, echoing the orders of

a long line of officers, a line that probably went back to the Bronze Age, if not further.

Viren, the sailmaker chief, got his orders to look for the new holes and patch them. He groaned but said nothing.

13.

Silver went into a room in the tail section and down a ladder. Confusion and panic predominated in the main passageway, but work was being done. All the cabin doors had been removed and thrown out. White-faced passengers were carrying out the chairs and beds now. Even the doors to the control room had been removed. Silver, having entered via a ladder in the tail section, could see the lower part of the entranceway through the smoking room, the navigation room, and the bridge. An armed man stood at the doorway of the smoking room.

Walking forward, he found out that one door still remained, that on Jill's cabin. It was opened enough to reveal a short chunky man with a bushy black beard and a fringe of bristly hair around his bald pate. He held a rifle. The interior of the cabin was dark.

"Are you Kapten?" Silver said.

"Yeah. What's it to you?"

"I'm Captain Silver. You've been informed that the ship's in grave danger."

"Sure." Kapten grinned. "That's quite a show you're putting on. You had me fooled for a while. But not any longer. Them bums, the frogs, and that Hooke, they made you do it, didn't they? So I'd get sucked outta here and—blammo!"

For a moment, Silver was speechless. Then he said, "This is for real! We may fall into the ocean any minute! Everybody's got to pitch in and help! And every bit of excess weight *has to be* thrown overboard!"

Kapten spoke, apparently to the men behind him. "Ain't that something? I told you it was all a trick. He sure puts on a good act, though, don't he?"

There was no use wasting time arguing with this man, a splendid example of what Mark Twain called "invincible ignorance."

Jill's voice came from the darkness. "Greatheart! Operation Odin!"

Silver wanted to protest, but he dared not. She had decided to take action that might result in her being killed. Not to mention himself. However, she must have a good reason for this desperate move.

Kapten half-turned. "What's this? Operation Odor? Shut that chick up, Punchy."

Strange cries burst from the room. A black cloud suddenly struck Kapten's head from behind. He screamed and batted with one hand at the thing.

Head down, Silver charged. His shoulder rammed into the door, which struck Kapten and sent him rolling. Silver pitched forward onto the deck, spun on his side, and grabbed Kapten's beard. He jerked with all his strength.

A man, yelling, his head also covered by a black cloud, tried to run out of the cabin. He stumbled over Silver and Kapten and sprawled on the deck, his body halfway out into the passageway.

Kapten, bellowing with pain and anger, was up. Then he was diving for the rifle, the barrel of which was revealed in the light from the passageway. Silver couldn't get to Kapten fast enough, but two clouds, feathers flying, swooped onto him. The beaks and the claws of Huggin and Muggin pecked and tore at him. Kapten yelled, "My eyes! My eyes!" and he dropped the weapon.

Silver yelled, "Huggin! Muggin! Retreat!"

The light came on. Silver, rising with Kapten's rifle,

saw Jill standing over a man's prostrate body. An automatic pistol, butt reversed, was in her hand. Beyond her were the two raven cages, hanging from stands on the bulkhead. Their doors were open.

"That was pretty dangerous, Jill," Silver said. "Downright foolish."

"I was desperate," she said.

"Well, it turned out all right." He grinned. "Those birds certainly responded on cue."

As he spoke, the huge ravens fluttered from the edge of the bed and settled down on his shoulders. Silver spoke to them, and they flew back to the bed.

Kapten, holding his bleeding face, got to his feet. Silver told him to get into the corner. The man who'd fallen over him groaned. Silver got him up and shoved him toward the corner. The man from whom Jill had snatched the gun was still unconscious.

Flaherty came in grinning. "Sure, and what's this?"

Silver explained, then said, "Throw their weapons overboard. Get some passengers to strip this cabin. Put these creeps to work."

Kapten said, "You'll pay for this, you jerk! I'll get you!"

Silver whirled on him. "It may come down to deciding who's going to be thrown out so we can lose weight. You'll be the first candidate if you don't cooperate!"

Kapten croaked, "You can't do that! I got my rights!"

"We're in international waters. The only law here is the captain's, and I'm in command."

"Yeah! Tell that to those frogs and that butch!"

"They don't love you either," Silver said. "Jill, are you able to help out?"

"I'm a little shaky, but I'll be all right. I'll take the guns and the ammo and get rid of them."

He paused. "Sweetheart."

Jill smiled wanly. "Okay, sweetheart. I've been doing a lot of thinking. The Hoowards and that steward must've been paid by Daddy to frame you. But I won't really know until they confess, will I?"

"They will. Or I'll wring their necks."

After throwing the captured weapons and ammunition overboard, Silver pushed his way through the mob to the bridge. A man holding a rifle stopped him at the entrance to the control room and frisked him. Silver bellowed for Hooke, who came waddling to the doorway. She was very short, very broad, and looked like Santa Claus minus the beard. Minus also the twinkling eyes. They were mean, tinged with scare. And Santa Claus never wore pistols nor carried an automatic rifle.

"Let him in, Anko."

The windscreens had been cranked down. The electronics crew had gutted the control console and thrown out its contents. They were unscrewing the bolts securing the console to the deck. All the chairs had already gone overboard.

Silver was amazed to find that there were only two robbers left. Ronan, the Breton hostage, sat in a corner, scowling.

Hooke said, "What was that shooting about?"

Silver told her. She looked at him narrow-eyed. "You sure you didn't hide them rifles?"

"I thought about it. But I'm the one who gave the order to get rid of all weapons."

"No, we don't," Hooke said, walking toward him, her belly shaking like a bowl of jelly. "You're going to get this tub onto land. Otherwise, I'll shoot you—if it's the last thing I do."

14.

"That'd save me from drowning by a few seconds," Silver said. "And it would be the last thing you'd do. If you're hanging on to the guns because of the platinum and iridium, forget it. They went overboard when the ship rolled."

Hooke looked stunned. Then she burst into tears.

"You mean it?" she said, sobbing.

"Ask Luzel."

"I wouldn't trust that crook. He'd try to keep it for himself."

Silver bounced into the air as an especially violent gust struck. "No, he's seen the damage and he knows what a mess we're in. Now, get rid of those guns."

"Not me, mister. Not even if Luzel's gang throws their blasters away. If we get to land, we'll need them. Old Hooke ain't going out without a fight."

Silver said, "At least chuck the rifles. You can get by with your pistols. I tell you, every ounce gotten rid of means a few more minutes of life."

Hooke wiped her eyes with a big, dirty handkerchief. "Yeah? You really mean it, don't you? Okay. If Luzel does the same."

Luzel finally answered. Silver told him what had happened, then gave the phone to Hooke.

There was a long discussion, punctuated by bursts of profanity from Hooke. Somebody, Flaherty probably, had ordered the stewards to make sandwiches. Agocelli staggered in under a huge tray holding sandwiches, cookies, glasses of milk, and several bottles of booze and wine.

"This is the last supper," Agocelli said in a shaky voice. "We're throwing the trays out and the cutlery, after everybody eats. From now on, if you want food, you'll have to go to the galley to get it."

Silver said, "I'll take a couple of ham-on-ryes and milk, steward."

Agocelli came toward him but stopped several feet away. His arms shaking under the strain, he held the tray out to Silver. Apparently, he did not want to get within hitting distance.

Hooke snatched two sandwiches with one hand and a bottle of Duggan's Dew of Kirkintilloch with the other. Stuffing half a sandwich into her mouth, she chewed savagely for a minute, then washed the food down with several ounces of the scotch.

"Say, Agocelli," she said, "things ain't turning out the way we hoped, are they?"

Silver said, "What's this? What do you mean?"

Hooke took another massive bite. Mayonnaisse streaked her chin and lips.

"No harm telling you now."

"No!" Agocelli cried. "You promised to keep quiet!"

"Aw, what the hell's the use now? Anyway, I ain't taking you with us. The metals're gone; your usefulness is over. Yeah. This little creep sold you out, Silver. He smuggled our guns in for us. Really held us up on the price, too. That's the kind of jerk you got working for you."

Agocelli paled and retreated a few more steps.

Hooke laughed, spewing food down her front. "He snuck the guns in long before the ship took off. Had to bribe a guard to do it, though."

Silver, glaring, said, "Agocelli was working for somebody *else*, too. He was in a frame with the Hoowards to bust up my marriage."

At that moment, the bridge deck tilted up. For a second, Silver thought it was an updraft. It wasn't however. The nose-engine gondola had been cut off by the laser. Now Salmons and his gang would hasten with their equipment to the tail, over a quarter of a mile away, and would sever the support struts of the engine gondola there.

The phone rang. Silver, nearest it, answered. Luzel, panting, said, "What are your demands?"

Silver told him that Hooke would agree to throw away the rifles if the Breizists did the same.

"How would we arrange that so nobody is holding any rifles back?"

"I know how many each party has," Silver said. "I'll collect them. I'm an impartial agent."

"Yes, but what if we gave you our rifles and then she refused to surrender hers?"

Silver sighed, and said, "A good point. Very well. I'll stand by in the observation deck. Each gun can be brought alternately to me. First one of yours, then one of hers. No, make that simultaneous. Since there's two of them and five of you, your man should bring in all your rifles and her man will bring her three. Miggleton left his when he became your hostage."

He added, "Then I'll count them and throw them out."

"I don't like it, but I can see the gravity of the situation, no pun intended."

Silver called Hooke to the phone. She talked a minute, then hung up. "Okay, Captain, you get to the observation room."

The transaction took ten minutes. As one of Hooke's men, carrying three clipless rifles, came down the passageway, one of Luzel's, burdened with five, approached from a point equidistant from the control room. Silver took their weapons and cast them out the port. The two, their hands on the butts of their holstered pistols, backed away from each other.

During this time, the tail-engine gondola was cut loose. The dirigible was now close to a horizontal attitude.

The rigger C.P.O. reported that the fuel tanks had been released. Cutting was now being done on the fore starboard transmission gear and propeller strust.

Viren, the sailmaker chief, reported that three cells were completely patched. But he had nineteen holes to go.

"You sound like you're playing golf," Silver said.

The ship's doctor called as soon as Silver hung up.

"I'm sorry. My patient, you know, the hostage, just died. It's not my fault. He was too far gone. And my surgical equipment . . ."

"I know, Doc," Silver said. "Just get rid of everything in the sick bay. And I mean everything."

He hung up. Hooke said, "Who was that?"

Silver hesitated. If he told her the truth, he might be, in a sense, responsible for her hostage's death. On the other hand, if Ronan were killed, he could be thrown out and the ship would have that much more lift.

He said, "It was the doctor. He wanted to know if he should throw his medical equipment overboard."

Dawn came, bringing light but little relief. The sailmakers had just found two holes in the cells they had unaccountably missed in the first inspection. The vessel was only fifty feet from the waves when the last of the ten engines was jettisoned. The ship responded by rising to an estimated six hundred feet.

Telling Hooke that he was going to see if he couldn't get more food brought in, Silver went down the passageway. Most of the passengers were lying down on the deck of the observation room or in the main smoking room. They huddled together as if for comfort.

He checked on the doctor, to make sure that Miggleton's corpse had gone out. The doctor complained a little about having to drag it out to the tail and rolling it out a hatch without any help. Silver said, "You could stand a little exercise, Doc."

He went to the port catwalk and walked down to a point opposite the big container caught in the wires. He paused to consider it. Should he get rid of it now or wait a little longer?

And then he was lifted up, curving backward and sideways as if he were a diver leaving a springboard. His shoulders smashed into the hard metal of the catwalk. A great cracking noise drowned out any others that might be made.

15.

When he finally regained all of his senses or most of them—some seemed to have been lost forever—he was able to reconstruct what had happened.

Another vicious downdraft had gripped the airship and hurled it toward the ocean. It had also twisted the framework again. He had been launched from the catwalk. As his luck had it—it couldn't be all bad, could it?—he had not been precipitated off the catwalk and so become food for the fishes. Speaking of which, they could not be too far away. Ocean water was lapping against the catwalk, occasionally surging up and wetting his back.

Standing groggily, he looked around. The container was now floating on the water, which was almost washing over the top of the main passageway. The impact of the crash had dislodged it.

He started to groan with pain, but, seeing Jill standing on the platform, he gave a cry of delight. She pushed through the people on it and came down to greet him. They put their arms around each other and wept.

"The crash knocked me out," she said, "but the water rushing into the cabin woke me up. I fought my way up to the tail section. A lot of people got out, though I don't see how."

Greatheart looked over her shoulder through a huge tear in the covering. The sea was comparatively smooth; the sun shone unhindered by clouds; the storm was over.

But their ordeal was by no means over. They were down in the ocean, kept afloat only because of the gas cells. The ship's metal skeleton had been twisted and damaged to such a degree that it might break apart at any time. Though the surafce of the ocean, judging from the rise and fall, consisted of long, low rollers, the prolonged action might separate the aft and fore parts.

They had no means of notifying ships or shore stations of their location. Which, in any case, they did not know except in a general sense. If the navigational satellite was still malfunctioning, it could be some time before they were located and help could arrive. By then, they could be under the ocean.

The first thing he did was to check on the food and water. There was enough in the aft section, in the crew's stores, to last them two days. Then he checked on the survivors. Amazingly, there were forty. Four, however, had broken legs; three, broken arms; one, a minor concussion of the skull. All, including himself, were badly bruised and suffering from various degrees of cuts.

Apparently, de Rioux had been among those who'd drowned. His secretary and two bodyguards had been trapped with him.

Siskatoo had not made it out of the control room.

He was not happy to find that Luzel and three of his gang were among the living. Nor that Hooke and one of hers were limping around. All of the kidnappers, except Kapten, had died. Nor was he gratified that the Hoowards and Agocelli looked healthy, discounting their frightened faces, skinned knees, and various contusions.

The only two who had not lost their pistols—wouldn't you know it?—were Luzel and Hooke.

Amey, the doctor, did the best he could for the people with the broken limbs, but it wasn't much.

Silver made sure that the electrical generating equipment was still working and that the laser cutter and certain tools were still available. After this, he got everybody on the catwalk. Addressing them from the platform, he said, "We may drift to Easter Island, that is, Rapa Nui. Perhaps, a ship might pick us up. But we may sink before that happens, and we're short on food and water. So, here's what I propose."

His audience was stunned. Finally, Hooke said, "You must be crazy!" A few echoed her sentiment. The others looked as if they thought his plan was desperate but agreed there was little else they could do.

During the long day, the airship looked like a broken but busy beehive. The riggers used the laser to remove the girders atop Cell No. 2. As these fell, they were diverted to one side by ropes attached to their severed ends. This prevented the thin cover of the cell from being damaged.

Meanwhile, the container was pulled out of the water and gotten onto the catwalk.

The cell was covered by a rope network. The ends attached to the lower girders were freed. The cell floated up for a short distance, then was held from rising on through the hole by wires placed through the bottom of the rope network. The ends of the wires had been run over girders and twisted around the wires.

Salmons returned to the container and with his laser cut off its upper portion. This was shoved into the sea, where it floated bumping against the side of the catwalk. Salmons then cut a series of holes about six inches below the open edge of the container.

A gang shoved the container into the water, where it was jockeyed around until it was directly below the cell. At this point Silver would have liked to place a circular piece of metal at a point below the cell and then attach the ends of the rope network to it. There was none available, and he had no means of making one. The laser could cut a strip from a girder, and it could heat parts of the strip soft enough to be curved. But the laser could not weld the open ends of the piece together, and the welding equipment had gone overboard long ago.

Instead, the ends of the netting were looped through the holes in the sides of the container and tied.

A length of rope was attached to the automatic valve on the bottom of the cell. Its free end dangled to a few feet within the deck of the container. If the rope were pulled upon, it could open the valve, an arrangement made possible by Salmons, though undreamed of by its designer.

Though he was exhausted, Silver had enough energy to feel pride when he looked at the completed vessel.

What he saw was, in effect, a free balloon.

It was rough work, but, hopefully, it was adequate.

Everybody was exhausted from emotional drainage, physical battering, and lack of sleep. He let most of them lie down while food and water were brought out of the crew's galley.

"Eat up. Drink up," he said, giving them an example. "This is the last of it."

After half an hour, a silent time broken only by the moans of the hurt, he got the ambulatory to their feet.

A section of a ladder had been cut, one end tied down to the catwalk, and the other end run out over the container or "basket." The riggers carried pieces of metal of varying weight into the basket and arranged them along the sides. There were to be used as ballast.

Next came the badly injured. They were assisted or carried over the ladder or even dragged, not without some complaints, over the ladder and handed down to the riggers. After this, all but two riggers climbed out. The others stayed to help the passengers in.

Huggin and Muggin, the ravens, flew onto the edge of the basket, where they perched.

Meanwhile, Silver had passed word through the crew to line up on the catwalk ahead of the passengers. He took a place in between the two groups. If Luzel or Hooke thought this was a peculiar boarding arrangement, they did not say anything.

This might have been because they were watching each other too intently. At no time did they take their eyes off each other, and they managed to keep a good distance between them. Moreover, their hands never left their pistol butts.

Luzel now stood up at the foot of the ladder to the platform. His men, armed with crowbars and metal saws, stood behind him. Hooke stood on the crosswalk to the right of the platform.

"Okay, Captain Silver!" Luzel shouted. "I have an...."

"Just a minute, Luzel," Hooke said. "I got something to do before we take off. Agocelli, you dirty, double-crossing fink! You put the shiv in my back, and what's more you stuck it into Luzel, too!"

"What do you mean?" Luzel said.

"I mean, I found out that he not only smuggled in guns for me and Kapten, he smuggled them in for you, too! He took money from all three of us, knowing we was bound to shoot each other. I call that triple-crossing, not double. What's more, he probably took money from the captain's wife's old man to frame him. So that makes it a quadruple-cross!"

She snatched the pistol from her holster and aimed it at Agocelli. The steward, his ferret face twisted with horror, screamed, "Please, Captain, don't let her do nothing to me! I confess! I confess! I was in on the frameup with the Hoowards! But if you save me, I'll testify in court that you was framed!"

"It'd serve you right if she did shoot you," Silver said.

He spoke to Hooke. "Come on. Put that gun down. You're not judge and jury. He'll get what's coming to him when we get back to the States."

"What do I have to lose?" she cried. "I'll be in the slammer for life if I'm caught, but I ain't going to be. No, I pays my dues, and sieving rat-finks is one of them."

Agocelli backed away, forcing the crew behind him to retreat. Silver was also pressed back. There was no way he could do anything about Hooke except talk to her. She was beyond his reach. Anyway, even if he had been close to her, why should he risk his life by jumping her? He wasn't going to get killed trying to save that piece of slime, Agocelli.

Hooke's gun bellowed. Agocelli, lifted up and spun around by the force of the Magnum .375, disappeared over the other side of the catwalk.

A second later, Luzel's automatic boomed. Hooke was knocked backward into her colleague, and both went down. Neither got up. Apparently, the bullet had gone through both of them. The woman's pistol had flown out of her hand and dropped into the water.

Luzel, pointing his weapon at the crew in front of him, said, "I was waiting for a chance to get her. She was a mad dog, an irresponsible killer."

He backed away. "And now," he said, "comes the denouement. It's obvious that we cannot afford to take you people along. If we get to Rapa Nui, you'd tell the authorities about us, and we'd be jailed. And eventually we'd be guillotined in Paris.

"But if there are no witnesses, then we will just be poor devils who survived the crash of a zeppelin at sea.

"Besides, the fewer there are for the balloon to carry,

the more chance it has of reaching land."

Passengers cried out; many wept. Luzel, waving his pistol, shouted angrily. "I do not like to do this! But it is necessary for patriotic reasons! My men and I must not be kept from advancing our great cause! I hope you understand, even if you cannot fully sympathize."

Silver, hidden by the crew in front of him, stood on one leg, a hand gripping a crewman's shoulder to support himself. Jill swiftly rolled up his left pants leg. He lifted the leg, and she turned the plastic member to remove the neural connections. Two complete turns unscrewed the leg.

"I could leave you on this floating hulk so that perhaps you might drift to land or be picked up by a boat . . ."

"Ship, dammit!" Flaherty said.

Luzel glared at the Irishman. "You will be the first to swim for it.

"Now this grieves me, but it is a matter of necessity, of historical pressure, of inevitability."

Mrs. Hooward screamed, "We'll drown! Or be eaten by sharks!"

"Then you can make an existentialist choice of your fate," Luzel said. "Very well. Mr. Flaherty, you will jump into the water and swim through that breach in the hull. Land is due southeast of us, perhaps a hundred miles away. Or so you told me."

"Thanks for the directions," Flaherty said. "You scum!"

"The patriot must expect abuse," Luzel said, smiling. "Go ahead, Mr. Flaherty. I don't want to shoot you. But if I have to in order to set an example for the others, I will."

Silver had by then adjusted controls in a groove on the inner side of the plastic leg. He held the end of the thigh

in his right hand while Jill's finger poised above a button.

"Now!" he bellowed, and he threw the leg over the heads of the crowd in front of him.

Spitting a narrow, blue-white flame a foot long, it rotated in an arc, the end of which was Luzel.

The Breton froze just long enough for the missile to strike him. Unfortunately, the thigh-end hit him. But as the leg bounced off his chest and flopped over the catwalk, its flame turned at him. In effect, a hot foot gave Luzel the hot foot.

The Breton jumped back, screaming, and he fired at the plastic leg. By then, Flaherty, head down, bellowing like one of the bulls of Cooley, was charging. The top of his head rammed into Luzel, who folded. His automatic fired twice, but it was pointed away from the crowd. Over he went, Flaherty on top of him.

Close behind the second officer came the crewmen. They leaped over the two strugglers and bulldozed the other Bretons backward.

Silver had gotten word to his men that they must act when he gave the signal. He had no idea when or under what circumstances. He just knew that a showdown would come. Luzel would not let them have a chance to survive.

The battle was furious but brief. Flaherty wrenched the pistol loose from Luzel's grip, and it slid into the sea. The burly Irishman then proceeded to choke the Breton until he became unconscious.

The five Breizists hurt a few of the crewmen, though not seriously. Then they went down under a barrage of fists and feet.

16.

Jill retrieved the leg and turned off the flame. Greatheart resecured it and then got things going swiftly. The

Bretons were dragged upon the platform and their hands and ankles bound with rope.

"We'll be long gone by the time you work yourselves loose," Silver told the now conscious Luzel. "I don't want you to be able to interfere with our ascent. I won't wish you good luck."

Luzel groaned and spit out a tooth.

"If we reach land, I'll send a ship out for you. Maybe you'd better wish *me* luck."

"Either way, I die."

"Then you have an existentialist choice of your manner of death."

The boarding took fifteen minutes. Silver got into the basket last. He looked around, then opened his mouth to order the men stationed at each corner of the basket to cut the restraining wires. Jill put a hand on his shoulder and said, "Are you really going to leave those men here?"

"I've been wondering if I should," Silver said. "It goes against my grain to do it, but they *are* dangerous."

"Yes," said Jill, "but you've allowed Kapten and his men to come along. And they are just as bad."

Silver looked at the kidnappers, who sat on the deck, their hands bound before them.

"Okay. I was really hoping someone would argue with me about Luzel."

There was another delay while the Breizists' feet were unbound and they were roughly muscled into the basket. Luzel cursed him while this was going on.

Silver said, "Your gratitude overwhelms me. Now, sit down in the middle there and don't annoy me at all. Otherwise . . ."

He made a gesture as if he were throwing ballast overboard.

The wires were cut. The cell, looking not at all like the layman's conception of a balloon, resembling more a wrinkled elephant skin hung up to dry, rose slowly. Some of the passengers cheered; others looked as if they were going to be sick.

The balloon rose straight up until the upper one-third had cleared the hole in the top of the zeppelin. Then, as Silver had expected, it moved forward. And it stuck.

Though the airship was being moved by the wind, its speed was slower than the air outside the hull. The wind had pushed against the upper part and now only the up-and-down movement of the ship in the waves would free it. Knowing this, he had had the girder ends wrapped in covering taken from a cell.

Some of the passengers asked why the balloon was not moving. Silver ignored them. The balloon would have to free itself; he could do nothing to aid it. If it did not get loose, then it would have to be brought back down. He'd pull the release valve cord, and the balloon would settle back. And they would be back where they had started.

Well, yes, he could do something.

"Throw out two more pieces."

Over they went, splashing in the well below.

Suddenly more buoyant because of the loss of weight, the balloon shot up. Passengers and crew cheered. But Silver, Flaherty, and Moon leaned out over the side of the basket. As the balloon sped up and out, it would drag the basket along. Here came the end of a girder, inserting itself between ropes. The three pushed against the girder just above them, and the basket swung back. Just enough to free it. For a second, the basket scraped against the girder end, tearing off the wrapped cell-covering. But not before Silver saw that the girder had not been thoroughly covered. A thin edge of metal had projected beyond the fabric. There was a chance that the thin skin of the cell had been ripped. If so, it would have been better to have stayed on the AZ-49.

Looking back at the zeppelin, now dwindling as it fell behind and below, Silver estimated the wind speed. It sould be around a spanking twelve miles an hour. Number 3 on the Beaufort scale. A gentle breeze.

They were on their way, but to where?

An hour passed. As the helium in the balloon expanded due to lessening atmospheric pressure, the balloon became rounded. It would continue to rise until it reached pressure height, at which point the valve would open automatically. But it could not be allowed to go so high. Everybody aboard would die of oxygen starvation before it attained its maximum ascent. As soon as breathing became difficult, it would be necessary to release some helium with the cord.

After that, the balloon would fall. It would do so slowly, but nevertheless, unless checked, it would descend. Only Silver's skill could keep it up beyond its natural rate of fall. And the situation would be complicated, though possibly improved, by temperature inversions, updrafts, and downdrafts. And by his aptitude at estimating ballast jettison.

"We must be at about ten thousand feet," Silver said. "It's hard to judge."

A few minutes later Flaherty said, "I think I see land. It could be low clouds on the horizon, though."

"If it's land," Silver said, "it could be Rapa Nui. Or maybe one of the islands closer to Chile, Sala-y-Gomez, or San Felix, or Juan Fernandez, one of those islands. Maybe even Chile. I don't know. There's no telling how far that wind blew us since we lost our instruments.

"But if we are at about ten-thousand-feet altitude, and if that is land, then it's about one hundred and seventeen miles away."

A half-hour passed. Silver, using his wristwatch, estimating the distance between wavecaps over an estimated

mileage, tried to calculate their velocity.

"I make it between thirty-five and forty miles an hour," he said to Flaherty. "The wind's stronger up here."

"Yes, but it seems to have gotten stronger on the surface, too," Flaherty said. "Look at those waves."

Silver did not bother. He was too intent on his figuring.

"If the wind keeps up, we'll get to that land, if it is land, in about three-and-a-half hours, maybe four. Just pray that the wind keeps its direction. If it shifts, it could blow us to one side."

"The balloon'll stay up that long, won't it?"

"Sure!"

A half-hour passed. The land, or the clouds, swelled slightly.

And at the same time it became evident that the waves were getting larger.

Silver's heart turned over like a cold motor with a weak battery.

The balloon was losing altitude.

He went around the basket, leaning out to look above. The enormous bulge of the semisphere made it impossible to see any holes in the upper part. It was easy to see that the bag was deflating, however.

His inspection finished, Silver said, "That girder must have torn a hole. Okay. Get rid of four of the larger pieces of ballast."

Flaherty did so. The balloon rose again, then started to settle down. Two more pieces went over the side. Since it was difficult to conceal the reasons for the sudden activity, Silver told the passengers not to panic. Some of them went into a fit anyway.

Mrs. Hooward yelled, "It's all your fault!"

"You could have stayed behind," he said. "I told you

about the dangers."

He looked around. "Flaherty, untie those men. They're going to need their hands, and they're too outnumbered to give us any trouble.

"Now, everybody throw overboard anything you're carrying or wearing except your underwear. We need all the lift we can get."

He removed his wristwatch and flipped it over the side. Huggin, the raven, left his perch, disappearing from view.

Most of the people obeyed him quickly enough, but Mrs. Hooward and two other passengers seemed reluctant. Silver urged them on. Mrs. Hooward plucked a pearl necklace and a tiny jewel box from between her breasts. Another woman wept as she threw out a diamond necklace and a wristwatch which she had hidden in her bra. A man, scowling, cast his wallet and two jeweled rings over the side.

At that moment, Silver was startled by Huggin's landing on his shoulder. He turned his head to see his wristwatch dangling from the raven's beak.

"He must have dived after it when you threw it out," Jill said.

Silver removed the watch and cast it over again. His left hand held the bird's legs, restraining him from repeating the feat.

"Say, what about the crows?" a passenger said. "They weigh *something*."

The man was right, except about his identification of them as crows. Silver called Muggin to his other shoulder and spoke to the two birds, pointing at the clouds ahead. After some croaking protests, they obeyed. He watched them wing toward the dark mass on the horizon, wondering if they would be the only survivors.

Another half-hour. More and more ballast hurtled toward the sea, which seemed to rise toward them depressingly often. Silver tried to measure out the lost weight sparingly. The higher the balloon rose, the more helium escaped because of the difference in pressure.

Another thirty minutes. More ballast was tossed. Two more hours passed. And the last piece of metal was dropped.

But now, the clouds were not clouds. They were land! *Mountains!* Hills, anyway.

Grinning, Greatheart Silver announced the news. Everybody cheered.

Ten minutes later, his spirits chuted from high to low. The balloon was sinking again and so swiftly that it would be in the ocean many miles from land.

Nobody cheered.

"Okay, everybody. Off with your underwear. Every last stitch."

To set an example, he removed his T-shirt and shorts and dropped them over the side. A few people protested, though not vigorously.

Mrs. Hooward, looking malicious, said, "Off with it, Silver."

"What? I'm not wearing anything, as you can plainly see."

"Your handy-dandy, razzle-dazzle, flame-throwing electro-mechanical member. Your plastic leg."

Greatheart stuttered with rage. "But, madame, I can't walk without it."

Flaherty said, "Logically, she's correct, sor."

A number of passengers seemed to agree.

He shrugged, "All right."

A moment later he sailed the leg over the edge. His eyes were dimmed with wetness. It was almost like losing a part of his body. Hell, it was just that. He could get another one, but it would put him in debt for years. At that thought, the tears did flow.

By then the balloon was falling even faster. The land was three or four miles away, and the basket would touch water in about three minutes.

"And no more ballast," Silver muttered.

Flaherty said, "Sor, your permission to leave the vessel. I'm a strong swimmer, Captain, and the seas ain't so rough, ayther. I can make it."

"That's a noble thought, Flaherty," Silver said. "But what about the sharks?"

"I don't see any. Anyway, if I don't do it, we'll all be battling sharks soon enough."

"Go, and God bless you," Silver said, choking.

"Sure I always was glory-happy."

Two minutes passed. "We're almost ready to hit," Flaherty said. "Wish me luck, Captain."

Over the edge went Flaherty. Silver watched him fall feet-first and enter upright. The Irishman emerged grinning, waved a hand at them, and began swimming strongly. The balloon was rising—for the moment.

17.

Silver watched, sweating from more than the westering but still hot sun, as the coast slowly drew nearer. The balloon began dropping again. When it was two miles from the surf-pounded beach, it would strike the water. For a little while the wind would blow it along with the basket tilted. Then it would fall to the surface, and water would enter the basket. Eventually, the basket would go under, and there would be thirty-two people in the water. Ten of whom couldn't swim at all.

Then Moon, the chief electronics officer, made the offer. "Captain, I'm not a bad swimmer myself. I'll go next, if the situation demands it."

"God bless you, too," Silver said.

A moment later, she went over the edge, falling about

ten feet. Immediately, the balloon rose.

But four minutes later, he felt compelled to call for another volunteer. Sparks said he would go, though he wasn't exactly eager.

"You coward!" Mrs. Hooward said to Silver. "Why don't you volunteer?"

"Madame," Silver said, "and I do mean 'madame,' I'm the captain. The captain is always the last to leave a vessel in distress. It's an ancient tradition. Besides, my lack of a leg would handicap me too much."

Sparks sat on the rim of the basket, one hand gripping a rope, facing Silver. "Tell my wife I love her, even if she is hell-on-wheels to live with. And tell her there's a checkbook taped to the back of the Maxfield Parrish picture in the living room. I got a hidden account. Only don't tell her if I make it. She'd kill me."

"I promise. And go with my blessing."

Sparks let himself off backward, like an aqualung diver. The balloon soared up. But not for long.

Jill called up from below. "Are we going to make it?"

Greatheart shook his head.

"I'm going next," she said, "and don't you dare say no. You know what a great swimmer I am, sweetheart. I'm also a coward. I was waiting for someone to volunteer. But I guess they aren't going to."

He squeezed her and kissed her cheek. "You're no coward. I am. I just don't think I could make it, though, and that'd be a useless sacrifice."

"I know. Well, so long, baby. I love you."

Jill seemed to be in no difficulty, and there were no shark fins visible. She'd make it.

A few minutes later he asked for more volunteers. This time, since the coast was only half a mile away. Salmons and four crewmen went overboard. The balloon rose swiftly, and presently it cleared the beach and the low hills behind it by a hundred feet and the higher hills by forty feet. Below it spread a valley strewn with rocks. Some of the rocks, he soon recognized, were the towering carved stone heads which made Rapa Nui so intriguing.

The balloon began to settle again; and the figures at the other end of the valley became more distinct. The large ones were stone heads staring from a hillside across the valley. At the base of one was what appeared to be a sacrificial ceremony. Hundreds of scantily clad Polynesians were dancing around it foolishly to the beat of drums and the tootling of flutes. A woman was stretched out on a stone block. By her stood a feathered man wearing a high feathered headdress.

Silver wasn't alarmed at this grim sight. Around the dancers were a number of cameras and chairs for the chief actors, the director, and the producer. Extras stood by; an actress was sitting on a chair while a woman added touches of makeup. Beyond a low hill was an army of tents, vans, and trucks.

Silver called down. "Everybody get to the other end! We'll be landing in a moment. The basket will tip over, so I want your weight to be on that side. Now, don't panic. Just hang onto the rim. The balloon'll drag us a little ways. But thank God there's plenty of help to grab us."

By then the movie company had seen the approaching intruder. They all stopped dancing; the drums and flutes were silenced; everybody was looking up. A man, probably the director, was running out toward them, waving them away.

As the balloon got nearer, Silver could hear the director's screams. "Go away! Go away, dammit! You're ruining the scene!"

"Sorry," Silver shouted. "We can't do a thing about it."

"It's ruined, ruined! I'll have to shoot the whole thing over!"

Silver could see by now what was going to happen. The basket was going to hit the upper part of the stone head.

"Brace yourselves!" he called out.

The stern, weird profile of the ancient rock spread out before him. He ducked. The next moment, the basket struck with a loud noise. He was half-stunned. But he felt the basket tilting, and then he slid forward. Behind him, shrieking, came most of the occupants. He went first, falling out of the basket, scraping off skin against the coarse volcanic stone and landing with a thump that seemed to jar his teeth loose on the ground.

Others fell on him, knocking the breath out of him. And, as he found out later, cracking several ribs. Fortunately, they did not all strike him.

Through a haze of confusion and pain, he saw the basket, suddenly relieved of many bodies, snap to an upright position, as its edge slid off the statue's chin. And the balloon carried it on past the head and up.

Not everybody had been tipped out. Mr. and Mrs. Hooward must have hung on with all the tenacity of the thoroughly terrified. Their pale faces looked despairing, and their screams rose—along with the rapidly ascending balloon.

Then the director was standing over the scattered pile of squirming, groaning humanity. "I'll sue! So help me, I'll sue."

"You idiot," Greatheart said faintly, just before fainting, "don't you know what a scoop you just made?"

18.

He was right. The movie company—Famous Artists Resplendent Teledramas—sold the films of the landing to the news networks after the story of the AZ-49's ordeal became known worldwide. Moreover, the producer bought the exclusive rights to Silver's personal narrative while Silver was still in a daze, not sure what he was signing. He was shafted on the deal, but he was able to buy another bionic leg with the money.

All this came out later. In the meantime, Silver was joined in the hospital by Jill, Flaherty, and the other crewmen who had swum for it. Both the Silvers were out of bed in two days. They moved into the Hilton Rapa Nui, expenses paid by the film company. Jill phoned her father, who was delighted that his daughter was safe and delirious with ecstasy at not having to pay a huge ransom for her. As for the ship and its cargo, the loss would be covered by insurance.

Micawber had a few painful moments, however, when Jill accused him of trying to break up her marriage. He denied it, of course. Unfortunately, there was no way of verifying Agocelli's confession through the Hoowards. They had been picked up by a ship twenty miles east of the island and taken to Los Angeles. There they disappeared, no doubt assisted by her father.

Jill said, "I really told him off. I swore that if anything fishy like that happened again, I'd automatically assume that he was behind it. And he'd never see or hear from me again."

"That's a fate to chill the blood," Greatheart said. "Come here and warm it up."

Later, Jill said, "Daddy promised me you'd get a new command as soon as you were on your feet. He didn't like it, but he knew what'd happen if he tried to make out that you were negligent in losing the ship."

"That's great," Greatheart said. "After that mess, I'm sure life is going to be one sweet song. I've used up all my bad luck."

Some are born with bad luck; some achieve it; some have it thrust on them. Silver seemed to have attained permanently all three conditions. For the reason why, see the next episode:

Greatheart Silver
in
The Great Fog
or
IN OLD NEW YORK: 1934

GALACTIC

ARTHUR BYRON COVER • RALPH REESE

INTRODUCTION

Galactic Gumshoe
a Franklin Davis thriller
by Arthur Byron Cover
Illustrated by Ralph Reese

If they burst into BPVP's office today and demanded a hostage for an insane asylum, I'd yell, "Cover! Take Cover!"

I wouldn't be referring to a safety precaution, either.

I mean, this guy has to be nuts. Take Art Cover's Hugo-nominated first novel *Autumn Angels* (Pyramid, 1975)—*that* was a real looney-bin. Crawling birds, indeed! Or how about *The Platypus of Doom* (Warner, 1976)? I mean, whoever heard of doom-oriented platypuses? (Platypi?) This Cover is obviously using a guava melon for a brain, nu?

Not quite. Art knows a good deal more about what he wants to say-do-write than what his titles let you think. *Autumn Angels* has depth and humor. *The Platypus of Doom* has a glossy cover. *Galactic Gumshoe*, the final feature of this book, has two monsters for your money—and a private dick living in the Seldon Cessation, way in the future.

This story is alternately low-key and low-brow in its humor. It's a fun read and an idiosyncratic introduction to Cover's shamus-is-outrageous series. *Franklin Davis*, the dick in question, has appeared in *Platypus*, and although this adventure may be a bit atypical for *W.H.*, any later appearances will slide more comfortably into our mode of fantasy.

In the meantime, peruse the pages of this story for some

remarkable, really remarkable, illustrations by Ralph Reese, a fantasy illustrator who is best known for his work at *National Lampoon* and for *Marvel Comics*. The sheer linework of these pieces have left such talented graphic storytellers as Jim Starlin and Neal Adams with smiles on their faces. Drawing on a set of influences ranging from Wally Wood to Howard Pyle, Ralph has come forth with some tight, funny and evocative artwork.

A gumshoe, for those of you unfamiliar with the phrase, is a detective (usually private). For more information on this and an answer to the question, "What has feet, slime and a headache?" please turn the page.

GALACTIC GUMSHOE
by Arthur Byron Cover

My story ended in 1963; it renewed its option in 2678 Seldon Cessation, approximately two million years after mankind began colonizing the galaxy. My name is Franklin Davis, and I'm a private eye, a shamus, a gumshoe, a peeper, the only hard-boiled dick in the universe. I could have become a spaceman, a miner, a pirate, a historian, a lecturer, a soldier, or a basket case, but investigating the indiscretions of faceless nobodies was all I knew, so I was stuck with it.

I'm six-foot-three; I weigh two hundred pounds, some of it muscle, some of it fat; I have curly blonde hair, heavy eyebrows, blue eyes, a tan complexion, and a nose which has been broken six times. My smile is mildly sardonic, but women in this sector of the galaxy prefer their men subtle and debonair, so I altered it after many nights alone practicing to meet their standards. I wear green corduroy slacks, a light green jacket, a white shirt, and a thin black tie. My wing-tip shoes have holes in the soles, my mirror sunglasses have golden wire-rims, and my white snap-brim hat needs dry-cleaning. I designed my laser to resemble a .44 Magnum.

For a time I lived on Rakish, the tackiest planet in the galaxy. Its lush, thick jungles were populated by bothersome insects and even more bothersome cowardly carnivores who swallowed people whole when they crept upon them in their sleep. The huge yellow sun hung like a five-hundred-watt naked bulb in the dark blue, cloudless sky. It rarely rained, but when it did, the people rushed for shelter to avoid the acidic raindrops. There were five great cities on Rakish; I lived in Carnelia, the capital, a burg constantly beset by heavy fog, minor earthquakes, and three volcanoes emitting eternal columns of soot in the sky. No matter what, I couldn't escape the eternal pollution problem, though the government had begun planning to cap the volcanoes after King Henry's mother died ten years before her time due to the foul air.

There was no reason for mankind to colonize Rakish. No one could make a fortune there because the planet had no decent farmland, no rare metals, and no tourist attractions. People settled there because of manifest destiny. Man was created to swarm over the galaxy and to use it as a stepping stone to the universe. I spent many evenings with cigarettes and a bottle of cheap wine trying to find some flaw in the logic supporting the belief and I couldn't, so I reluctantly came to accept it. Besides, private eyes traditionally don't question society. They fight for realistic concepts of justice and for the happiness of a few innocent faceless nobodies. They're perpetual martyrs who find suffering more attractive than fortune, spiritual fulfillment, and peaceful afternoons sipping lemonade beside the swimming pool. That's me. That's what makes me so mean.

It started out like any other day. I woke up in my sparsely furnished one-room flat in the slums of Carnelia. I examined my bloodshot eyes and my rugged, angular features in the cracked mirror. I shaved myself with soap and a dull blade, cutting myself only once. I had no tissue, so I let the blood run until it clotted. Since I had lost my toothbrush, I pressed the paste on my finger and rubbed it over my teeth. Telling myself that I would have to do my laundry someday, I dressed. My quick breakfast consisted of a hard-boiled egg left in the refrigerator. I love hard-boiled eggs. They remind me of me.

I walked through the narrow city streets, just as I had on many other average days, because it was the only way I could get to my office. There were a few spaceships, planes, automobiles, and four-legged beasts of burden to carry people around, but these were too expensive for working-class heroes. Carnelia proper was only five square miles anyway, and I could get wherever I wanted to go by walking. The stone buildings were very slender and tall; the population was close to a million. The stench of garbage and sewage assaulted my sensitive nostrils. Children wearing rags ran past me as they played tag or chased their buddies with the intention of beating them up. Purple dogs descended from man's best friend on Earth sniffed about. The brick pavement was cracking, crumbling, and I saw several senior citizens who hadn't watched their step trip and balance themselves just in time to keep from falling.

Humming "Rock Around the Clock," one of my favorite songs, I took a small detour and entered the drugstore near the white concrete twenty-story building containing my office. At the snack counter I purchased four stale doughnuts and two styrofoam cups of black, steaming, foul coffee. That took care of the last of my credits. Being a hero isn't a profitable business. My rent was due in a week, and I didn't know how I was going to pay it.

Rather than take the elevator, which probably wasn't working anyway, I walked up the creaky wooden stairs in the back of the building. The plaster on the walls was decaying and falling off. The naked lightbulbs were twenty watts; I had to take off my mirror sunglasses and slip them in my shirt pocket. Even then, I almost tripped over a rat descended from those who had stowed away on spaceships. Precariously holding my coffee and doughnuts, I kicked the rat down the stairs. It lay there, stunned. It wouldn't mess with The Kid again.

My office door was unlocked because there was no point in locking it; I had nothing left to steal. The twenty-story walk had exhausted me. I put the doughnuts and coffee on my wooden desk, took off my jacket and holster, and then laid down on the couch, folding my arm across my eyes. The office was ten square yards. Huge balls of dust were piled in the corners. My desk had no drawers (someone had stolen those before I had moved in, many years ago) and my filing cabinet had no files. The creaky springs in the couch made it uncomfortable, but I was too tired to move. The walls were so thin that I could hear the strange dance instructor next door praising a student—probably a bow-legged, knock-kneed little girl who was so uncoordinated that she couldn't walk in a straight line, much less dance.

It was strange. With my eyes closed I could almost imagine that fateful day in 1963. I was almost back home. I was one of the many people who had taken time off from work that afternoon to watch the president and his wife and the governor ride through the city. Then I was just another faceless nobody in the crowd, although I had quit the Texas Rangers and had opened my own office five years before. It was comforting to be one of so many, to be unimportant, and yet to feel warm as the president rode by. I felt that we were close personal friends. I believed he smiled at me, just before he turned away from the crowd and faced the road ahead, just before he reached to his throat. I saw his head bow and I think I was the first person in the crowd, including the president, to realize what had happened. I saw him jerk back when the bullet penetrated his skull.

As Old Bill had said, time was seriously out of joint. I had seen many violent things in Texas and Virginia; I had been the leading man in some; but never before had the sight of murder (which is always shocking and surreal no matter how accustomed you grow to it) numbed me so completely. I was horrified. When the First Lady picked up a piece of the president's skull and tried to put it back on his head, I felt my gorge rise and I looked away. I saw what appeared to be a rifle briefly reflecting sun on a hilltop. Then the glow was gone.

To this day I'm not sure if what I saw was only a figment of my imagination. I could have gone zonkers right then (and still be zonkers right now, my experiences of life in the far future only a delusion of my cracked brain while I sit in a white room in that special place for zonkered people), but again, I'll never know for sure. I ran up the hill with all the considerable speed I could muster. When I reached the top, I glanced back and saw that no one had followed me; everyone's attention was riveted on the president's body; the car was surrounded by Secret Servicemen, tourists, and other foolish gawkers. I heard a car door slam on the other side of the hill. I saw a 1951 Mercury spurting huge puffs of black smoke from its tailpipe slowly pull away from the curb, as if the driver had become bored and was going home.

Fervently wishing I had brought my cannon, I took my first step down the hill. The tingling began at the nape of my neck and in the space of a second had spread all over my body. I floated in darkness, surrounded by the twinkling of stars. I held my hands to my eyes, but my hands were transparent; through them I could see the swirling of galaxies and the void of infinity. I was immersed in what should have been a mystical experience, but my spirit did not feel fulfilled and at peace while it was being transported to some other plane. Instead I felt insignificant, frightened, with absolutely no control over my destiny . . . and I in fact *had* no control. For I had entered a time vortex which sent me spinning, spinning, spinning through eons piled upon eons. I didn't know it then, but my second step would take place in the far future.

The entire incident didn't seem distant now. With a bit of imagination, I could pretend that I was back in Dallas working on a thorny case. But reality could not let me forget for long that I was in the future. My dirty window was cracked open, and I heard members of a religious cult chant, "Hare Seldon, Hare Seldon" twenty stories below. If for no other reason, I couldn't forget that I was in the future.

I sighed. I sat up. I suddenly felt very homesick. It was no way for a hero to act, but there was nothing I could do about it. Being careful not to spill any steaming coffee on my hands, I pried the plastic cap from one of the styrofoam cups, opened the window further, and tossed out the cap. It sailed halfway toward the building opposite before it dropped toward the street. I tasted the coffee and winced. At least it would keep me awake. Every time I pondered the unusual circumstances of my life, I wanted to go to sleep so I could forget the whole matter. I tasted the doughnut. It was like eating dirt. If the coffee didn't keep me awake, my stomach spasms would.

Someone knocked at the door. As I sat down in the swivel chair behind my desk, I said, "Come in. Everything's copasetic."

"I know. Space Patrol scientists inspected the premises last night to minimize the possibility that I would contract space leprosy."

I recognized her immediately as she walked into the room, slowly closing the door behind her. I couldn't hear it click shut. The long blonde hair stacked on top of her head made her look like a lemon ice cream custard. Her pale skin appeared as soft as velvet; she had put rouge on her cheeks so no one would mistake her for one of the walking dead. Her mouth was wide; not unexpectantly, it

was covered with glistening pink lipstick that looked as if it were impossible to smear. Her nostrils flared as she sniffed at the odor of dust; evidently she hadn't been told everything to expect. She was five-foot-five; she weighed a hundred pounds, maybe a little bit more but almost certainly not less. Her legs were a tad short for my tastes, but her figure was just right. She wore dark green slacks sprinkled with glitter, a tight red sweater, knee-high black boots, and emerald earrings. She looked every inch an aristocrat, and with good reason.

I couldn't see the two soldiers of the Space Patrol standing outside my door, but I knew they were there, taking time out from persecuting the innocent. The young lady was Lurleen, the oldest princess of Carnelia. I had seen her on holovision many times. She had impressed me as a native person whose main goal in life was to be entirely artificial. Perhaps she was only trying to fulfill her social obligations as a princess. I'd hoped so, for it was difficult to reconcile the shallow woman she had become with the athletic youth who had been champion of the mock gladiatorial tournaments for three years running. Until recently, she had been one of the leading lights of my fantasy life.

Greeting her with my mildly sardonic smile and gesturing toward the couch, I leaned back and planted my feet firmly on my desk. "Sit down. This isn't the palace, but it's my castle, as the saying goes."

Placing her hands on her hips, she appraised me as if I was a cheap watch. She stood with her legs apart, as if she had been a fashion model from my era posing for a famous photographer. She made no move to sit. "Then you are aware of my identity?"

I leaned back further and formed a church steeple with my hands. "Of course. I watch all the quiz shows."

She smiled, causing two dimples to appear in her

cheeks. "I have never participated in a quiz show on holovision. You must have seen me on something else."

"Funny. You don't look like the type who makes news. Go on, sit down." When she did, I continued, "Why don't we get right down to the heart of the matter and see if anything worthwhile develops?"

"Do not rely on it, Mr. Davis," she said coldly. Turned slightly sideways, she sat with her knees together and her back arched. She had an interesting profile; her nose was small and her cheekbones high. "I have come to your offices on a matter of the utmost importance. I assume I can depend upon your discretion?"

"Everyone can, including royalty. But what have you done to smear your good name?"

Under her rouge her cheeks turned red with anger; I hadn't thought it was possible for her to have any color. She glanced toward the door, apparently considering having me arrested for insubordination. It wouldn't have worked. Twice before I had met members of the family; they were both jerks and I had let them know in no uncertain terms. Neither tried to arrest me after I beat up their bodyguards without working up a sweat.

"I have committed no indiscretions, but I repeat, I do require *your* discretion. Do I have it?"

"Sure, toots."

She winced, but continued as if she had put my answer completely out of her mind. "As you know, my father has built a mead hall which he has christened Mead Hall. In this structure he gathers his friends and they drink and feast until they drop from exhaustion."

"They could do that at the castle in the middle of the city, couldn't they?"

"They have in the past, but Mead Hall was erected for the sole purpose of having an enjoyable evening. There is not the slightest possibility of suddenly being burdened with a detail of government."

"Yes, I understand. That can certainly be a problem when you're smashed."

"Mr. Davis, under different circumstances parrying clever quips with you would be immensely entertaining, but at this very moment brave men might be dying because you are here in your office while your services are required elsewhere."

"That could be, lady, but I can rattle off several incidents when men have bit the big one because your old man had a hangover and couldn't be bothered with *his* job." Sometimes I'm a dynamic revolutionary.

"This is not a political problem," she said. "This is a matter of life and death."

"Your father's life and my death?"

"Please. Allow me to elucidate on the situation and you will reach an understanding."

"Sure. I've got nothing but time. Would you like some coffee?"

She nodded no. Her hands on her knees, she looked away from me as she spoke. Her story, such as it was, had an air of unreality due to the soft, musical tones of her voice. She spoke as if her old man's lackeys had carefully rehearsed her the night before. Betweeen sequences she often paused to take a deep breath; she exhaled as if the fate of all mankind rested on her frail shoulders. It was a ridiculous attitude, typical of royalty. She said:

"My father searched all over the immediate vicinity for the proper location for Mead Hall. He wanted the surroundings to be as dynamic as the structure itself. Unfortunately the only location satisfactory to him was near the three volcanoes which pollute the air, near the mysterious black castle of his deranged foe, Cochineal.

"A few months ago a hideous monster began attacking Mead Hall. I wish I could describe it to you, but I have never seen it. Those who have witnessed an attack have given conflicting reports concerning its appearance. However, all agree that its size is incredible and its strength is extraordinary. Evidently the monster is pained by the songs and the laughter emitted from Mead Hall. It groans and screams with the sound of every laugh, every voice, every drop of spilt wine striking the floor. Covering its ears, it tries to muffle the noise. According to the words men have heard the monster speak, all it wants is the eternal rest of a boring, uneventful life spent sunbathing and surfing at the beach. I am positive that you have become acquainted with many people who possess an identical desire.

"However, Cochineal controls the monster's mind. Perhaps the beast could obtain the peace it so fervently desires if Cochineal would only allow it. The Space Patrol has theorized that Cochineal broadcasts the sounds of Mead Hall to the monster wherever it is; even if it fled to the other side of the planet, it would suffer. The monster has no free will. If it were able to slay my father, then Mead Hall would fall into disuse and silence. But Cochineal will not allow the monster to slay my father, only his friends and guards. Cochineal wants my father to suffer.

"Mr. Davis, you must help us. The consensus is that you are the proper man to put the monster out of its misery."

Thinking that I would rather put King Henry out of his misery, I tapped my fingers on the desk. It was getting hot outside; the sun beat mercilessly on the city and I happened to be sitting directly in its dull, irritating rays. I would have pulled down the shade, but a few months ago, in a pique, I had disintegrated it with my laser. The landlord hadn't replaced it yet, though he promised to the first of every month.

"Lurleen, why hasn't your old man split the scene?"

"Pardon me?"

"Why hasn't your old man vacated the premises? Seems to me that would save a lot of lives without any effort on my part."

"Mr. Davis, surely you are jesting. Do you realize the expense constructing Mead Hall required? Why, it cost the taxpayers of Carnelia a gigantic fortune! Under no circumstances can my father allow Mead Hall to go to waste."

"That's what I thought you would say."

I turned around and stared out the window, gazing at the three distant volcanoes, unable to see Mead Hall or Cochineal's black castle. It didn't take too much guesswork to determine why King Henry wanted to keep the affair secret. Chances were that a few of the people killed by the monster were decent, hard-working government chaps taking a well-deserved night off in a place where they could eat and drink all they wanted for free. When the news leaked (an inevitability), the Carnelians' suffering would be eased if they knew that the perpetrator had been brought to justice. I turned back around and faced her. She stared at me with wide, glassy eyes; now she looked like an automaton, but I forgave her for it.

"Okay, baby, I'll talk to your old man."

"A simple yes or no that I can relay would suffice."

"There's the simple matter of my fee. Great heroes don't come cheap."

After I stood up, I put on my holster and jacket. I had circles of sweat on my shirt under my arms. I placed my mirror sunglasses on top of my head and held my white snap-brim hat in my left hand. Only slightly regretting not taking the remainder of the stale doughnuts and black coffee with me, I opened the door for her. Not even nodding curtly to acknowledge my gesture, she passed me, her eyes riveted to the floor ahead of her.

Sure enough, two stone-faced soldiers of the Space Patrol with black hair and pot-bellies stood outside my door. They wore the traditional black uniforms of all secret police; their shirts were so tight that when they inhaled I thought the fabric would rip. They glared at me as if they had ordered a well-done hamburger and I was very, very rare. Their eyes were four blue steel balls; when they scowled; which happened every time they accidentally looked at me, it was a reflexive scowl. Fuzz always do that. Irritates me no end, but there's nothing I can do about it.

Since I'm a brilliant private eye wise to all the scams that petty dictators use to maintain their positions of authority, I realized that these soldiers weren't the fighting furies they were cracked up to be. Otherwise King Henry wouldn't have needed me. I could have punctured the soldiers' confident balloons with ease, merely by muttering a phrase here, by insulting their tactics there, by spitting on the sidewalk and daring them to arrest me. But I don't get my kicks by killing overgrown babies.

We took the stairs because my earlier deduction had been dead on; the elevator didn't work. Outside the building Lurleen and I followed two steps behind the soldiers; it's a clever technique employed by bodyguards who don't realize that their clients could be shot in the back. There was a very real possibility of a holovision critic offing Lurleen so he wouldn't have to watch her any more. The streets weren't as crowded as usual; the few people about avoided looking at me; perhaps they thought I had been arrested and they were depressed because they weren't able to help me. So much for social activism.

The soldiers guided us to a pneumatic gold automobile with a hinged glass roof, enabling it to serve as a

door. The automobile was so ugly I couldn't believe it.
The edges had jewel studs; the seats were red corduroy;
the console had glittering red lights which were definitely
not functional. Lurleen and I sat in the rear. The front
seat was pushed back too far; consequently my legs were
uncomfortable. No one said a word. I was extremely
aware of Lurleen's presence, particularly of the way she
looked out the roof, pretending to scrutinize the surroundings. She resembled the Lurleen of old more than
the mature, distant princess; she had slumped down in the
seat, resting her right knee against the front backrest and
hooking her left ankle around her right. She appeared
bored and depressed (her lower lip protruded slightly) as
if she was thinking of a hundred better things she could
do rather than escort a genuine hero to Mead Hall. For
some reason this disturbed me.

The soldier in the driver's seat was a real flamer.
Rather than slow down for pedestrians in his path, he
honked his horn; he smiled as they scurried out of his
lane. I think he wanted me to be nervous, but frankly, I
was bored.

In ten minutes we were out of Carnelia proper; we
entered the suburbs. I visited the suburbs only when I was
working on a case; if I had had any friends, I wouldn't
have had them there. Carnelia's middle class was unin-
teresting, consisting of dull people who cared about beating the rush out of the city and what was on holovision
and little else, while paying lip-service to such respon-
sibilities as raising children, government policies, and the
philosophical concepts men live and die by. No wonder
Lurleen's old man had such an easy time of it; if he had to
answer to anybody, it was to these dullards.

All the houses were uniform; each was brick, one-
story, rectangular, with white shutters, white doors, and
white roofs, and without attics or basements. Each house

was built in the center of an area of fifty square yards, with long macadam driveways, whether or not the family owned an automobile. A few houses had stables, but they all looked alike too. Although I knew intimately every alleyway in the city, I always got lost in the suburbs; I was famous for, among other things, ringing the doorbells of the wrong houses.

As I watched the houses and yards file past like dominoes on display, I became aware of Lurleen's eyes upon me; I didn't have to look to know that she was staring at me, but I looked anyway because something inside me wanted to. I felt strangely satisfied, as if an unknown yearning had been quietly answered, when I learned she was, indeed, staring at me. I guess I had caught her off guard, because she stammered before she finally asked me, "Why have you never attended my father's parties? For years he has desired to meet you. Yet you have never acknowledged a summons."

"I guess they must have gotten lost in the mail."

"Do people really believe you humorous?"

"Some people do."

"I suppose it takes—how do they say it?—all kinds."

I smiled, without a sardonic trace to be seen.

Lurleen sat up and said, "I too have desired to make your acquaintance. When I was younger, I faithfully followed your exploits."

She wanted me to reply, but I couldn't think of anything to say because I didn't know what I felt. I was afraid that any reply, regardless of my natural eloquence, would be disappointing. I pursed my lips and simply looked at her. She turned her head away and resumed her former position, but not before I saw her lips turn upward in a knowing smile. What the smile knew, I had no idea, but I consoled myself with the thought that not all revelations are unhappy ones.

Thirty miles from Carnelia, Mead Hall was on top of a barren, golden mountain (gold was cheap on Rakish; the people thought brick was more attractive). At the northern foot of the mountain was a field of red poisonous grass and perfectly safe yellow flowers; a dense green jungle was east; Carnelia was south; and to the west was the base of a tremendous craggy mountain range, much of it gold. Cochineal's castle and the three polluting volcanoes were the four major landmarks of the mountain range. Mead Hall was magnificent, an incredible conglomeration of columns, doorways, arches, flying buttresses, statues, gardens, gates, walls, purple guard dogs, and more. It was over a hundred yards tall, over a thousand yards long, over five hundred yards wide, on a plateau forming the mountain top. The exterior of Mead Hall was built almost entirely of the rarest stone on Rakish—gray balm. The drab sunlight, dulled by the volcanic soot in the air, caused the balm to sparkle like a spider web glistening with dew at the coming of dawn. As we drove on the bumpy road up the mountain, I was nearly overcome with the beauty of Mead Hall despite myself. It was too bad that all the work that had gone into building the thing hadn't *meant* something; as it was, Mead Hall was a monument to the energetic waste of man.

Cochineal's castle, which was only three miles from Mead Hall and rested on an even higher mountain, did mean something—evil. The stone was pitch black; the long drawbridge was lowered, allowing minions access from one cliff to another; huge black birds (spies? guards?) hovered near the turrets. A volcano was near the castle; apparently Cochineal felt he had nothing to fear from nature.

Lurleen and I got out at the front door, leaving the soldiers to park the automobile. I bet myself that even the servants' entrances were gigantic here, for the front door was thirty yards high and twenty yards wide. It wasn't exactly aesthetically pleasing, but it was impressive. On the door were gold carvings of demons, devils, witches, warlocks, and werewolves, and other historical members of the Rakish aristocracy. They were stabbing or kissing each other. Or both. Those were strange carvings.

I wondered how we were supposed to get in; the door had no knobs and no knockers. Lurleen walked three steps ahead of me, as befitted an intellectual princess of Carnelia; yet I could not fail to notice that she walked with a bounce in her step totally out of character with the cool official representative who had greeted me in my office. I suspected (with pleasure) that the young gladiator who had grown up wanting to meet me had still wanted to meet me. She had treated me in the manner expected of her while presenting the offer. The door mysteriously opened when I thought she would walk smack into it.

Inside we wandered through several endless golden hallways with red rugs, paintings, columns, weapons, racks, servants scrubbing floors, soldiers standing guard, and potted plants, one of which I sidestepped because it wanted to eat me. Lurleen giggled like a four-year-old. I would have utilized my mildly sardonic smile, to show her that I possessed the ability to laugh at the unfortunate circumstances of my life, but she became cold quickly, the perfect princess, as if she had committed an indiscretion against social mores. Fascinating.

Eventually we arrived at a pair of flat, shiny, wooden doors, as large as the first pair, but with huge knobs; at least I knew how to open them. Stopping, Lurleen looked at me with a delightful, playful glare in her eyes. Whether or not she was acting her preordained role escaped me, but it was readily apparent to my trained eye and to my amazing ability to judge character that she was enjoying telling me without a word that I was expected to open the door for her.

One of my talents which has kept me alive this long has been my ability to become paranoid in any situation. Back on Earth, circa 1961, I had become involved with a client who was having trouble with the CIA. I had inadvertently learned many of the common practices that agents of governments for, by, and of the people use to keep free citizens in line. Carnelia's government was worse than the CIA; I can't get more derogatory than that. I expected to feel an electric shock capable of burning me to a Kentucky Fried crisp if I grabbed the knobs, all part of the Carnelian government's never-ceasing program to test and to accidentally kill those who can help it the most. I took off my sunglasses and slipped them into my jacket pocket. I withdrew my laser and fired it at the hinges of both doors. One, two, three, four, five, six, just like that; I had melted them all before either door could sway or dangle.

Falling backward, away from Lurleen and I, the doors landed with a tremendous thump against the soft green rugs lying on the golden floor. A lot of astonished people standing near the doors had barely missed being crushed. They stared at me as if I were Seldon himself, returned to life. I felt like an idiot who had just bet his home, his wife, his children, and his collection of bubble gum cards on Dewey; there had been no trap or test; Lurleen had only been giving me an opportunity to be a gentleman for a change, that was all. But since I had begun a grand entrance, I had to finish it. I spun my laser on my right forefinger and holstered it with one smooth motion like an old cowhand. I bowed, motioning Lurleen to enter before me. She didn't move. Her act had completely folded, and she gawked at me as I sauntered into the banquet room; I nodded and smiled and waved to the people. Either she was fascinated by the sight of a raving lunatic, or she dug me the most, like I was beginning to dig her.

The banquet room was approximately one hundred yards on each side; the dull rays of the Rakish sun shone through the glass roof. I had expected to see the banquet room filled to the brim with voluptuous serving ladies and cushions on the floor and bowlfuls of grapes and swimming pools, like the Roman homes I had read so much about in my high school Latin class. There were a few voluptuous serving ladies, but they were outnumbered by the ugly serving ladies. The spartan banquet room was clearly a man's sanctuary, and women such as Lurleen who could enter as equals, as comrades, were rare indeed. Although the green rug was soft enough to sleep on and the walls were gold, the banquet room didn't look like millions of credits had been squandered on it. There were no couches, no holovisions, no tablecloths, no dying flowers in glass pots. On the walls were animal furs and stuffed animal heads. The long wooden tables sat at least fifty people each, counting both sides; they were laid end to end in ten columns, until they reached a rise in the floor upon which sat the king's favorites. The wooden chairs had no cushions; the same was true of King Henry's golden throne.

From where King Henry sat he could see perfectly everything that occurred in the banquet room. He inspected me intently as I sauntered. He was a grossly fat man, weighing nearly four hundred pounds, with a round, cheeky face and hairy eyebrows topping his seven-foot frame. He had a huge red moustache, and the scattered strands of red hair on his dome needed combing. His meaty fingers were at least an inch in diameter. He wore a green robe and leather sandals. He wasn't wearing his crown, but he was such a big man that he didn't need to;

you couldn't miss him, no matter how much you wanted to. Apparently he liked my entrance, for he giggled, just like his daughter, and mumbled something to the man on his left.

The man on his left was Peter the Advisor, who was personally responsible for many of the social ills plaguing Carnelia. He was so skinny that I bet myself his elbows could rip his tacky blue-and-yellow-striped shirt. He wore black boots, blue jeans, and a silver watch powered by a solar battery. He was six-foot-one; he had blond hair and a smooth face reminding me of a baby girl. His deep-set eyes seemed to be constantly shadowed by his forehead; his cheekbones were high; he smiled a lot, showing off those pure white teeth. The only things missing were fangs and whips, and I'm sure he had those hidden in an appropriate place. He spoke first, in a reedy voice which would have been laughable were it not for the self-confidence dripping like maple syrup from his words. He said, "And this is the champion who's going to kill that hideous monster? He doesn't look capable of stepping on a bug without breaking his ankle."

I stuck my tongue into my cheek, then moved it to the other. I pretended to size him up, but actually I had quit long ago because I had reached the point of diminishing returns. I said, "Flake off, birdbrain."

Peter's eyes widened. He turned to King Henry to say something, but King Henry was laughing too hard to pay attention. So he said to me, "Listen, you perversion, I'm a powerful man in Carnelia. I have influence. You be nice to me."

"I'll think about it, wimp." I'm such a witty guy.

"You're not listening." He drank a purple liquid from a brass cup. Touching his napkin to his lips, he said, "You could make a whole slew of enemies by putting yourself on the wrong side of me. If you want this assignment, you better apologize."

"Where's your right side? Behind you?"

By now King Henry was laughing so hard that he sounded like thunder; he slapped his knees and bent over as far as his massive stomach would allow him. When he calmed down enough to cease rumbling, he looked at Peter; then he immediately started laughing again. I had never before met a man so easy to please.

Peter licked his lips and held his head high, looking at me by lowering his eyes. "Mr. Davis, I've been studying your record. You claim to be a native of the past; in fact, you say that where you come from, Seldon hadn't been born yet. This leads me to conclude that you're quite insane."

"Maybe I am. But I've got the right tool for the job," I said, patting my laser under my jacket.

"On top of that, I don't think your record is very distinguished."

"Shut up, Peter!" said King Henry in the manner of a father ready to pound his son five feet into the earth. He looked at me and grinned. "I like you, boy. Will you kill this monster for me? I'll make it worth your while."

"I might."

"You see?" said Peter, turning to his boss. "I told you he was a smarty."

"Be silent, you cretin!" said King Henry.

"I'll kill the monster only for the right amount of kale," I said.

Peter stared at the glass roof and crossed his arms. "You're an overrated has-been."

"Oh, yeah?" shouted someone near me. I turned to see a man of about forty with silver hair slicked back into a ducktail stand up and point at me. "This is the same man who cracked the Nefarious Sutherland Murder Mystery. It had baffled the Space Patrol for months, and he just stepped into the storm and waltzed off with the answer."

"And with a handsome fee," I added, though actually all I had waltzed off with was a kiss on the cheek from my beautiful, poor, and married client. Otherwise I would have treated her to a holomovie.

An old man to my left stood up and said, "And who hasn't heard of the interesting Case of the Missing Space Leper? It baffled the greatest minds of our government—both of them—until Mr. Davis inspected the premises and deduced that the space leper had been living in the walls of the house for ten years, without anyone so much as suspecting that something odd was going on when they heard those mysterious thumps in the night."

I smiled at Peter. I had gotten paid for that one.

A middle-aged man I had almost struck with the doors stood up in the rear and said, "And he tracked down Father Flambeau, the killer no one had heard of before and who no one has heard of since."

"And he solved the Paradox of the Empty House Full of Dancing Men!"

"And he exposed the illicit practices of the devious officials who covered up the Creature from Beyond Infinity Caper!"

"And he invented baseball!"

That was the clincher. No one could argue with that. I received a spontaneous standing ovation. I lifted my arms, acknowledging their outburst of appreciation for my cultural contributions to the planet. King Henry and Peter the Advisor were silent; evidently they preferred to remain aloof from such activities as applauding. When I lowered my arms, the applause ceased and business continued as usual.

"My fee is two hundred credits a day plus expenses. If I don't stop the monster, you just have to pay for my funeral."

King Henry stared at me. "That's outrageous! I'll pay you a hundred and fifty a day!"

"Nope. I won't take less than two hundred and fifty."

It was Peter's turn to stare. It was the first thing I had seen him do well. "Sire! Sire! His price is going up! He's not worth that kind of kale!"

"Sire, I feel compelled to disagree. If anything I'm undercharging. I'm worth much more than three hundred credits a day and if you keep haggling, I'll prove it."

Peter opened his mouth to speak, but an unsubtle slap on the wrist from King Henry, a resounding clap which echoed throughout the banquet room, stopped him. Peter said, "Ooh!" King Henry said, "We'll accept your generous offer. And I, in turn, will offer you a seat and a hot meal, free of charge. George!"

"Yes, Sire?" asked a waspish man three seats to King Henry's right.

"You've work to do in Carnelia. Do it."

"Yes, Sire. Right away, Sire. I'm going away right now, Sire. Yes, Sire," he said as he walked with a bent back from the raised level.

I took my seat, placed my hat beside my plate, and prepared to dig into the hot stew an ugly serving lady was scooping into a bowl so clean I could see that I needed a haircut. King Henry patted his knees. "Lurleen! Lurleen!" he boomed out like a drunken radio announcer speaking into an overmodulated microphone. "Come here, girl! I say, girl, come here!"

Lurleen ran up and over the table and jumped into her father's considerable lap, putting her arms around his neck and kissing him full upon the lips. I thought I was going to die.

"How's my little girl today?"

"I'm fine, Daddy. How's my big bad old Poppa?"

"I'm fine, sweetheart. Now why don't you run along

and let us men get down to some serious banqueting?"

She ran along. She almost knocked over a servant trying to help pick up a door so it could be put back where it belonged when she turned to blow a kiss at the raised level. It was impossible to accurately ascertain the identity of the recipient of the kiss. King Henry beamed; Peter shrugged and looked uncomfortable; and my bloodstream doubled, boiled, and troubled. I swallowed a portion of my stew; it was good, but very hot, and I chased it with a swig of ice water.

I never became used to the stew during that long, interminable meal which did nasty things to my waistline. I must have drunk twenty glasses of ice water and eaten thirty chunks of ice while listening to boring conversations and jokes even worse than mine. After a while I didn't pretend to think the jokes were funny, and around sunset I got tired of insulting Peter. I had run out of names to call him anyway.

As the sky darkened, as one of Rakish's four moons glowed through the glass roof, the laughter and chatter of the feasters became forced. A more undistinguished group of men I have never met. They talked of dull things—why prices weren't rising high enough, farfetched solutions to the space leper problem, the earned run average of the most overrated pitcher on the planet. When the time had come for them to discuss what had been on their minds all along—the impending arrival of the monster—they stuck to their dull topics with the tenacity of a G-man refusing to cop to an error. Instead of trying to overcome their fear with the support of their comrades, they pretended their fear didn't exist. They squirmed in their seats, licked their lips, wiped sweat from their brows, drank too much alcohol, breathed heavily, laughed nervously, and indicated their fear in so many other obvious ways that soon I too was afraid. I couldn't remain unaffected by their contagious fear.

I realized, as the air cooled and an unpleasant odor vaguely reminiscent of sweaty gym socks caressed my nostrils, that I hadn't seen the monster; they had. Perhaps they had good reason to be afraid.

Gradually all conversations diminished, and except for a few hushed remarks between men confident that they wouldn't die that night because they hadn't the night before, the banquet room was silent. Outside the wind whispered, its sound muffled by the balm and gold walls. Thick clouds rolled across the sky; it was a rare sight, one I hoped I wouldn't experience without the protection of the glass roof, chemically treated, I presumed, to withstand the acidic raindrops of Rakish. Peter, who had been glaring at me all day when I wasn't rewarding his attention with piercing barbs, sat sullen, his arms crossed, his eyes half-closed; he seemed to be wishing that he were in a dream from which he could awake at the moment of his choosing. King Henry's hands rested on his massive stomach as if he were holding gas inside a balloon about to burst. He seemed as unreal as Lurleen's recent appearances on holovision. He stared directly at the doors the servants had finally fixed, but if he was aware of the sights and sounds surrounding him, I couldn't tell it. Clearly he was completely wrapped up in his thoughts of the monster, and I couldn't blame him. After all, if I couldn't do the job, he would be stuck with the bill for my funeral.

At nine o'clock King Henry stood up. The veins of his neck protruded; I thought they would explode due to the strain that standing put on his heart. He inhaled deeply, surveying the banquet room with all the majesty he could muster. Surprisingly, he could muster considerable majesty. He inhaled several times before he finally spoke, in the voice of a general who, while not overjoyous that he was staying behind the lines, wasn't exactly unhappy about it either.

He said, "Gentlemen, if this night is like all others, the monster will arrive soon. We should retire to our homes or our sleeping quarters and allow Mr. Davis to do his job." He jabbed Peter on the shoulder; the alert advisor had fallen asleep. "Come on, boy! Wake up, boy! Let's get out of here before we lose our skins!" Then he looked at me. His face was grim, but beneath the cold veneer of his eyes I read intense concern. He turned his gaze away from he; he pretended to watch his host of friends slowly file out of the banquet room, but occasionally I caught him sneaking a peek at me. He was wondering what I was doing and how I was taking all this.

The answer was: not bad. I was still afraid, a little bit on edge, and though you never get used to that sort of thing in my line of work, you learn to live with it. My feet were propped up on the table; my jacket was unbuttoned; I had a toothpick I was putting to good use. I grinned a lot.

Nevertheless, I could have used a few appropriate parting words such as "We're counting on you" or "We know you can do it" or "Call when you get there." I didn't get one final word, not even a final glance. King Henry was the last person to waddle out of the banquet room; when he closed the door behind him, he didn't look back.

I was alone, patting my laser. They had left all the lights on. That way the monster would know where to find me. Since there was nothing else to do, I waited.

I sat at the table until my legs became stiff, about to go to sleep, and I had to pace the banquet room just to stay limber. I walked as quietly as possible; I didn't want to disturb the silence; I wanted to be part of it. Spilt wine and milk dripped through the cracks in the wooden tables onto the floor; each drip shattered the silence I tried so desperately to preserve. Flies buzzed about chunks of leftover food; they landed, twitched, and left in search of more. The air seemed filmy, as if I were looking at the banquet room through a curtain hiding me in another world. When I inhaled, the air's dank smell increased; it became more and more distasteful. There was no silence; there were no socially redeeming features in the banquet room; there was nothing for me to become part of.

I would have been happy to continue brooding all night, but my incredible survival instincts surfaced. The odor increased to such an intensity that an inner sixth sense told me that only the monster could be responsible. The smell became so awful that every time I inhaled I wanted to vomit.

Nausea and an innate sense of the dramatic commanded me to walk to the front of the banquet room and face the doors. When I was thirty-five yards from the doors I pulled a chair from a table and put my right foot on the seat; holding my laser in my right hand, I bent over and rested my right elbow on my knee. I was ready. Nothing could stop me now.

I waited.

Finally the odor increased a final time. The door creaked open. I saw a huge red eye peeking in. It seemed to be on fire. When it saw me it widened; I wanted to melt in order to forget the hideous experience of being its object.

I smiled. "Come in," I said. "Ever since I read your last story, I've been dying to meet you."

A rumbling growl sounding like boiling lava came from the throat of the eye's keeper. The monster breathed heavily, this time sounding like chalk scratching a blackboard.

My smile widened. I thought my mouth was going to rip the cheeks off my face.

The growl climaxed with an ear-splitting roar as the monster pushed the door completely open. It stood there, looking at me, waiting for me to react. This monster was the most pathetic horror I had ever seen. It didn't have skin; it had glistening gray slime, some of which had clung to the door when it had pushed it open. The slime slowly crept down the door and rested on the floor; it quickly ceased glistening. New slime immediately formed on the monster's hand. The monster itself was over seven feet tall; it weighed over three hundred pounds, but I could tell from its throbbing sinews that it could lift four times its weight without wheezing hard. It was cast into a laughable approximation of the human form; its long arms reached down to the knees of its short, stumpy legs; its back was perfectly straight. It had two eyes, a mouth, fangs, a nose, and two webbed ears, but it seemed that they were put slightly out of place, off to the left or to the right. Green saliva dripped from the fangs; the mouth had thin red lips upon which slime crept; the monster constantly licked its lips, but the slime always returned. Its only clothing was a loosely fitting pair of red swimming trunks.

"You've come to the wrong place," I said. "The dating service is down the hall."

The monster glared at me.

"But if you're looking for a cheap meal, then you've definitely come to the right place." I gestured at the tables behind me. "We have piles and piles and genuine human leftovers, the most sought-after leftovers in the galaxy. Now don't look suspicious, friend. Sure you see flies here, and everybody knows flies are unsanitary. Well, these are *clean* flies we put here to increase verisimilitude."

The monster said, "Please keep quiet. I can't stand the noise. Everywhere I go there's the noise!" Its voice sounded like a four-axled truck on the New Jersey Turnpike.

"Yeah, I can see where you're coming from . . ." I replied. "Sometimes it's impossible to find peace and quiet. Sometimes I lie down to catch forty winks and the videophone rings. It's never a job, though—just some bill collector wanting credits I haven't got. Really gets to me, know what I mean?"

The monster's expression had already reached an extreme. "Please, stop it!" he cried again. "I don't want to kill you. I just know that if you don't stop it, I'll have to. So please. *Please*."

"I like to hear myself talk. Want to know what I think of Spinoza?"

Taking the only logical course of action open to it, the monster roared and charged at me, moving with an astounding quickness. I didn't even have time to aim my laser. Holding a chair in both hands, the monster swung it at me like a baseball bat. I was beginning to regret my cultural contribution to Rakish. Without thinking, I raised my arm to protect myself. My arm took most of the blow's force, sustaining little damage but shattering the chair. I fell down. I hit my forehead on the edge of a table. Warm blood ran down the side of my head, getting into my hair and screwing up my profile. Although the monster was capable of achieving a momentum, its reflexes were terrible. It had swung at me while on the run and it had lost its balance. Although it had tried to stop, to hit me again, it ran past me and into a table. Chunks of wood flew all over the immediate vicinity. It could have been chunks of me.

Somehow I had held onto my laser. The gash on my head was wider than I had suspected, for as I aimed at the monster turning to face me, a flood of red poured over my left eye. I felt sick.

I fired and missed. The crackling laser melted a six-foot-square area of golden wall fifty yards over the monster's misshapen shoulder. I felt sicker. I would soon pay the penalty for missing.

Dropping two shattered chair legs, the monster looked at the melted wall with what can only be called surprise and shock. It roared at me. I could barely see it coming for the blood in my eyes. I was becoming dizzy; I couldn't think straight. There was only one thing to do. I turned and ran as fast as I could, which wasn't very, and hoped that I would have a chance to clean up and take a good shot. The only reason I was able to stumble out of the banquet room was because it tripped over the chair I had left in its path. It was the dumbest personification of pure death and destruction I had ever seen.

I slammed the doors behind me. I heard the clattering of the monster trying to stand up. Apparently when it fell down it was like a turtle rolled on its back. Nevertheless, I didn't have much time.

I wiped the blood from my eyes, only to have more blood flow into them. I heard the monster screaming that all the noise of the chairs falling and breaking was driving it insane. It would have been an interesting soliloquy under slightly more favorable circumstances. I saw that the lights in the hallway were on, but that no one was there. Stumbling down the hallway, supporting myself by leaning on the wall, smearing blood on a painting by one of the great Rakish masters, I called out for help. I called out several times; no one answered. Dimly, I realized the obvious, what I should have known all along: Mead Hall had been vacated so I would be the only person making noise; the sensitive hearing of the monster would pick up a sound as insignificant as my breathing. The monster would be drawn to me no matter where I waited for it in Mead Hall.

However, my amazing deductive abilities were of no help in my immediate situation; I required every fiber of my muscular, quick-thinking, action-oriented brain. And believe me, I felt that all the muscles in my head had turned into energy-sucking fat. I was twenty yards down the hall when the sounds of the monster getting up ceased. I ran five more yards, almost using up too much strength and causing myself to collapse against a statue of a fetching dame; and then I patiently waited for the click of the door opening. When it came, I blindly fired my laser.

This time I didn't miss, but then again, I wasn't aiming for anything in particular. I fanned the laser all over the floor, crisscrossing it so the monster was trapped at the doorway.

"The pain! The pain!" the monster screamed. I thought that I might have accidentally hit it, which would have made me feel very wonderful, until it said, "I can't stand hearing the floor melt and the rug burn! I can't stand the smell! Please stop it or I'll kill you! Please! Please!"

The way things seemed to me, it was going to kill me anyway, so I continued firing my laser as I backed off. Finally I accidentally hit a column, cutting through it instantly. I then aimed my laser at the ceiling, again crisscrossing the white beam in a mad pattern. I was only vaguely aware of what I was doing. The ceiling—I don't know how much—collapsed. Through the blood in my eyes I saw that the monster was covered with debris—but certainly not dead. I knew that I had better cut out while the cutting out was good.

I cut. I had no idea where I was going. But the thought of my impending greeting with Saint Peter at the Pearly Gates supplied me with sufficient motivation; I summoned energy out of nowhere and ran and ran. It seemed that my legs were mysterious appendages grafted onto my torso. I found a small, regular-sized door and opened it. When I closed it behind me, I leaned against it, breathing heavily, fighting off my dizziness. I wanted to rest, but I realized that the monster's amazingly acute hearing would lead it straight to me sooner if I remained in one spot rather than moved.

I wiped the blood from my eyes, and it's a good thing that I did, because if I hadn't, my first step would have sent me plummeting down a long, wooden staircase. I was in no condition to take that kind of punishment. By now my shirt and jacket had absorbed much of my blood; I would have rejoiced that I was still alive if I had had the time. The only light was a naked thirty-watt bulb over my head. I couldn't see where the staircase led. I grasped the bannister, holding my laser in my other hand, and glided down the stairs like a drunken hobo on the verge of passing out. After a short time I was completely enshrouded in darkness and I felt like a ghost who couldn't quite make it back to the world of the living. Feeling ahead with my feet, I came to a concrete floor, but I still had no idea where I was. I discovered that sometime during the action, I had lost my hat; I wondered if I would ever be the same.

I leaned against something round. It was a barrel. A spigot tried to worm its way into the small of my back. I reached out and felt another barrel. I had found heaven; I was in a wine cellar. I didn't want to make any more noise than possible, but feeling quite fatalistic—an unfortunate character trait of ace detectives in a jam—I slumped to the floor. It was time for ad-libbed first aid; I turned on the faucet and cool wine poured on my head. I grimaced. It was the only way I could think of to prevent an infection and to preserve my health if I lived through the night. My head burned. I touched my forehead. A huge portion of my scalp had been ripped open; some dermis was holding on by a strand; I wondered if it would stick to my skull if I folded it back into place and pressed down real hard.

There was no doubt about it. I was a sick man. I couldn't even summon the strength to turn off the faucet. I leaned against a barrel resting on a stand. Sliding sideways to avoid the wine pouring from the barrel above me, I slipped out of my jacket and ripped a clean bandage from the bottom of my shirt. Trying to lift that very, very heavy bandage to my head, I passed out.

I felt the touch of the monster. I might have been awake, but I don't know. The touch was slimy and cold, but it didn't descend on my head with the force of a meteor, crashing into my skull and sending bits and pieces all over the wine cellar. The touch was tender, and despite the coldness of the fingertips, it sent warmth through my brain. My face broke out with sweat, but not with the sweat of fear.

"You've stopped. You've stopped," said a terrible voice softly. "I'm glad you stopped. The others—they never did and I had to kill them." The fingertips moved slowly over my head, and then they were gone. "You may speak, but please, please, speak softly. It has been so long since anyone has spoken softly to me. My mother—she screams, nags, and repeats herself, but I must always run from her because it would be wrong for me to kill my mother. The others—I could kill them because it was right."

By now I had opened my eyes, but I could see nothing in the total darkness. The fatigue was gone from my body; I felt as if I had awakened from a refreshing nap and was preparing to take a cold dip in a swimming pool. I sat up, keeping my laser at my fingertips on the floor. I instinctively rubbed my scalp. My hair was an unruly mess, but I was well. The monster had cured me.

I hadn't expected the monster to have a reassuring bed-side manner. In fact, I hadn't expected to be able to expect anything. The fortunate turn in circumstances almost renewed my faith in the ethical structure of the universe. Moving as quietly as I could—my body wasn't even stiff—I scooted out of the puddle of wine. If I had been my usual witty self, I would have asked the monster to clean my shirt and press my pants. Private eyes always laugh in the face of death.

I hated to turn down my fee, but I couldn't possibly kill the monster after what it had done for me. I whispered, "How can . . ."

"Speak lower, please. My ears hurt so. Everything hurts my ears so."

"How can you heal people?" I asked, whispering even lower. "I've never heard of anything like this."

"It's a talent I was born with. It's because of my special talents that I kill. The people make me do it with their infernal singing and laughing and dancing, but I'm not responsible. I must stop the noise or it'll drive me insane!"

"All right! I believe you. You don't have to belabor the point."

"You understand? You don't want to hurt me?"

"Of course not. Why should I?"

"Because I kill your kind."

"They're my species, but they're not my kind."

"But I bear them no malice. It's because of the pain, the pain that drives me mad. I don't know if life's worth living because of the pain. What do you think?"

The monster was more intelligent than I had supposed. Not everybody picks up instantly that private eyes are the modern cracker-barrel philosophers. "Life's always worth living. Ask any space leper."

"My fate is worse than theirs. At least they can enjoy the sonic pleasure of beautiful singing, of music, of great oratory. To me, all sounds are discordant noises. I love the beach, but the pounding waves drive me insane, I tell you, they drive me insane! Life isn't worth living! I can't bear any more pain! Each moment causes me an infinity of agony! Please, kill me! Kill me! It's the least you can do for someone who has saved your life!"

The monster may have been intelligent, but it certainly wasn't logical. "Look, son, calm down. Talk to me. Think about it. No matter what your problem is, we can work it out. What's your name?"

"Mother calls me Mac."

"Tell, me Mac, isn't there anything you can do to filter out the sounds of Mead Hall?"

"Don't you think I haven't tried? Everywhere I go I hear those noises! Everything I do—fails! There's only one solution: you have to kill me. Fire your laser into my heart."

"I don't want to kill you. You're my friend."

"Friend?"

Before I could elucidate further on the matter. Mac shifted his weight and shuffled his feet. I no longer thought of him as "it." I had been extraordinarily dense in refusing to pity his plight previous to our conversation. He was still ugly, even in pitch blackness; and he stank—his odor reminded me of a moldy dishrag; but I understood something of his soul.

"*Friend?*" repeated Mac. There was a trace of hope in his terrible, rumbling voice, but also a deepening sense of anxiety. Something was wrong. I imagined him looking wildly about, expecting to find an item which wasn't there. "They're coming," he said.

"Who?"

"The king, his daughter, their entourage, and those

idiotic soldiers. They're opening the doors. They must think one of us is dead. Can't you hear the doors creak open?"

"Frankly, no."

"Their incessant pounding on the floor? Their breathing? I can hear every word they're saying! They won't shut up! It's bad enough that I have to listen to the horrendous thumping of your heart, but I can't bear all that noise! You up there! Stop or I'll have to kill you!"

I still couldn't see Mac, but I heard him stumbling about, accidentally bumping into things. I imagined him holding his hands over his ears and tossing his head back, vainly attempting to shut out the noise. But suddenly I stopped feeling sorry for him; I stopped being grateful to him for healing me; I felt like a maggot, but there wasn't anything I could do about it.

"Please, stop it!" he screamed. "I don't want to kill you, but I will!"

Hoping that he couldn't hear my fingers tightening about the butt of my laser, I decided to make a last-ditch attempt at humanity. I wished that I could move, but even the sound of my pants rubbing against my skin would have infuriated him more. "Mac! Cool it! You've got to calm down! Control yourself!" I'm afraid that I raised my voice too loud, but he didn't seem to notice.

"I can't, friend, I can't. I've tried controlling myself, I really have! But how can I control myself when they don't stop making that noise?"

"Isn't there anything I can do? I'm going to do whatever I can. I'm going to help you, Mac, understand? If you hold on, I'll help you."

"No! No! I can't stand it any longer! I'm going to kill them now!"

What he was going to do to those deadheads didn't bother me as much as the knowledge that Mac would find Lurleen in the crowd. As he climbed the stairs, I picked up my laser and, guiding my aim by his sounds, fired. I would have crisscrossed the beam, since the technique had worked so well before, but the thought of finding the light switch and then seeing poor Mac chopped into fifty throbbing, slimy pieces was too much for me to bear. I turned off the beam when he screamed the most hideous scream I had ever heard, when he sounded like he had gargled with acid, when his voice became so terrible, so eerie, that I had difficulty accepting that anything alive could emit such a painful, chilling roar. I heard him collapse on the stairway; I heard steady spouts of blood or slime pour from his body and splash on the stairs and drip onto the floor below. Again, I couldn't see him, but I imagined him turning to look at me with a shocked expression on his loathsome face as he tried to stand up.

He said in a low, tender, amazed voice, "I thought you were my friend."

"It was a case of conflicting loyalties."

Mac didn't bother to respond. He roared and charged up the long flight of stairs. Gradually his footsteps faded, and I heard the soft, dim slam of the distant door. I closed my eyes in relief. Soon I stood up and felt around the walls until I found the light switch. I flicked it on.

After my eyes adjusted to the light, I saw Mac's left arm lying on the stairway. My laser had burned through it just below the shoulder. Its edge was charred and smoking; his hand was balled into a fist. I looked away, walked to a barrel, turned on the faucet, leaned over, and drank. Much of the wine missed my mouth, trickled down my chin, and mingled with the mixture of wine and blood on the floor. I drank until I almost became sick. I shut off the faucet, kept my hand on it, and looked at the floor, concentrating on my eternal search for a good reason to move. I never found one, but I moved anyway.

I holstered my laser and picked up his arm. It weighed thirty pounds; the slime oozed between my fingers; it smelled like poor Mac had already been decaying for years. At the top of the stairs I opened the door and stepped into the bright hallway.

King Henry had his arm wrapped around Lurleen; she was almost swallowed by his fat. They wandered up and down the hallway, staring at the bodies of soldiers and civilians lying around. Medics administered first aid to those who looked like they had a chance. I glanced beside me. A young soldier was crumpled near the wall; his neck was broken; a thin red line of blood ran from his forehead. He seemed to be about twenty.

A trail of Mac's blood or slime (I'm still not sure what to call it) led through the bodies, toward the banquet room and out again, then toward the front doors. It had been quite a battle.

Standing at the doorway, I wondered what I should do next. I knew I should have said something by way of announcing my presence, but anything I said would have sounded stupid. I had already experienced more than enough violence for the evening, and to see evidence of more made me want to go home and bang my head against the wall until I suffered amnesia. Then I saw Peter walking about, inspecting the damage done to the dead and wounded, rubbing his hands and trying unsuccessfully to conceal his grin. He had delighted in the carnage though his opinion would have been different if Mac had gotten ahold of him. I bet myself that I knew what kind of books were in Peter's library. I knew that I would have to write myself a check in the morning when I saw him pick up a finger someone had misplaced during the battle. He held it tenderly in both hands while staring at it with an inane smile, then slipped it into his pants pocket, obviously unaware that my sharp eyes had noticed his activities. Then, grinning to himself, he walked toward a member of the entourage; as they spoke, his face softened and became etched with grief and nausea.

My muscles stiffened and my face turned red and my teeth gritted so hard that I was afraid the enamel would break; I couldn't stop trembling. Without a thought in the charred residue of my brain, I charged toward Peter; screaming at the top of my lungs, I shook Mac's arm at him. It took Peter a couple of seconds to realize that, for once, he was what all the shouting was about. Opening his mouth, he pointed at me, as if his dainty forefinger could have possibly warded off an accomplished madman like me. Before he could take a step, I walloped him with Mac's arm. He fell over backward, his limbs spinning everywhere like the blades of a windmill struck by mortar fire; the momentum of my swing carried me forward, and I almost stepped on him twice; and Mac's arm broke in half, leaving a smear of slime on Peter's temple. I stood over him, holding the upper half of Mac's arm; I breathed hard, as if I had just ran a four-minute mile in thirty seconds.

"Frankie, my boy, my good old boy!" boomed a royal voice behind me. King Henry, his arm around Lurleen, waddled as fast as he could toward me. Lurleen smiled at me with a blank expression she normally reserved for holovision commentators. However, King Henry was so overjoyed that when he slapped me on the back, I felt like I had sunburn. "Am I glad I hired you!"

"Are you really?"

"Of course, of course! You killed the monster in one day!"

I gestured at the carnage around me. "The monster doesn't act dead."

"Oh, it will be. The way it was bleeding and screaming

was a sure sign of approaching death. It did a lot of damage to my men, but in less than five minutes. It was in a hurry to go somewhere to die."

I wanted to collect my fee and leave, but first there was something else I had to do. "Where can a guy get some shut-eye in this joint?" The vigor Mac had granted me had faded; I needed a week's sleep.

King Henry answered with such generosity that I got the feeling he had defeated the monster himself. "Bill here will take you to your quarters." An old soldier standing near us nodded. "And I'll see you tomorrow at breakfast, won't I, Frankie?" He was like a little kid anticipating the arrival of a brand-new toy. I wondered if he would break my wheels and toss me down the stairs.

Assuring King Henry that tomorrow I would join him in what was left of the banquet room and allowing my eyes to linger on lovely, mysterious Lurleen one last time before surrendering to exhaustion, I dropped Mac's arm and turned on my heel, following the old soldier. For some reason I couldn't forget the hollow thunk Mac's arm made when it struck the floor, or the callous way I had tossed it near Peter's head. It seemed disrespectful to poor Mac. I wondered if I really would be able to sleep.

The soldier led me through more hallways, up stairs, through large dens and recreation rooms, and through still more hallways. I wondered why King Henry couldn't afford elevators; I wondered why he hadn't indulged in one of those teleportation devices that had come out recently. Perhaps he was trying to rough it. Many of the recreation rooms—full of bars, pool tables, ping pong tables, pinball machines, easy chairs, and coffee tables upon which were stacks of magazines from the far corners of the galaxy—looked as if they hadn't been used since the hall had been constructed; there were no flicks of ashes in the ashtrays, no wads of candy or chewing gum wrappers in the trashcans. Not once did the soldier speak to me, not even to congratulate me on my stunning victory. When we came to my room, he opened the door for me, allowed me to brush past him, and left, silently closing the door behind him. I was alone.

My room was immense and gaudy, just what I had always wanted. The room was two hundred square yards. The soft red rug was so thick that I was afraid I would accidentally step into a pool of quickfiber and would forever be lost to the sight of all mankind. Gold ornaments and priceless paintings decorated the red walls. One painting in particular impressed me; it was of a hideous red beast rising from the earth, surrounded by columns of fire; the beast had two horns, glowing yellow eyes, and long white fangs; upon its head was a gold crown. King Henry's tastes were the strangest of any person I had ever met. There were four five-foot statues in the room, statues of warriors with swords drawn.

I could have easily spent, oh, three or four minutes inspecting my quarters, but I was too tired. I threw my jacket on a chair, not caring that the blood and wine would stain the green velvet, took off my holster, wiped my laser clean with a handkerchief I found in the top drawer of a dresser, stripped to my light blue boxer shorts, reminded myself to search for my hat in the morning, turned off the lights, and crawled into the large circular bed with white blankets and white sheets in the center of the room. I was so tired that I was dizzy, almost sick. When I closed my eyes I was spinning. But I slept.

I don't know how long I slept, but finally I tossed and turned, trying to escape my nightmare. I woke.

Instinctively I groped at the thin, small hands wrapped around my throat. I gasped. The hands felt like flexible bundles of wire. I was vaguely aware of the hundred pounds sitting on my stomach, of the knobby knees puncturing my gut, forcing breath out of me, but not allowing any to come in. I slipped my hands under those choking me and shoved them to the right and left with all my might. When someone is choking you, the thumbs are the weakest point of your attacker's grip; the thumbs can't resist pressure pulling them apart, which is the tactic I used in my defense. That successfully accomplished, I followed through; since my attacker's arms were spread apart, since he was looking down on me, his face was unprotected; I gave him my best punch. I experienced extreme satisfaction as I felt tender lip being crushed against the hardest, longest teeth I had ever struck; I felt like I had punched out a lion.

My attacker recoiled from the force of my tremendous blow. I sat up and pushed my foe off me and onto the floor. I had no idea who I was fighting, but it was somebody weird, because his eyes glowed in the dark.

I leaped out of the bed and onto my attacker; I beat him blindly, hitting him wherever I could. One reason I beat him blindly was because I couldn't see a thing; my room didn't even have a nightlight. My attacker made his first sound when I punched him in the throat: an indignant, squeaky wheeze that sent a rush of hot air and saliva into my face. I had six tiny third-degree burns before I quickly wiped the liquid off my face, burning my palm in the process. The breath of my attacker was asphyxiating; the smell reminded me of sulfur. Both characteristics sent me into a frenzy; I beat him wildly, even as I realized that the tiny, sharp claws which had cut into my neck when he had been choking me were now trying to rip up my face and chest. I wouldn't give my attacker a chance to do any more than that. As soon as I believed that I had done enough damage to whomever or whatever was attacking me, I grabbed two pointed ears and lifted the head several inches, bringing it down to the floor as quickly as I could.

With a forceful motion that took me completely by surprise, my attacker shoved me off him. I rolled on the floor and wound up in a crouching position, facing those eerie glowing eyes. My attacker, consumed by a wild bloodlust, charged, snarling and (I imagined) readying to claw out my eyes. My right hand felt the marble base of a statue. I slipped behind the base and shoved the statue off the base and toward my attacker. The statue missed; like a drop of mercury, my foe had avoided it. But it did him no good. The base weighed only thirty pounds; it was thin enough for me to grab and lift with ease. I swung it, aiming toward those glowing eyes. I missed the head because my attacker moved, but I got him on the chest. I heard several ribs crack with a noise reminding me of fire-crackers popping.

I crouched and tried to catch my breath. My victim lay there on the floor; his glowing eyes stared blankly at the ceiling. He wheezed and groaned. My knees felt fresh blood on the carpet, comparatively little of which was mine. I wanted to vomit. I turned on the lights.

My victim had stringy black hair, a flattened nose with large nostrils, small breasts, and coarse green skin. *Her* arms and legs were thin but strong. Her face was battered; blood flowed from various cuts on her cheeks, on her skull, and through her nose. She wore a yellow blouse, a red skirt, black stockings, and a plain gold ring on her finger. Two high-heels laid near my bed. On a chair was an ugly white Sunday-go-to-meeting hat with plastic flowers and fruit on top of it; next to the hat was a Teflon frying pan which evidently she was going to use before she decided to kill me with her bare hands. A cool wind blew into my room; she had climbed in through the window.

She summoned up strength and rolled over on her side,

reaching toward me, straining to touch and cut me, but she couldn't move the rest of her body and she was putting too much pressure on her chest, and so she rolled on her back, admitting defeat. I walked to her. I stood over her, being careful not to stand where she could easily scratch or kick my legs.

"You're Mac's mother, I take it?"

"Take it and . . ."

"Why did you try to kill me?" I tried to sound very indignant, but looking down at the poor creature made me nauseous. Her every breath caused her to spasm in pain. It was terrible, hearing her struggle to breathe. One eye was puffed up so much, so bloody and torn, that I couldn't see it. She had given up on life; she didn't care to fight anymore. Not that I could blame her. I felt pretty much the same way.

"My name is Agnes," she answered. "You know why I'm here, you bully."

"I'm not a bully. These days it's no disgrace to defend yourself if a woman tries to kill you."

"What are you babbling about?"

"Nothing. Forget it."

"Soon I'll have no choice, thanks to you, the murderer of my son. You killed my son, you burned off his arm, and now he's dead, thanks to you."

I turned away from her. Sorry that I had switched on the lights, I sat down, covered my mouth with my left palm, and tried not to look at her. Tightening the muscles of her jaw, she tilted her head so I would have to see her face. From her mouth dripped several huge drops of blood. I hoped the rug stains would be permanent. "Don't blame me," I said. "I'm just a poor, lonely warrior who isn't responsible for the ethical structure of the universe. As a harried private investigator trapped in a world I didn't make, I'm upholding the struggle for human dignity in the only way I know how. It's not my fault Mac killed people."

"Do you honestly think pretty speeches are going to make me feel better?"

"It's been known to work, lady. Why did Cochineal pick Mac for this job?"

"Cochineal always considered his son a barrier between us."

"Pardon me, but did you say 'his *son*?' "

"Did I stutter?"

I inhaled deeply. This case was beginning to take on ramifications I hadn't suspected. I had been laboring under the mistaken assumption that once I killed the monster attacking the Mead Hall, I could go home and pay my rent for a change. But no amount of kale could ever have provided me with the proper incentive to bump off Cochineal's wife. However, while my mind was feverishly racing to figure a way to get out of the mess alive, I was dying of curiosity.

"Uh, pardon me, perhaps you don't like to answer personal questions, but how did you and Cochineal meet?"

Agnes coughed up blood. I was afraid she would expire before she answered. "We met in Cochineal's laboratory."

"That sounds romantic. Were you his assistant?"

"No. I was his product. I was designed to be the perfect mate. He had sent his spies all over the galaxy, in search of a woman who deserved his wonderfulness. When no one could find one, he decided that if he wanted somebody to love, he would have to make his own somebody. It took him three years, Seldon Time, to produce me, but after he was finished, he dug me the most."

"Am I to assume that although Cochineal didn't care if his son lived or died, he feels quite differently toward you?"

"Yes. Mac burst into Cochineal's mysterious black castle so he could tell me how much he loved me before he died. Cochineal was unimpressed and wasn't particularly interested in avenging Mac. However, he promised that great woe would descend upon those who harmed me in my quest."

"Oh, no."

Before she could eloquently state the obvious remark, Agnes convulsed one last time and expired. I sat there for several minutes, trying to figure out what to do. The only thing to do was wait. Believe me, it wasn't easy. After a short while of that, I couldn't help but notice that Agnes smelled like she had been dead for six months; she looked like it, too. She was rapidly decaying. I grimaced, fumbled for a phone, and dialed room service.

"Yes, may we help you, sir?" inquired an old man on the screen who sounded like he was speaking through a tin can.

"Yeah, you sure can, you poor bozo. I'm Franklin Davis, the private dick in the hero's suite."

"Yes, we know very well who and where you are," he replied, looking as if I had insulted his intelligence.

"Well, I need four strong lackeys with colds to lug out a body. It seems that the monster's mother tried to choke me to death."

"Oh dear, sir! Are you all right?"

"Everything's fine, Jeeves. Just send up those lackeys. Oh, yes—and send up two ham-and-cheese sandwiches on rye, with plenty of mustard and mayo, an order of fries with catsup, a tossed salad with blue cheese dressing, some potato salad, a taco, a glass of cold milk, and a cup of hot black coffee. You got that?"

The old man repeated my order and asked if there was anything else.

"Has anyone in the vicinity spotted Cochineal during the last hour or so?"

"Well, I should most certainly hope not. Since you killed the monster, Mr. Davis, Mead Hall has become the safest place on the planet. The Space Patrol has seen to that."

"That's what you think, buster," I said. Then I switched off and opened a few windows; I didn't want any of that odor around while I ate. When the lackeys finally came, they were perturbed at the odor and shocked at the corpse. They didn't like touching it.

Five minutes later, just as I had closed the windows because most of the odor was gone and because blue boxer shorts aren't famous for the protection they provide against cool breezes, my meal arrived, carted in by three beautiful women who would have been honored to spend the night. I would have let them, too, if I hadn't been saving myself for Miss Right.

Ten minutes later when I sent my compliments to the chef, I felt like my old self, whoever he was. As I stood looking out the window, sipping coffee, the night's events already seemed like a dream. I put on my torn, bloody shirt. My laser was in my holster, draped across the bed, where I could leap for it instantly if a sudden danger popped up. And I was expecting one to pop up. I hoped it would soon, because I was nervous and tense. The pale sun was rising and for a moment the sky was light blue; oddly enough, there were a few clouds on the horizon, clouds made bright red by the sun, and I hoped that it wouldn't rain. I reflected on how tough it was to be a shamus. Just once I wanted a nice, neat case where there was a murder, five suspects, twenty motives, and a solution from left field.

After a time I became tired of waiting; I wanted to get the whole thing over with. I thought of Cochineal. I calm-

ly set my coffee cup on a table, strapped on my holster, put on my jacket, and walked out of the room. I had planned on walking to the front door without speaking to anyone, to finish the case without making a big deal out of it. That way if I died, I would be less humiliated afterwards. To get out of Mead Hall, you need a map. I spotted a servant and had him guide me out, making a detour to pick up my hat, which the chef had appropriated as a souvenir. All great heroes should do battle in uniform.

Outside I felt my mirror sunglasses in my jacket pocket. Miraculously, they had survived the punishment. I walked out the main gate, veered toward the mountains, and with my mind blank, amazingly free of thoughts, made my way toward the mysterious black castle.

Walking down the golden mountainside, away from Mead Hall, was easy; all I had to do was keep my feet from working too fast and I maintained my balance. Walking up the next mountain was a problem, because it wasn't gold, because the upper layers of the soil were dust and loose rock, and there were no plants to hold onto. Soon I found a gulley leading up to a section of boulders and gray slate, and then it became simpler for me to make my way. After I climbed off the second mountain, I saw paths, beaten down by animals, which ran around and over several mountains.

If I had an emotion during the early portion of my trek, I don't know what it was. I realized that I should have been reviewing my life and judging myself, but I had always considered my life worthy only of pans. There was no point in belaboring the obvious. I should have had the feeling that I was totally alone, but after a time, when the rock became dark brown and black, when a thin fog of volcano soot began blowing past me toward the city, I felt that someone was near. Those old survival instincts acting up again. Being paranoid in defense of your life is no vice.

I clung to the irrational hope that if I talked to Cochineal, perhaps he would grant me a reprieve. True, I had killed his true love, but he could always build another one. With my luck, he would be a man of principle. Already I was becoming too tired to put up a good fight; as I walked upward, my leg muscles tightened and strained. The volcano soot didn't help my breathing any. I had stoically accepted my demise when I turned a bend and saw Lurleen sitting on a rock, facing me.

She sat with her right leg crossed over her left, leaning backward, resting on her palms like a pinup girl. She wore the same outfit she had yesterday (it seemed to be ironed on her body), but with the addition of a stun pistol and holster strapped about her hip and a knife strapped to her right boot. At her side lay a heavy broadsword which I had seen her wield effortlessly in a tournament a few years ago. The breeze fanned a strand of blonde hair over one eye; and for several instants her image had an eternal quality, as if she had been sitting on that rock forever, like a statue somehow come to life. Her first movement was a slight, incredibly sexy upturning of her lips, and her eyes seemed to glisten (doubtless caused by the soot) as I stood still, pondering what my first words to her should be. They were hardly memorable. I said, "What are you doing here?"

"Waiting for you," she said softly.

I repressed the urge to click my heels in the air. "How did you know that I would be here?"

"This is the only path to Cochineal's castle. When I learned about Agnes from the chef, I knew where you were going to go. During my childhood, when Cochineal and my father had a much more stable relationship between them, these mountains were safe for play and exploration; and so, in your parlance, I took a shortcut."

"Terrific. That's very touching, sister, but it's time for you to wiggle home. These mountains aren't safe for exploration any more."

"Which is precisely the reason for my presence. You are exhausted; you require my assistance."

"Whether or not I need it is immaterial; I don't want it."

Lurleen shrugged and looked away, toward the black castle and the black birds flying above it. I didn't need any great insights into the human condition to know that she was essentially unimpressed by my objections.

"I was also aware that you would belittle my offer," she said. "I suppose that men whom women throw themselves at invariably become insensitive louts."

"Hey, it's nothing personal."

"A private investigator of the meanest abilities would have realized long ago that I am capable of taking care of myself. Not only am I able to chop off limbs with this sword, but the blade itself is equipped with many bizarre weapons, all of them more sophisticated than your primitive laser."

If I had thought about what I was doing next, I probably wouldn't have done it. I walked to her, sat beside her, and turned so I could grab both arms. She leaned forward. "That's not the point," I said. "I don't want you in any situation where you can get hurt. It's not good for my peace of mind."

"What about my peace of mind? I will feel much more self-assured and confident of my control of my destiny if I am beside you. Why not grant me the same privileges you grant yourself?"

"That has nothing to do with it. Logic is . . ."

"Immaterial. I know." She leaned closer. "Then what

are you trying to say?"

"I love you."

"And I have loved you for years. It is truly satisfying to live in the world of my dreams."

We kissed. I guess saps like me are always sentimental old fluffs on the inside; that's why my imminent danger seemed so far away, so inconsequential, as I realized that I too was living in the world of my dreams.

"All right, cut the PDA!" said a rude voice.

Lurleen broke away from me and pushed her hair back into place. "Well, *really*!" she whispered.

The voice had emanated from a holocamera hovering three feet above the ground. It was equipped with an antenna, flashing lights, a microphone, speakers, and other artifacts of the machine age, all of which fulfilled only decorative purposes as far as I was concerned. "You're on holovision now," said King Henry through the wonders of modern science, "so conduct yourself in the prepubescent fashion expected of public figures. And you, Frankie, I'm surprised at you, mixing business and pleasure, being involved with a woman, climbing down from your ivory tower. What will it do to your image?"

"I'm not worried. I can't find enough work anyway, so what difference will a little less make?"

"Humph," said King Henry's metallic voice. "Are you sure you don't love my daughter only because of her social standing? Forgive my bluntness, but you don't know who you can trust these days."

"Basically, Sire, I just crave her bod."

"My social standing, like logic, is immaterial," said Lurleen, "because I have grown tired of pretending to be someone who cannot take pleasure in a little 'PDA' now and then. After Franklin and I do away with Cochineal—that is, after we discharge our obligations to you—we will close my account at the Universal Bank and use my funds to pay for our travels around the galaxy. We will lead a life of adventure, will we not dear?"

"Yeah. Sure. If you say so." I smiled. Visions of the pitter-patter of little feet echoing in Mead Hall faded. Lurleen was certainly an optimistic young woman; as of yet, I had had no indication that I would survive the coming battle, and already I was exploring the universe. Lurleen stood and picked up her broadsword; she pointed the formidable weapon at the holocamera. "And what is the purpose of *that*?" she asked.

"Why, when the chef told me that you were following Mr. Davis, I called in the holovision networks. Your PDA has been broadcast all over the planet. So will your victory. A member of the royal family taking part in a battle with the great Franklin Davis and ridding me of my most annoying enemy at the same time will be excellent public relations."

"What if she dies?" I asked.

"Oh. Well. There's a five-second delay. If she gets into a situation she can't handle, we'll shut off the broadcast and make a few excuses for her disappearance until we can dig up a clone or something."

"You think of everything, don't you?" I asked, somewhat superfluously.

"You have to take these things into consideration when you're a king," answered Henry pompously.

Standing the point of her blade on the earth, Lurleen leaned on her sword. She threw her shoulders back and spread her feet apart. She ignored the holocamera, staring and speaking directly at me instead. "Franklin, dear, we should continue. Doubtless Cochineal is preparing to greet us appropriately, and the longer we tarry, the more preparation he will have an opportunity to make."

It took me a while to figure out what she was saying, but eventually I understood it; I hoped she wouldn't talk like that all the time.

This time, as I walked toward the mysterious black castle, there was no question as to the identity of the emotion in my heart. Despite the knowledge that my joy could become pathetically brief, I felt that I had entered a delightful limbo. Even the soot had cleared up, and the three volcanoes were filled with the quietness of doom. The only noise was caused by the crunching of our feet on the loose rocks and, occasionally, by the blade of Lurleen's broadsword as she accidentally allowed it to drop too low. The holocamera silently followed us, the very fact of its presence preventing my left hand from resting lower than upon the small of Lurleen's back.

Soon we came upon a flat level approximately fifty yards square, bordered by sharp rocks jutting upward, causing the entire area to resemble nothing more than a desolate tiny valley, though the tips of the rocks formed the top of the mountain. Lurleen whispered to me to be cautious, but we did not slow our pace. We might have if we hadn't been on national holovision, but fame sometimes does strange things to people. The silence became oppressive as we walked the valley; even the crunching of the rocks under our feet got on my nerves. I had definitely left that delightful limbo, so soon after having entered it, and now wished that I were alone; I knew that the time for action would be soon, and if I had been alone, I would have had the freedom to act exactly as I chose within the perimeters of the situation. However, it wouldn't have surprised me to discover that Lurleen was thinking the same thing.

Without warning, we heard what resembled the magnified rustling of dried leaves; but there were no trees or other plants about. We stopped, and Lurleen's free hand tightened around my arm. When I looked about, I saw the holocamera behind us retreating to the entrance of the valley. I wondered if the showdown had been arranged in advance; and for a terrible instant I suspected that Lurleen had been a part of the conspiracy; but when she remained by my side, my worst fears were abated. I was oddly calm when I learned the cause of the rustling: the black birds who had been flying above the castle, walking up the opposite side of the jutting rocks, flapping their wings to maintain their balance, until they rested at the top, staring at us, waiting for some unknown signal to be given before they attacked. Each black bird had a wingspan of approximately thirty yards, which they showed off by spreading their wings as if they were preparing to take flight. Their cylindrical ears resembled those of bats, though they belonged (perhaps distantly) to the aves family. Their clawed feet were a shade lighter than their feathers; and they would have been totally black had it not been for their glowing yellow eyes, which seemed to penetrate deep into our souls as we stood motionless, waiting for one (or all) of the giant birds to make the first move.

Slowly, trying to be as casual as possible, I moved my right hand into my jacket, unsnapped my holster, and kept my hand on my laser. Lurleen released me and held her left hand on her stun gun. We were afraid to move too quickly; we didn't want the birds to start something we would regret later.

At the exit of the valley appeared Cochineal; I don't know how he appeared there, because neither Lurleen nor I saw him do so; he was just there. I couldn't see how he was dressed because his glittering black cape was wrapped about his body, accentuating his demonic pose. He was bald, ageless, with a round, clean-shaven face and thick black eyebrows which rose to points near his temples. I doubt if he had altered his grim expression once during his life (except, perhaps, to whisper sweet nothings into Agnes's ear). He examined us as if we were an undesirable culture on a slide under a malfunctioning microscope. Finally he spoke.

"I've long been an admirer of your exploits, Mr. Davis."

"Thank you. It's not often that I get to meet such an illustrious fan."

"It's extremely unfortunate that we had to meet under such circumstances, but since nearly everyone I come into contact with has those sentiments, I suppose it's not surprising."

I swallowed something; I think it had been manufactured by my saliva glands, but I wasn't willing to take a chance on it. Lurleen's expression was blank, devoid of emotion, as if she were facing a contingent of reporters armed with boring questions. She scowled. I reasoned that since at the very least she would be familiar with Cochineal's *modus operandi*, it was possible she had a good reason for scowling. That was the only warning I had previous to the bolt of green light shooting from Cochineal's eyes. The man had augmented his humanity with some very sophisticated weaponry. Before the bolt could strike us, Lurleen lifted her sword and pressed a tiny button on the hilt; and from the blade flowed a yellow bolt which collided with the green one less than ten yards from us. The shock was devastating, tossing Lurleen and myself to the ground like wadded pieces of paper; because she had been holding the sword, Lurleen took the brunt of the shock; I was merely stunned, with the breath knocked out of me. I rose to my elbows after an eternity of struggling; and I saw Cochineal smile grimly.

"So you were prepared for my bolt of mystical force," he said without passion, as if he was a teacher preparing to spank a habitually mischievous child. "We shall see

how you fare against more direct methods."

I had no idea what could be more direct than a green bolt of mystical force, but I had no intention of finding out. I fought to my knees and reached for my laser. Then I saw it ten yards to my left. Three yards to my right was an unconscious Lurleen, with her sword lying at her feet. I would have dived for my laser, but a shimmering yellow glow began radiating about Cochineal; hesitation might prove inconvenient. I rolled toward Lurleen and picked up the sword before I came to my feet. I squatted and pointed the sword at Cochineal. There were several tiny green studs on the hilt; and my fingers lingered over them as I waited, hoping to make Cochineal think that I had some expertise with the weapon.

The glow increased until it smothered him; it expanded and rose. I squinted; for several moments I expected Cochineal to materialize near me; I believed that the yellow glow was but a distraction. Then as I realized that the glow was the essence of Cochineal himself, the outline of a dragon took shape in the air. Had he materialized in his new form, he would have been ten yards long, with a triangular mouth equipped with sharp fangs; his ears would have been two large flaps and his feet would have had three claws apiece.

But he did not materialize.

I pushed a button, firing (as Lurleen informed me later) an electronic disruptor beam which sent the vibrations of Cochineal's atoms askew. He screamed, but to my ears it was only a wistful whisper of no discernible origin. I could not be sure *where* or *into what* our nemesis was heading. For a few silent minutes, I stood panting, one eye on Lurleen, and one on the air where Cochineal had floated. Then I took a breath. He had obviously vanished. I had little interest in following.

When I stood straight, my legs trembled; I was afraid

that I would collapse. Lurleen groaned and shook her head; still holding her sword, I helped her stand and then retrieved my laser. Instead of appearing relieved, she was nervous; beads of sweat formed on her forehead as she stared at the grim black birds perched on the rocks. One bird flapped its wings, and we expected it to fly either away from us or toward us; yet it had only been attempting to balance itself. Its yellow eyes, like those of its fellows, stared at the battleground below as if the events which had transpired there had been beyond all comprehension. Lurleen rested a hand on my shoulder; she smiled weakly as she said, "Franklin, my dear, what course of action is open to us now?"

"Baby, if I knew that, we would already be doing it."

The holocamera at the entrance to the tiny valley began floating toward us. King Henry's voice blared forth, shattering the fragile silence. "Well, congratulations! That was a marvelous battle, brief, yet not too succinct . . ."

"I don't have to listen to this dreck any longer," I said, forgetting about the impending danger of the birds as I raised my laser and fired it directly at the holocamera. The beam fizzed through it, disintegrating the center, causing it to crash and break into pieces against the rocks. "Frankie, how impolite . . ." crackled a speaker just before I disintegrated it in its turn.

"An extremely judicious procedure," said Lurleen. "And the birds did not move."

"They may not. We might as well leave and force their hand rather than stand around and wait for them to attack."

"I wonder," said Lurleen as we slowly, cautiously walked from the valley on the mountaintop, "will the birds follow Cochineal's orders after his disappearance, or will they rejoice in their freedom?"

We never knew, for the birds remained perched on the rocks until nightfall when, shielded by darkness, they flew into space, never to be seen on Rakish again.

AFTERWORD

I was born in Grundy, Virginia on 1/14/50, and four years later my parents moved to Tazewell, Virginia, in the Appalachian Mountains. Though the area is coal mining country, I've only been in a mine once, and that was in Kentucky. I also saw another mine several years later, but I didn't go in. As Harlan revealed for all the world to see in his introduction to AUTUMN ANGELS, I discovered literature through Flash Comics, and those old stories (approximately 1959 to 1963) are the very foundation of my creative mind. Green Lantern, Atom, Hawkman, and the Justice League also did their part (these are the Julie Schwartz edited magazines of the time). I didn't discover the glories of Stan Lee until 1972, when I returned to comic reading in a big way and bought up all the back issues I could get my hands on. I've read every kind of speculative fiction in bulk, and my tastes include an unholy love for Russian and South American writing, even though, comparatively speaking, I've read very little of that sort of thing and know only one language, and that just barely. Rock music and classical music profoundly affect my thinking in ways I can barely express, though I've no musical talent and don't know the first thing about playing an instrument. I graduated from Virginia Polytechnic Institute and State University in 1971, an English Major with minors in history and theatre arts; from there I attended the Clarion workshops in New Orleans and Seattle ('71 and '72, respectively). At New Orleans, I met Harlan Ellison, who has befriended and influenced me: Harlan is one of the few people whose personality and example have influenced me, though I hasten to add that I learned not through imitation. Harlan taught me to, ah, "be true to myself" and follow my own instincts in writing, wherever they would take me. He also bought the first story I sold, and of course he edited AUTUMN ANGELS for Pyramid. I keep writing from becoming a boring occupation by giving myself full leeway to surprise myself; quite often I'm shocked (sometimes pleasantly) at what I write and say.

I shouldn't be saying this, but *Galactic Gumshoe* is a failure. That's nothing odd, since all my stories fail in the final evaluation. In this instance, I don't want anyone to think that I didn't do my best, because I've rewritten it three times. I rarely rewrite more than once, if then (thus giving my critics ammunition and my admirers—both of them—good cause to believe I don't try enough). Nor does it mean that I don't love the story; after all, it is one of my metaphorical children.

What I do like about *Galactic Gumshoe* is the smart-ass quality of the narrative, the smooth prose (save for a few passages), and the way it glorifies in its punk existentialism. Nevertheless, the character of Franklin Davis fails; he should be more, much more, than he is. The plot should deal with the ultimate revelation of character, as Raymond Chandler said, rather than with just punching the bad guy's ticket.

In other words, I caught all the paraphernalia, but none of the soul, revealing little of Davis and the tormented spirit I have in mind for him.

Despite all this hedging, I do love *Galactic Gumshoe* at this writing; and I might even enjoy reading it in print. (For obvious reasons, my opinion of my work in print loses its pretensions of objectivity.) This will probably be the only Davis story that will be primary adventure.

I might as well conclude these rambling thoughts by revealing the nature of my ultimate game-plan, especially since this will be the only opportunity I'll have for a while.

In case anyone is wondering about Franklin's background, they can investigate my cycle of horror stories, which is a combination of Faulkner and Lovecraft. This may prove frustrating since a) I haven't written that many yet; b) only a few of those have been published; and c) there's only one reference to Davis so far anyway, and that story hasn't been quite completed. But hopefully over the next five or six years everything will become clear to those who care, and then I can figure out other universes to conquer.

End of plug.

POSTSCRIPT

From here, *Weird Heroes* will return to the *second* volume in our mini-series *Quest of the Gypsy*. Those of you unfamiliar with this continuing saga by Ron Goulart with Alex Nino art, are directed towards *WEIRD HEROES 3*, the first *Gypsy* book. It's a highly entertaining blend of mystery, science fiction and humor, bringing out the best of both Goulart's talents and Nino's impressionistic line.

Following the Gypsy title (*WH 7*) in October, will be our second new anthology in November. The line-up for that book should delight the best of our fans and the hardest of our critical readers. Stories by Maxwell Grant, Kenneth Robeson, Michael Moorcock, Ben Bova and J. Michael Reeves.

Maxwell Grant and Kenneth Robeson? Yes! As the premier new American pulp, *Weird Heroes* has been granted the right to print an extraordinary lost classic of the heyday of the pulp hero magazines. In this set of unpublished tales, Maxwell Grant and Kenneth Robeson write stories—*mysteries*—featuring themselves as characters! To top it off, the Grant story is written in the Robeson style and the Robeson story in the Grant style! It's an extraordinary venture into fantastic fiction and it will be right here in November!

To top off the next anthology, we will be introducing a new series, *Kamus of Kadizar*, by the talented J. Michael Reaves. Those of you unfamiliar with J.M.'s prose will find the first KAMUS story to be a tantalizing blend of Raymond Chandler and Edgar Rice Burroughs, placing a hard-boiled 'sword and sorcery' character on an alien planet and letting the cultures clash for themselves. Kadizar and its city of Myriad may go down as the most entertaining and alluring of all the new *WH* series, especially since it is illustrated by Steve Hickman, who did not only the cover to our left, but the upcoming *WH 8* cover, too.

The second cycle continues—Hickman, Reaves, Chaykin, Bova, Russell and more. If you have any trouble finding them, contact John Rutledge, Direct Sales, Pyramid Books, 757 Third Avenue, New York City 10017.

GYPSY RETURNS!

The incredible QUEST OF THE GYPSY continues its way along a path of unknown danger with *EYE OF THE VULTURE*.

This seventh volume of *Weird Heroes*, available in *Oct. '77*, is the second book in the epic series of the wandering hero and his winged antagonist, the vulture.

Journey to Africa with Gyp and his two companions, Annabelle and the scoundrel Walpole, as they search for clues to a 55-year-old puzzle!

EYE OF THE VULTURE

About the Contributors

Ron Goulart, Edgar-award-winning author, has written over seventy-five books, including three non-fiction titles on popular fiction. Among his best known science fiction novels are *After Things Fell Apart, The Hellhound Project* and *What's Become of Screwloose?* He currently resides in Connecticut.

Carl Potts and *Terry Austin*, fantasy illustrators, and cartoonists are natives of California and Michigan, respectively. Potts has produced comics for *International Insanity* and *Charlton*, in addition to numerous commercial jobs for Continuity Associates. Terry Austin has "inked" over a hundred comics for various American companies, including *Green Lantern* for DC Comics and *Captain Marvel* for Marvel Comics. He moonlights as a science fiction illustrator. As a team, Potts and Austin have produced *Shinbet*, and a child, Gregory, age 4.

Ben Bova is a novelist, lecturer, and editor of *Analog Science Fiction—Science Fact* magazine, the most widely read and influential science fiction magazine in the world. He received the Science Fiction Achievement Award (Hugo) for Best Professional Editor for four consecutive years, 1973, '74, '75, and '76. The author of more than forty books of both fiction and non-fiction, Bova has also been a working newspaperman, an aerospace executive, a motion picture writer, and a television science consultant.

Craig Russell, a native of Ohio, is a fantasy and comics illustrator best known for his work with Marvel Comics. His influences range from Mucha to Steranko, and he favors classical music. His recently released portfolio of continuity graphics, *Chimera*, has been widely acclaimed as a classic of fantasy panel art.

Edmond Hamilton, widely respected fantasy author, is

responsible for the classic science fiction pulp series, *Captain Future*. He is perhaps best known for his legendary *Star Kings* and, to comic readers, for his evocative and stimulating *Superman* stories of the fifties and sixties, often illustrated by the unsung, talented Wayne Boring. Edmond Hamilton resides alternately in California and Ohio, with his wife, writer Leigh Brackett.

Philip José Farmer is the author of numerous award-winning stories and novels. His *Riverworld* series has a cult following in both America and Europe and his sexual, surrealistic fantasies have been recognized internationally as ground-breaking, if bizarre, experiments in a historically sexist and cliché-burdened field. He has written biographies of *Doc Savage* and *Tarzan* and is widely respected as a pulp historian of the first caliber.

Tom Sutton, popular cartoonist, illustrator and painter, is also a filmmaker. In his spare time, he resides in Newburyport, Massachusetts. His credits include *Schlomo Raven* (Pyramid), a detective comedy; *Planet of the Apes*; Marvel Comics; Warren Comics; and various visual aid materials. Tom has been a cartoonist for *Stars and Stripes* and an art director in Boston for an educational firm.

Arthur Byron Cover, who currently lives in California by way of the South, is one of the most original new writers in science fiction today. His three books include *The Sound of Winter* (Pyramid), *Autumn Angels* (Pyramid), and *Platypus of Doom* (Warner, cover by Neal Adams). He is currently working on a new novel for Pyramid Books.

Ralph Reese, award-winning inker and illustrator, has two books, *Son of Sherlock Holmes* (Pyramid) and *One Year Affair* (Workman) to his credit. A resident of New Jersey, he is a contributing artist to *National Lampoon*.

Byron Preiss, editor/producer of the innovative *Fiction Illustrated* series of adult graphic novels, began his editorial career with National Periodical Publications for whom he developed the *EDU graphics* reading program. From there he went to the Children's Television Workshop, where he acted as writer/editor on books tied to the popular *Electric Company* television shows. This work and *EDU graphics* were exhibited at the J.F. Kennedy Center in Washington D.C.

In California, he was head writer for an innovative ABC game show for children which stressed concepts in visual thinking. The show aired in 1975.

His company, Byron Preiss Visual Publications, Inc., has developed educational and fantasy graphic story materials for a variety of publishers and organizations, including *The Model Cities Program* and *The Children's Hospital*. They produce two series for Pyramid Books, *Weird Heroes* and *Fiction Illustrated*. The former is a showcase for a new style of "pulp" fiction; the latter has been acclaimed as an important step forward for the comics medium.

Preiss is the author/editor of ten books, including a juvenile, *The Silent e's From Outer Space*, and a detective comedy, *Schlomo Raven*. He has a BA from the University of Pennsylvania and an MA in Communications from Stanford University.